TruthStone

THE TRUTHSEER ARCHIVES
BOOK I

MIKE SHELTON

TruthStone
Copyright © 2018 by Michael Shelton
2nd edition © 2020

ISBN: 0-9987935-4-x
ISBN-13: 978-0-9987935-4-2
Library of Congress Control Number: 2018900579
Salem, Oregon

Cover Illustration by Christian Bentulan
https://coversbychristian.com/

Map by Robert Altbauer
www.fantasy-map.net

For More information about Mike Shelton and his books
www.MichaelSheltonBooks.com

mikesheltonbooks@gmail.com
www.MichaelSheltonBooks.com
https://www.facebook.com/groups/MikeSheltonAuthor/
https://www.facebook.com/mikesheltonbooks/
http://www.Twitter.com/msheltonbooks
http://www.Instagram.com/mikesheltonbooks
https://www.pinterest.com/mikesheltonbooks/

ACKNOWLEDGEMENTS

There are so many people that go into writing and publishing a book. First and foremost I would like to thank my daughter Danielle who helped me out tremendously in this series by doing research and giving me guidance and direction in regards to the stones of power that you will read about.

I want to thank my new illustrator for this second edition, Christian Bentulan. He really did an awesome job! Robert Altbauer continues to amaze me with his maps. You can see a color version of it on my website.

The editors at Precision Editing (Heather, Crystal, Julie, Lisa) are really amazing and continue to help me stay organized in my thoughts, give me direction and corrections when needed and make my book more polished.

Lastly on this page, but always first in my heart is my wonderful wife, Melissa who continues to encourage, love, and support me in this wonderful endeavor of creating and writing stories!

-Mike-

BOOKS BY MIKE SHELTON

WESTERN CONTINENT BOOKS:

The Cremelino Prophecy:
The Path Of Destiny
The Path Of Decisions
The Path Of Peace
The Blade and the Bow (A prequel novella to The Cremelino Prophecy)

The Alaris Chronicles:
The Dragon Orb
The Dragon Rider
The Dragon King
Prophecy Of The Dragon (A prequel novella to The Alaris Chronicles)

The Dragon Artifacts:
The Golden Dragon
The Golden Scepter
The Golden Empire

The Wizard Academies:
Mark of the Medallion
Search for the Medallion
Power of the Medallion

GEMSTONES OF WAYLAND BOOKS:

The TruthSeer Archives:
TruthStone
TruthSpell
TruthSeer
The Stones of Power (A prequel novella to The TruthSeer Archives)

MAP

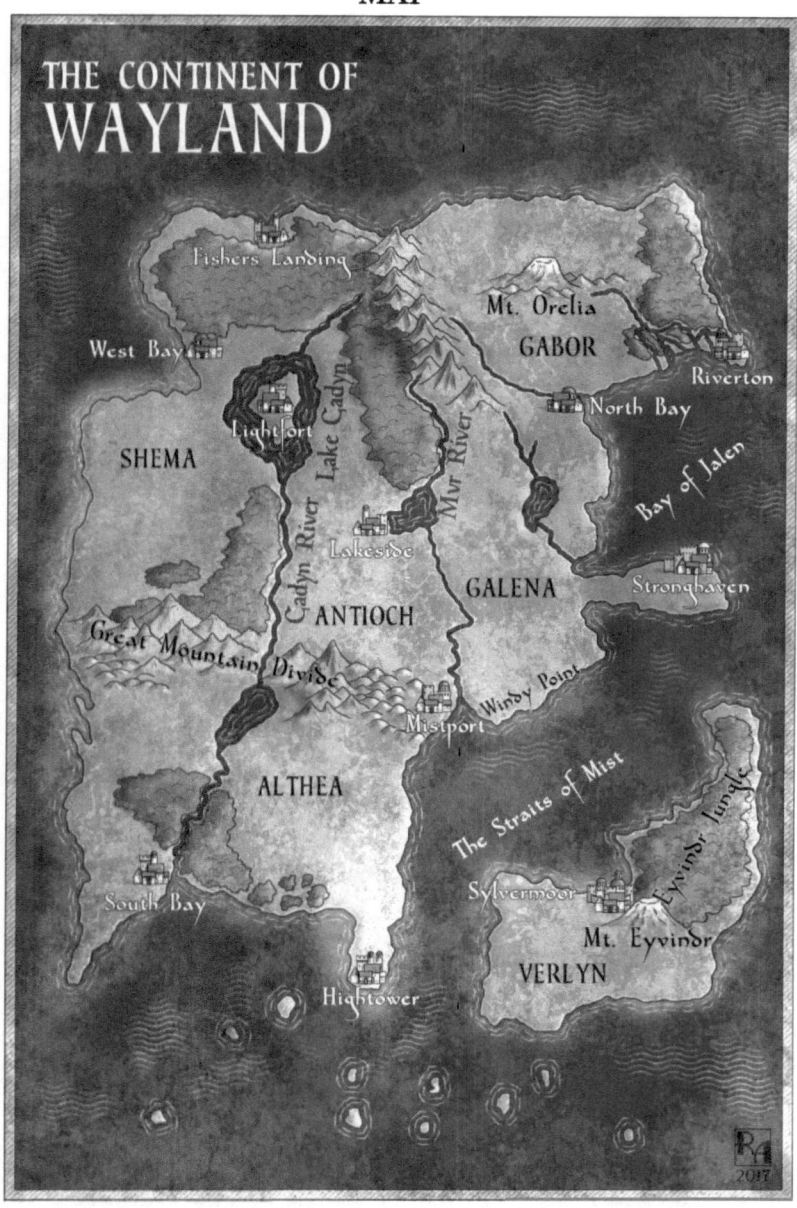

See Color map at www.MichaelSheltonBooks.com

STONES OF POWER ON WAYLAND

TruthStone—Moldavite—Green

IntelligenceStone—Labradorite—Blue—Kingdom of Galena

StrengthStone—Red Jasper—Red—Kingdom of Gabor

SpeedStone—Garnet—Orange—Kingdom of Antioch

HearingStone—Celestite—White—Kingdom of Althea

HealingStone—Azeztulite—Pink—Kingdom of Shema

CHAPTER ONE

Someone was watching her—Shaeleen was sure of it. Stopping at the edge of the market place she rose up on her tiptoes, and tried to look out over the crowd. Cursing her height once again she thought she saw a flash of a dark cloak and someone duck out of the way, but she couldn't be sure.

Returning her focus to the task at hand, Shaeleen's loose brown hair flew around her face as she turned her head to the right and left, her light blue eyes scanning the vendors in the crowded marketplace of Stronghaven. She didn't have a lot of time.

As a ruse to her father she agreed to pick up some lace for her mother. The real reason for her venture that day was to get to the palace's practice yard, where all the young men would be training for the upcoming spring competition.

Her skin prickled and she whipped her head back around searching for the reason. Two people with dark cloaks seemed to disappear back behind a vendor's booth, but she lost sight of them. It was noon, and the crowds were thick.

Shaeleen turned back around and found the shop that sold her mother's lace. She took a step in that direction, but her nose began to twitch and she stood up on her toes once again. She smiled and moved forward. This time something else had caught her attention.

The aroma of freshly baked sweets filled the air, and she pushed through the crowd. All thoughts of the lace or of some mysterious people following her faded to the back of her mind. Squeezing between two large men she finally spied the source of this delicious smell.

I need to have one.

She fished in her pocket for a few coins and thrust them into the hands of the baker. It would be a quick diversion, and then she'd be off to watch her brother, Cole, practicing his sword.

As she stuffed the sweet roll into her mouth, she glanced around the marketplace, still feeling that someone was perhaps following her. Nothing was obvious at the moment so as she continued through the marketplace she thought about her brother.

Cole was almost two years older than her own fifteen years, and though they did have similar blue eyes and slightly upswept brows, nothing else was the same. Shaeleen had smooth brown hair, while Cole had black shaggy hair. She was short and thin, but he was tall and broad-shouldered. She was fun-loving and carefree, while he was more quiet and thoughtful and had an impeccable track record of doing what was right and obeying the rules: something Shaeleen found quite boring.

But, with all their differences, she loved Cole fiercely and looked up to him. It was she that had talked him into competing this year, which he would've never done on his own.

Reaching the edge of the crowd, someone with a dark hooded cloak - similar to what she had seen moments before, came from Shaeleen's left and fell down on the ground in front of her.

"Are you hurt?" Shaeleen asked, kneeling down to offer help.

The person shook their head and peered up at Shaeleen, the hood sliding back. Shaeleen gasped and put her hand over her mouth.

"Don't be afraid," the old woman said in a quiet voice. Her long, white hair hung straight around her slender face, and she peered hard at Shaeleen. But it was the woman's upswept ears and pale blue eyes—a similar eye color to her own and her brother's—that clued Shaeleen in on the woman's heritage. A heritage that Shaeleen had always wondered if she and her brother shared with those from Verlyn—though mixed and weak it would have to have been. Only her eye color was similar to the woman's, but that was enough to stick out in a nation with predominately brown and green eyes.

The woman was obviously not from the kingdom of Gelena but from Verlyn, an island off the southeast coast of the continent of Wayland. An island where the descendants of elves lived and, if believed, where the magic in Wayland had originated.

Shaeleen's heart pounded. She'd seen the people of Verlyn from a distance before, but they were usually aloof. The woman's face held wrinkles that had been chiseled into her delicate features over many years. She lifted up a gnarled hand toward Shaeleen's cheek, and it took all Shaeleen's will to not move away.

"What are you doing in the market today, my dear?" the old woman asked, stopping her hand just short from actually touching Shaeleen.

"Buying lace for my mother, ma'am," Shaeleen said, instantly suspicious of the woman.

As a man came running up next to them, the woman cleared her voice loudly and seemed annoyed. He moved more quickly than Shaeleen had thought should be possible. The power of speed came from Antioch, but the man didn't look like he was from there.

"Keeper," the man said to the woman. His long, brown hair hung down loosely over his brown leather vest and dark green shirt. Next to his leather pants hung a silver sword, on which his hand rested. His blue eyes continued to roam the marketplace.

"We need to leave," he added. "They have followed us here."

The woman looked up at the man then returned her attention to Shaeleen. "I do not see any lace with you, child. Are you sure that is where you were going?"

Shaeleen blushed and felt guilty at lying, something that had lately become easy to do to her father and mother. Without admitting her guilt, she changed the subject by saying, "Let me help you up."

The woman brought her other hand out from behind her back and placed it in Shaeleen's outstretched hand to accept the help. As she did so, the woman pushed something into Shaeleen's palm.

Once standing, the woman brought Shaeleen's hands together, wrapping both of her own wrinkled hands around Shaeleen's, squeezing them tight around the object. A soft, green light appeared around the edges of their hands, and something strange and peculiar raced through Shaeleen's body, increasing her heart rate and stimulating her mind.

"What are you doing?" Shaeleen said as she tried to pull her hands free. But the woman held strong and looked Shaeleen in the eye.

"Take it," she said, her voice hoarse and low. "You are the one to save all the stones. Their magic is fading. You have been prophesied."

The man with the sword moved to grab the old woman's elbow. "Keeper Melindra, we must leave!"

Melindra turned to the man. "We have a few more moments, Galen. You just watch out for trouble."

Shaeleen couldn't follow what was going on. What had the man called the woman again?

A keeper!

The only keeper Shaeleen knew about was the keeper of stones from her history books. Shaking her head, she couldn't believe this crazy woman was one of *those* keepers. But the woman was from Verlyn, so something was going on that Shaeleen couldn't quite figure out.

A sound in the crowd alerted Shaeleen, and she turned to look. Through the swarming shoppers in the marketplace, she saw three men approaching. They had the same slender builds and facial features as Melindra and Galen. Shaeleen had never seen so many from Verlyn traveling together before.

The three men were turning their heads from left to right, glancing down each row of vendors, searching for something—or someone. Shaeleen took a step back as she realized they must be searching for Melindra.

The old woman followed Shaeleen's eyes and then seemed to stiffen. "Go," she croaked. "Don't let them see you."

"But..." Shaeleen tried to speak. Then she felt something in her hand. She had almost forgotten that the woman had given her something. She slowly opened her fingers and found herself looking at a small, green stone. It was beautiful and sparkled in the sunlight, holding her transfixed for a moment. This couldn't be what she thought it was. That wasn't possible.

She turned, to give it back to the woman, for she couldn't accept such a gift, especially from a stranger. But, by the size of it—a little smaller than a chicken egg—she'd guess that her entire family could live forever on its worth, and its value was worth much more than gold or silver if it was indeed what she thought it was. Shaeleen's mind raced momentarily with the possibilities of wealth it would bring if she could sell it.

But she finally shoved the stone back toward the woman. The old woman pushed Shaeleen's hand away.

"It is yours now, but not for the riches."

How could the woman know what I had been thinking?

"I..." Shaeleen tried to speak but felt a tightening of her chest.

"Don't deny it, child," Melindra said sternly. "Those types of thoughts will only cause you pain."

This is crazy. Why did she give me this gemstone? This is...

"Moldavite, a TruthStone," Shaeleen whispered.

"Hush, child. You don't want people hearing that, do you?"

All Shaeleen could do was shake her head. Once again she asked herself, *Why is the keeper giving me a TruthStone?* Only one TruthStone was given to each kingdom—over two hundred years ago. How could there be another?

"What is your name, child?" the woman asked.

"Shaeleen," she said, glancing from the stone to Melindra and then over at the approaching men once more. They were closing in but still hadn't seen Melindra. And they would be upon them in less than a minute.

"Well, Shaeleen, you now have a life ahead of you that you had never supposed. Be careful. Be true. And don't doubt yourself. Kings and queens will clamor for your attention, and lords and ladies will want to be your friends. You will know the ones to trust."

Shaeleen shook her head. *No. No.* The nobility paid her little attention. She was only the daughter of a carpenter, a father she loved dearly, but one that surely wasn't a lord. Glancing into Melindra's eyes confirmed the truth to her: it was a TruthStone she held in her hand.

"How?" Shaeleen whispered out loud. Then she covered her mouth. The three men were only a dozen feet away by now. If they turned their heads only slightly, they would see Melindra and Shaeleen.

"Go!" Melindra said. "Go quickly, and keep it hidden for now. You must also gather what is left of the others." Melindra then pulled a small package out of her dress pocket and shoved it into Shaeleen's other hand. "These men would kill you for the truths you now hold."

Once again Shaeleen knew Melindra spoke the truth. She turned around and took a few steps into the crowd, away from Melindra and her guard, Galen. Before she could disappear into the crowd, Shaeleen turned back and watched as one of the men grabbed Melindra.

"Where is the package, Melindra?" she heard one of the men ask as he roughly checked for it on Melindra's body. A small wisp of blackness seemed to hover over the man's hand.

"It is gone," Melindra said without looking in Shaeleen's direction.

The other two men spread out into the crowd, looking for what Melindra had just given to her. For once Shaeleen was glad she was short. She peered back through the crowd, and as a woman and her son moved to the side, Shaeleen caught Melindra's eye one last time. Her look seemed to hold compassion and understanding. Then she twitched her head, ever so vaguely, as if telling Shaeleen to run.

And so she did. Crouching low, Shaeleen ran through the marketplace crowd as fast as her young legs would carry her. Holding up her skirt with one hand and holding the gemstone and small package in the other, Shaeleen swerved in and out between merchants and shoppers alike. As she did so, she overheard snippets of their conversations.

"I'll give you two silvers for that," a shopper said to a vendor. "It's all I have."

Shaeleen was hit by a gut-wrenching pain, and she knew the shopper was lying.

"This fruit was just picked yesterday," another vendor said. "It's as fresh as can be."

Once again Shaeleen recognized the lie.

What's happening to me? Tears filled her eyes, and her breathing quickened, for she didn't want to know when other people were lying or not.

She finally emerged from the marketplace and found herself in a twisting alley between two old stone buildings, just outside of the practice yard. She stopped to catch her breath.

Putting the gemstone in a pocket of her blue, homespun dress, she gazed down at the package, barely the size of her hand, a dirty brown cloth tied around something harder inside. She turned it over and around a few times, moving her hands around the bundle. It felt like a book.

Shaeleen heard the sounds of raised voices and clashing steel from the practice yard and took a few steps in that direction. Glancing behind herself, to make sure no one was following, she put the package in a large pocket along with the stone. She felt bad for leaving Melindra like she had, but the woman had been insistent.

She continued walking with quick steps toward the practice yard. Maybe she wasn't too late to see her brother practicing. As she moved ahead, she slid her hand into the large pocket and felt the gemstone once again. It was cool to her touch.

A TruthStone? How could it be?

CHAPTER TWO

A short time later, Shaeleen climbed up the stone steps to a little-used balcony overlooking the practice yard outside of the castle gates. Nobles and commoners alike were practicing today in preparation for the upcoming tournament.

Holding her hand over her eyes to shield them from the sun, Shaeleen scanned the yard for her brother. Finally, she spotted him toward the back. He was sparring with another young man, who seemed about his same age and height, but with much finer clothes on. Both had dark hair, though Cole's was a bit longer and shaggier.

The yard held about fifty young men, with a few older gentlemen walking amongst them and giving them pointers. One older man stood with his arms crossed as he watched Shaeleen's brother sparring. The older man was nodding his head in approval, but Shaeleen didn't know if it was for her brother or for the one he was sparring with.

Both were of equal talent, it seemed, which said a lot for the other young man, as Cole at only seventeen had a natural affinity for weapons of all kinds. The two seemed to be moving in a similar fashion, as if calculating each other's next move before it was taken, but at a speed of thinking that was astonishing to Shaeleen. Back and forth they dueled, faster and faster, turning this way and that. Up high, down low. Sweat poured down the two young men's faces.

During the duel, Shaeleen moved around the balcony, closer to her brother. A few other onlookers—all young men— scowled at her but said nothing. Soon she stood merely twenty feet above him.

In a flash, the other young man moved more quickly than Cole and brought his sword up toward Cole's chest. Shaeleen's hand went to her mouth as her brother seemed to stumble back. But then she smiled at this ruse, for her brother had pretended to lose ground, only to come back at the last possible moment and bring up his practice sword inside of his opponent's, knocking it out of his hand.

She wanted to yell out praise to her brother, but she stopped short just as his opponent turned—Prince Basil, the heir to the throne of Galena!

Shaeleen gasped out loud, and all three men turned and glanced up in her direction. Shrinking back behind a column, she hoped they hadn't seen her there, for it was not proper for a young woman to watch the young men practicing. She peered again around the column slowly. The older man was congratulating her brother, then turned and had a few words with his opponent.

The young prince would soon be seventeen—and upon that day would become king in his own right, his father having passed away five years previously. Prince Basil's uncle, the current regent, would step down then. And, if rumor held true, the prince would also announce his betrothal then to a princess from one of the other nearby kingdoms, thereby creating a stronger alliance.

The prince continued to smile while talking to Cole and the older man. His dark eyes sparkled with strong intelligence. He pushed his black hair out of his eyes, and Shaeleen noticed a dimple on his right cheek. The prince was talked about favorably in Galena.

As Prince Basil turned toward Cole, his eyes flicked upward and found Shaeleen's. He held them for a mere moment, gave a twitch of a smile, then spoke to her brother.

"You are a fine swordsman, sir," the prince said. "We need good men like you in the Stronghaven Guard. When you are eighteen, come and see me."

Shaeleen smiled. Her heart lifted, and she felt the truth of the prince's words. She was happy for her brother. This was what their parents had wanted for Cole. They would be overjoyed to hear the news. Looking down at her hand, she realized she was holding the stone once again.

Cole bowed his head to Basil, his face serious, showing little emotion. "Thank you, Prince Basil. I was lucky today, that's all."

As Shaeleen felt the wrongness of her brother's words, her chest tightened and her stomach turned. *This will not do.* Pushing the stone back into her pocket, she shook her head, trying to clear away its effects on her. Cole must be lying in telling the prince he was only lucky today. It was a small lie, though, the kind she told to her mother and father all the time.

Why would such small lies cause me so much pain? They are just part of life, aren't they?

Her brother had walked off the practice field and now stood to the side, cooling down. He cupped his hands in a barrel of water and brought some up to his mouth.

"Cole," Shaeleen whispered from up above on the balcony.

Cole surveyed the practice yard around him and then looked upward. His mouth turned down, and his eyes darkened. "Shae, what are you doing here? You know Father does not like you sneaking around. And it's not proper anyways."

Before Shaeleen could answer, a young noble caught Cole looking up at her.

He pointed and said, "Hey, you there, girl, what are you doing here?"

Shaeleen tried to move back, into the shadows, but others had followed the young noble's pointed finger, and too many eyes were now looking her way.

"Get down from there," the young noble said, a frown creasing his forehead under his blond bangs. "No girls allowed."

"I was lost, sir," Shaeleen said. Then she grimaced in pain. It was all she could do to keep herself standing straight. *The stupid stone! I can't even lie myself without feeling pain.* She wasn't even holding it this time. She wanted to take it out and throw it down at the noble.

Cole turned to the noble, with his hands out wide, and said, "I'm sorry, sir. It is my sister. She likes to watch me practice."

Shaeleen nodded at Cole's admission, glad that he hadn't lied about this.

"Well, take her away from here, and make sure she doesn't return," the noble said. "Next time, she will be fined or put to work."

"Yes, sir," Cole said as he motioned Shaeleen down with a crooking of his finger.

He met her at the bottom of the steps. Pushing his hair out of the way, his light blue eyes smoldered in her direction.

"What are we going to do with you, little sister?"

Shaeleen smiled sweetly, shrugged her shoulders, and then broke into a laugh. "I saw you sparring with the prince. You did well."

"I did, didn't I?" Cole said, the small twitch of a smile forming at the corners of his mouth. Shaeleen knew he couldn't stay mad at her for long. "But I do think he was holding back."

Shaeleen braced herself for the pain, but it didn't come. Was the prince actually better than her brother? The power of intelligence ran through the royal family in Galena more than strength.

"That is something he would do, isn't it?" Shaeleen said. "I have heard he doesn't like to hurt anyone's feelings."

Cole nodded and motioned Shaeleen forward, away from the practice yard. "If he is as smart and kind as they say he is, he will make a good king—not like his twin brother, Calix."

Shaeleen nodded. She pulled Cole back to the marketplace and toward the shop to buy the lace—she couldn't forget what she had told her father she came here for.

"I have heard that Calix beats his servants and would like nothing more than to be the king instead of his brother."

Cole's face darkened. "I'm glad, then, that Prince Basil was born first."

Shaeleen yelled out in pain and fell to the ground. Her gut retched, but she did all she could to not throw up the sweet roll she'd eaten earlier.

Cole dropped to the ground next to her, concern written all over his face. "Shae, what's wrong? Are you all right?"

A few shoppers turned in their direction, but most continued walking on when they saw that Cole was helping her. One young girl stood and stared at them a few moments longer, but then her mother pulled her back into the crowd.

Shaeleen stayed silent for a moment, trying to figure out what had happened. Her stomachache had subsided, but a dull ache now lingered in her head. Her brother had been talking about the two princes, and something he'd said had triggered the pain. So her brother had lied about something—whether intentionally or not—and, knowing her brother as she did, it would not have been on purpose.

"Stupid stone," Shaeleen muttered under her breath.

"What did you say?" Cole asked, still down on his knees next to her.

"Nothing." Shaeleen shook her head and tried to stand back up.

Cole put his hand under her arm and helped her to stand up. She smiled weakly at him, but his eyes continued to show worry.

"I'm fine," Shaeleen told her brother. Then something caught her attention. Out of the corner of her eye, she saw one of the men that had been looking for Melindra still lingering around the marketplace.

"Quick. We need to go." Shaeleen grabbed Cole's hand and pulled him away from that stranger from Verlyn.

"Shae, what has gotten into you?" Cole asked as he tried to pull his hand away from hers. "You're acting strange—well, stranger than usual. Slow down."

Shaeleen continued to pull her brother through the crowd and away from the marketplace. Soon they found themselves on a smaller street leading from the marketplace to the merchants' quarter. Their shoes slapped against the cobblestones as men and women alike turned to look at the two young people running down the street.

Turning a corner, Shaeleen ran into a couple, a man and a woman dressed in fine clothes, who were arguing as Shaeleen plowed into them. The man put a hand out, against the side of a building, to keep from falling over. But the woman fell to the ground, her wide silk skirts tearing on the rough ground. Shaeleen jumped and barely avoided falling on the woman. And Cole pulled his hand away from Shaeleen's and stepped to the side.

"I'm—I'm sorry," Shaeleen stuttered after she had found her balance. She leaned down to help the woman up. The woman had tears in her eyes as she stood up, smoothed down her skirt, and then adjusted her blouse.

"See what you did?" the man said to Shaeleen and Cole. "You have made my lady cry."

Shaeleen's gut tightened up again. "I wasn't the one making her cry. That was you."

The man glared at Shaeleen. "How dare you?"

Cole walked up next to Shaeleen and said, "Let's go, Shae." Turning to the man, he said, "We are sorry. My sister was in a hurry." He dug a few coins out of a satchel at his side and offered it to the woman. "Please accept our apology for ruining your dress."

Shaeleen didn't move to go with her brother but turned to the woman. "Are you all right? Did he hurt you?"

"Shae!" Cole said. Then he whispered to Shaeleen, "Let's go. This is none of our business."

"He's right," the man said. "This is none of your business. Go home." He then reached over and grabbed the woman's hand. "My fiancée and I are quite fine."

Shaeleen felt the effects of a lie once again and tried to control the pain. Through gritted teeth, she said, "She is not your fiancée, and she is not *fine*." Turning back to the woman, she continued, "This man is a liar, ma'am. You would be better off without him."

The man jumped forward to stand in front of the woman, facing Shaeleen. His eyes bulged with anger, and she could smell strong drink on his breath.

"Shae!" Cole said again and grabbed her hand to pull her away. But she stood her ground for a moment and then let Cole pull her away. As they left down the street, she could hear the woman telling the man to leave her alone and that their relationship was over.

Shaeleen and Cole walked in silence another block. His shoulders seemed tight, and his eyes were dark. But he did not let go of her hand. Finally, she pulled it free and put it up to her head. The pain was killing her. Her head was pounding so loudly she wondered how Cole couldn't hear it too.

"What has gotten into you, Shaeleen?" Cole turned his head to the side and peered down at her. He stood about ten inches taller than her and had seemed to grow an inch a month for the past few months. He was now six feet tall, the same height as their father.

"Just don't say anything," Shaeleen said. "Don't talk. I can't handle it right now." Tears filled her eyes as she stomped ahead of her brother.

She couldn't live like this: every time someone lied—including herself—she felt pain. What kind of life was that? Everyone lied. It was how life was. You lied about how someone looked in new clothes. You lied when you were asked if you'd been hurt. You lied when haggling over prices for goods at the marketplace.

"You're crazy," Cole mumbled from behind her.

CHAPTER THREE

A few streets later, after continuing to walk in silence, the two siblings came to their home in the merchants' quarter. Their two-story home was made of stone and held a woodworking shop in the back. Their father had done well for himself in recent years. And he had been gaining recognition more recently for his skills as a carpenter in making custom furniture.

Shaeleen and Cole walked through the side gate and toward the back door. Their father was outside, planing a long board. He stopped and followed the pair with his eyes for a moment. Shaeleen tried to ignore him and headed toward the house.

"How did you two end up together?" Their father stopped his work and stood up, stretching his lean body. He wore a long, burlap apron over his serviceable cotton clothes. And his dark brown hair was full of sawdust.

Shaeleen groaned inside. In the last hour, she had learned to regret questions. She opened her mouth to tell her father that she had found Cole on the road home. But her brother seemed to have other ideas.

"She came to watch me practice," Cole said.

"Shaeleen!" her father called out and took a few steps forward.

Shaeleen turned to Cole, narrowing her eyes in anger. But at least she hadn't felt any pain. She cocked her head at her brother, but he shook his head at her as if to tell her to be quiet.

"I do better when Shae is watching me. She helps me to know my weaknesses," Cole said, stepping in front of Shaeleen. "She isn't feeling well now. She almost fainted in the marketplace. She needs to lie down."

Their father stopped mid-stride and glared from Cole to Shaeleen. Shaeleen opened her mouth again to speak but stopped as she realized that none of Cole's words had caused her any pain. He had explained everything in a way that was true.

She turned her head to look up at him. "Thank you, Cole," Shaeleen said, more for his foresight to not lie than for helping her get home. Turning back to her father, she said, "I do have a horrible stomachache and headache, Father. It could be the heat, I suppose."

Pain! She couldn't help her lies. She leaned over and grunted. So her father and Cole moved to her sides.

"Let's get her in the house," their father said to Cole. "You're right. She doesn't look well."

"I'll be fine," Shaeleen said. Then she pulled away from her father and brother and raced to her room—a room she shared with her younger sister, Alva, who was not there at the moment, luckily. She slammed the door, sat down on the edge of her bed, and then sobbed.

Shaeleen berated herself for lying again. She knew full well where the pain had been coming from. How had Cole told the truth so easily? Come to think of it, her brother *was* the more truthful one between the two of them.

Maybe he should have the stupid stone!

Shaeleen withdrew the stone from her pocket and threw it against the wall, chipping a piece of wood off and into the air. A light green glow came from the stone as it rested on the floor. She let it sit there, for she hated the way it had made her feel.

Scooting back, to lay her head against the wall, she felt something hard in her pocket. *The package*. She had forgotten about it. After having experienced the effects of the stone, she was hesitant to look at anything else the keeper had given her. But she untied the white string and slowly removed the brown cloth.

Inside was a small book. It appeared to be ancient, its leather cover cracked and fading. She ran her fingers over the cover and took a deep breath. Then she opened the cover and began to read the first page. The book was entitled *TruthSeers' Journal*.

As she flipped through the first few pages, she wondered what was happening to her life. She'd been perfectly happy just helping her mother out at home, being with her friends, and watching Cole practice with the sword. Anger welled up inside of her, and she brushed away a few stray tears.

Then she came to a chapter entitled *The Founding of Wayland*. Everyone knew that story. They had learned it early in school. King Wayland had had five children: two daughters and three sons. He had split up the continent between them and had given them each rule of one land—Shema and Althea to the two daughters and Gabor, Antioch, and Galena to the three sons. Each was also given a gemstone from Verlyn that was endowed with its own special magic.

Shaeleen tossed the book aside without turning any farther into its pages. It landed on the floor, its cover facing up. *TruthSeers' Journal.* She shook her head at the idiocy of it all. Could *she* be a TruthSeer? It seemed ridiculous—only one Truthseer per kingdom existed.

A soft knock sounded on her door and in walked her brother. She tried to kick the book away, into a corner.

"Shae, what do you have there?" Cole asked as he took a step toward her. Then he turned his attention to the wall.

Shaeleen cringed and jumped off the bed, diving for the TruthStone she had left so carelessly on the floor. She scooped it up and closed her fingers around it.

"Shae?" Cole's eyes went wide.

Shaeleen ran around him and closed her door with a bang, moving a chair behind it to make sure no one else could come in. Then she turned and glared at her brother, almost daring him to say anything else. When he stayed quiet, she huffed and sat back down on the bed.

"Why did you tell Father?" Shaeleen asked.

"I had to, Shae. It was the right thing to do and the only way to protect you." Cole walked closer and sat down on the edge of a small table next to the bed. "It worked, didn't it?"

"But how did you know?"

"I'm not dumb, Shae." Cole glared at her. "You know I can figure out things rather quickly."

Shaeleen grunted. "You definitely have some of the noble intelligence in you. Are you sure you're not hiding any Labradorite anywhere?"

Cole shook his head. "You know I don't have any. I'm not a noble. But you…" He stared hard at her hand. "You do have something there, don't you?"

Shaeleen opened her hand slowly. "Something that has only brought me trouble since the old woman gave it to me."

Cole started to reach his hand toward it but then pulled it back. "Is it…?"

Shaeleen nodded her head and then said in a quiet whisper, "Yes, Cole, it's Moldavite, a TruthStone."

"That's why you were hurting every time you heard or told a lie?"

Tears welled up in Shaeleen's eyes, and she brushed them away. "Oh, Cole, what am I supposed to do? You know me. I don't tell the truth very well. Maybe you should be the one to have it."

Cole stood up and shook his head. "Oh, no, Shaeleen. You have been given a great gift. Each kingdom has handed out bits of their gemstones for two hundred years, so magic abilities can pop up almost anywhere nowadays. But the TruthStone—there are only five of them, one for each kingdom. Whose do you have? And how did you get it? We have to tell Father."

Shaeleen closed her fist and put the gemstone in her pocket. As much as she hated the thing, she couldn't give it up—at least not yet. She needed to find out more about it.

"You can't tell anyone, Cole. No one, not even Father. Please," Shaeleen begged. "This isn't one of the five."

Cole rubbed his forehead with his fingers. "How do you get yourself into these messes, Shae? Can't you just leave things alone?"

"I didn't go looking for this, Cole." Shaeleen stood up, planting her hands on her hips. "She found me, a keeper from Verlyn, and she made me take it and told me I had to save all the other stones. Until I find out what that means and how to do it, you must tell no one."

Cole paced the room. "But, Shae…"

"No, Cole. Promise me," Shaeleen said. "Your honor can take this one hit…for me." She dropped her hands to her sides and lowered her head. "For me?" she asked, the words softer this time. Raising her head up, she met her brother's eyes. She knew her own were filling with tears once again. "Please honor my will this time."

Cole seemed to go through a quick internal argument. Then he eventually nodded his head once. "For now, I will, Shae. For now. But, if you are in danger or get into trouble, let me help you."

Shaeleen smiled up at her brother. "Thank you, Cole. You are a good brother."

Cole's lips curled up into a crooked smile. "You might need more than a good brother to get through this mess, Sister."

CHAPTER FOUR

"Shaeleen!"

Hearing her father shouting her name from his carpentry shop, Shaeleen closed the small book on her lap and let out a puff of breath into the warm morning air. The late spring was quickly turning toward summer so to stay cool she had been sitting under a sizable pine tree a hundred feet or so behind their home.

Shaeleen wrapped the book up and put it into a pocket inside her homemade yellow cotton dress, wondering, *What does he want?* For it was only the day after her confrontation with her father and her conversation with Cole.

She had just been reading about the history of the gemstones, much of which she already knew. But bits and pieces had added new light to her meager education. She couldn't bring herself yet to turn to the journal section in the back of the book. That was still too much to think about.

"Coming, Father!" she yelled out so he would know she'd heard him. He was a fair father, but not very patient when he wanted something.

As she entered the back of his shop, a small smile came to her lips. The scents of freshly shaved wood, varnish, and paint were as natural to her as the scent of the sea air, which surrounded the peninsula that Stronghaven sat at the end of.

Her father stood up from behind a newly finished bureau of drawers. The wood was exquisite in its shine, and the carvings at each corner were so detailed and delicate that Shaeleen knew it was one of her father's finest pieces yet.

"You've outdone yourself again, Father!" Shaeleen exclaimed. This was no false boast and therefore brought her no pain at all. Maybe learning to tell the truth would be refreshing.

Her father watched her with a brief look of concern. They hadn't spoken since the previous day, but he forgave easily. And his concern soon turned to appreciation at Shaeleen's words.

"I need your help today," he said. "This is the first commissioned piece for Lady Judith. I need you to go with me."

The words of Melindra came back to her—'Lords and ladies will want to be your friends'—and she groaned out loud.

"It won't be all that bad!" Her father laughed. "Afterward, we can take a walk on the shoreline and get a sweet roll for you."

Shaeleen laughed. "You know me all too well, Father." She did love something sweet. "I would be happy to go."

A twinge of pain throbbed in her temples at these last words. She turned to the side to keep her father from noticing. Well, maybe she wasn't all that happy to go, but she was willing. That should count for something, shouldn't it? Maybe that's why she was only feeling a minor pain in her head rather than the gut-wrenching heave in her stomach that she'd experienced the previous day.

"Go and tell your mother we're leaving."

Shaeleen ran into the house. But before seeing her mother, she went into her own room and shoved the book from her pocket into the back of her dresser drawer. She stopped for a moment and looked at the other wad of fabric there. *The TruthStone.* She reached her hand toward it and then stopped and glanced behind her. Finally, with little thought, she grabbed it and stuck it in her pocket. She didn't know why, but she felt drawn to have it with her. As she took it, she realized she had felt the pain of her own lie earlier, even without the TruthStone on her person. Was just being its owner enough to feel pain from lies? Either way, she felt better having it with her for now.

Shaeleen headed to the kitchen, where her mother, Gleda, and her younger sister, Alva, were making bread. She smiled at the two. They were so alike. Her sister was thirteen and almost taller than Shaeleen. Her coloring—a little darker than Shaeleen's—took more after their mother's. They seemed happy making bread—something Shaeleen had found quite boring and tedious.

"I'm going with Father to deliver furniture to Lady Judith," Shaeleen informed them.

Her mother looked up and smiled. "This is a big opportunity for your father. If this piece goes well, he will have made an inroad into the nobles' community: something he has been trying to do for years."

Alva turned to Shaeleen with flour speckling her face and apron. "Maybe you can befriend a noble's son, Shae." Alva's brown eyes sparkled as she laughed musically.

"Alva!" Shaeleen rolled her eyes. "Boy crazy at thirteen, are we?"

Alva blushed and got back to kneading her dough.

Shaeleen just laughed. But, as she stepped toward the door, the words of Melindra came to her mind once again. She stepped outside, frowning at the thought that she was being manipulated by the stone.

"Why the scowl, Daughter?" her father asked. He had brought the horse and wagon around back and was ready to load the piece of furniture.

"Nothing," Shaeleen said and then felt the familiar pain in her gut. But she had braced for it this time. Maybe that's what she would have to do—just get used to the pain—for her lies were only small and didn't hurt anyone.

She helped her father lift the furniture into the back of the wagon and then set blankets all around it before her father secured it with soft ropes so it wouldn't fall over. Then both of them climbed up on the seat, and they began the ride to the nobles' quarter. They waved at a few other merchants. Heading out with their own goods, a seamstress, a fuller, and an ironsmith joined them on the road that headed closer to the sea.

Soon she could see the white spires of the castle, reflecting the morning sunlight. The building was hundreds of years old and had been the ruling center of King Wayland's empire before he split it up for his children. Now it was the capital of Galena, a kingdom on the east side of Wayland, and people worked on the castle daily, keeping it bright and clean. It rose up six stories in the air, with the spires reaching even farther into the blue skies, and multiple balconies, walkways, and parapets stretched around its perimeter.

Shaeleen let out a breath of wonder.

"Someday you will see inside of it," her father said.

Shaeleen laughed. "That is doubtful, Father. What reason would the prince or regent ever have to meet me?" The old woman's words came back to her once again: *Kings and queens will clamor for your attention.*

"You're scowling again, Shaeleen," her father pointed out. "Seems to be happening a lot lately. Is something bothering you?"

Shaeleen was about to say no and deny that anything was bothering her. But she knew that, if she did, the pain would come once again. So, instead, she spoke the truth: "Just trying to figure out something."

"Well, let me know if you need any help," her father offered. "I've been through quite a bit in my life."

Shaeleen laughed. Her father had no idea what she was going through. *No one did.*

"I don't think you would understand," she mumbled back.

Soon the roads became smoother and the shops and homes nicer. Lawns began appearing inside fenced properties with oversized mansions settled back behind gardens and trees. Due to the sea air, most of the homes were a light color—white, yellow, or even a faint coral. The wagons that passed theirs held covered areas for the nobles to sit in. Some had drapes drawn closed; others enjoyed the morning sun shining through.

Soon her father slowed down in front of one of the larger estates. A guard stood at the entrance and asked their purpose.

Then they were directed to pull their wagon inside the property and down a smaller lane.

Shaeleen was mesmerized by the many bright spring flowers—highlighted by the round, purple allium blooms and crimson geraniums—and bushes cut into the shapes of dolphins and birds. She couldn't imagine anyone having so much wealth.

Pulling around to a side door, Shaeleen's father slowed the horses. When he and Shaeleen dismounted, they were met by a servant.

"The lady will attend you once the piece is inside," the man said. "It is quite too warm out here for her today."

Shaeleen knew that was a lie. Her head throbbed, but not badly. Lady Judith just wanted them to attend to her.

They took the furniture from the back of the cart and carried it carefully inside.

"In here, please," the servant said, directing them into a room almost as large as Shaeleen's family's entire home. It was a sitting room of some sort, filled with chairs and heirlooms, and had a beautifully constructed fireplace at its center.

Then the servant left to retrieve Lady Judith.

After waiting for about half an hour, Shaeleen finally stood up and started walking around the room, looking at artifacts and artwork that were more amazing than she had ever seen before.

"Shaeleen," her father whispered. "Sit down. Don't be snooping around."

"I'm not *snooping*. I'm admiring," Shaeleen said. "How can they afford all of this?"

Shaeleen's father shook his head and, with a laugh, said, "I don't know. But, if Lady Judith likes the piece, maybe we can drain some of this wealth from her and her friends."

As Shaeleen laughed with him, it felt good. She hadn't laughed much in the last day.

After another hour of waiting, the servant finally returned.

"I'm sorry for the wait, but Lady Judith has been detained on some business with her husband, Lord Gregory," the servant informed them.

Shaeleen felt a churning in her stomach, but different than before. The man wasn't lying, but there was more to it. She was sure he was holding back.

"Should we come back later?" Shaeleen's father asked.

The servant shook his head. "No. No. I don't think so. It shouldn't be much longer. I will have some food brought in for you."

"Thank you," her father said.

A few moments later, tea and biscuits were brought in for Shaeleen and her father. They ate in silence, for Shaeleen could tell her father was very nervous. This sale meant a lot to him.

Then Shaeleen could hear voices being raised, off somewhere in the house. She regarded her father, and he just shrugged.

After another long hour, the door opened again. It was the same servant. Shaeleen and her father stood, expecting to see Lady Judith behind him. But he was clearly frazzled and seemed not quite sure what to say.

Finally, he said, "Lady Judith sends her apologies, but—"

Before he could say anything else, a commotion ensued outside of the door.

"I've told you the truth, my dear," came a man's voice. "Have you told me the truth?"

These words made Shaeleen cringe, and the pounding started up again in her head. She tried to keep it from getting too bad.

A woman's voice followed: "Gregory, you are mad. I have not done anything wrong."

Then a man burst into the sitting room angrily. "Is this where you're hiding him?" Shaeleen stared at the man. *Is this Lord Gregory?* He was about ten years older than her father, but about three inches taller and at least a foot wider. He had graying hair and fleshy jowls, but exuded strength.

Coming up behind him with quick steps was the woman. *Probably Lady Judith.* Her hair was up, and she was dressed immaculately, in a deep green gown with a lighter green sash tied around her middle. Although she appeared to be about the same age as the man, the years had treated her much better than they had treated her husband.

Neither Lord Gregory nor Lady Judith seemed happy. And the woman's eyes were wet with tears. She stopped short in front of Shaeleen and her father.

"Is this him?" Lord Gregory said.

"Is this who, Gregory? What did you think this was?" Lady Judith snapped at him.

Shaeleen glanced back and forth between her father and the bickering couple. This was very awkward.

Shaeleen's father took a brave step forward and gave a short bow. "Sir and madam, I am Seth the carpenter. This is my daughter Shaeleen. We have brought the piece you commissioned, my lady."

Lord Gregory's eyes went wide, and his face reddened.

Lady Judith pointed toward the bureau drawers Seth had made and said, "This was to be a present for you, Gregory. Now I might just use it for firewood."

Shaeleen looked at her father. His face had turned as white as a ghost's, and he took an absentminded step toward his creation.

"L-Lady Judith," Seth implored with a slightly wavering stutter. "We can come back another day if that would be better."

"Another day won't make any difference, with my husband's dalliances. He has accused me of impropriety, when it is *he* that has been unfaithful."

Shaeleen doubled over and groaned. This was too much for her to handle. Too much in Lady Judith's statement had hurt her. *Too many lies.*

"What is wrong with her?" the woman asked Seth.

Her father moved to Shaeleen's side to see what was wrong. She took a few deep breaths and then stood up straight once again.

"I have done nothing wrong here," Lord Gregory said. "You accuse me falsely. It is you who has been untrue to me."

That was true. Shaeleen knew now that Lady Judith hid behind her own accusations. She realized the lack of pain in signifying the truth was as clear to her as the pain of a lie.

"I most definitely have not been unfaithful to you, Gregory," Lady Judith cried out.

Shaeleen almost fell over in agony, her father catching her just in time. She couldn't stand it anymore. "Stop it," she said. "Stop the lies. He is right. You have been unfaithful, Lady Judith."

All talking in the room stopped abruptly, and they all scrutinized Shaeleen.

She stared defiantly at the woman and then whispered, "It's true. Your husband is right, and you know it."

Lady Judith's eyes bulged wide, and spittle dripped out of a corner of her mouth as she said, "How dare you insult me in my own house. You have no right to interfere with our business. Out! Out of my house right now, and take that cursed piece of furniture with you."

Seth stepped forward and said, "My lady, I apologize for my daughter's outburst." He glared over at Shaeleen, disappointment and anger written all over his face. "Let me keep the piece here and return another day. You are correct: this is none of our business."

The woman turned to the servant and said, "Pay the man for the piece he has brought." Then, turning back to Shaeleen's father, she continued, "But don't bother returning. There will be no more business for you in my household or in any around mine. I will make sure of that."

The servant gave a purse of money to Shaeleen's father and then used his arms to shuffle the two of them toward the door. Passing by the woman, Shaeleen glanced up and was met with a feeling of vehement hatred. She couldn't find it in herself to apologize, but she did feel horrible for embarrassing her father. Before leaving the room, she also caught the eye of Lord Gregory. His face was harder to read. She thought there was a hint of relief and thankfulness there, but she wasn't sure.

Soon they were ushered out the back door and to their wagon. Climbing up next to her father on the seat, Shaeleen watched him grab the reins and give the command for the horses to move. Her father's jaw was set hard, and his eyes flamed with anger and disappointment for several minutes.

"Do you know what you have done to me?" he whispered about ten minutes later. His voice held such pain and hurt that Shaeleen couldn't bear to look at him.

She hung her head down and tried to control the ache in her gut. Tears filled her eyes, and she wiped them away angrily and berated herself for the earlier outburst. She got in trouble when she lied and when she told the truth. It didn't seem to matter.

Peeking out of the corner of her eyes, she saw her father's jaw begin to relax. The anger was subsiding—he was always quick to forgive. But did she deserve his forgiveness this time?

She would fix it somehow. She vowed she would.

CHAPTER FIVE

That night, Shaeleen sat in her room reading the *TruthSeers' Journal*. Alva had gone to sleep hours before, and the candle now burned low. There were some introductory notes about the gemstones themselves, but Shaeleen gave them only a perfunctory glance. She continued to turn the book's pages until she came to a section actually titled *TruthSeers' Journal*. With trepidation, she turned the page, wanting—and at the same time not really wanting—to read about the former TruthSeers.

Nothing was there. She turned a few pages more. But the entire rest of the book was blank!

What kind of book is this?

The TruthStone, which was in her pocket still, began to feel warm through her dress. She reached her hand in and pulled it out. A green glow spread out from the Moldavite stone and filled the room.

Alva squirmed around in bed and mumbled, "What are you doing, Shae?"

Shaeleen felt panic rising up within her, and she cupped her hand around the stone, to shield Alva from most of its light.

"Nothing to concern yourself with, Alva. Go back to sleep."

Alva mumbled again and then grew still.

Holding the stone in one hand and the book in the other, Shaeleen noticed faint writing appearing on what had seemed to be a blank page. She moved the stone closer, and the writing became more clear. So she flipped back to the first blank page and read it: *If you are reading these words, you are one of the rare holders of a TruthStone. For, to see these words, you had to have been given the stone freely by a keeper—and you are now named a TruthSeer.*

A TruthSeer? Shaeleen panicked. *No. No. Not me!*

Then Shaeleen felt a jolt of energy run from the stone into her hand and up her arm, spreading until it had expanded through all the corners of her body. This brought clarity of mind—the same feeling she had received when Melindra had first given her the stone—but now the feeling remained with her.

"Oh no," she groaned softly and dropped the stone on top of her blanket. The words on the page disappeared once again, and the stone's green glow diminished back to the normal dull shine of the Moldavite itself.

What have I gotten myself into this time?

Shaeleen wrapped back up the stone and the book, hiding them under her pillow, changed into her nightclothes, and then lay down to sleep. But sleep didn't come that easy. She tossed and turned as she thought about what being a TruthSeer actually meant. She eventually fell asleep, thinking about how her actions had caused her father trouble.

* * *

Early in the morning, as the sun peeked over the horizon, Shaeleen's eyes popped open, and she found that her hand was under her pillow, cradling the stone in her fingers. She knew now what she must do to fix the problem she had caused. She glanced over at her sister—who was still breathing deeply and would not be up for another hour. Shaeleen hoped no one else was up yet.

Quietly, she changed from her nightclothes into a tan cotton dress, tied her hair back into a ponytail, and slipped on a pair of serviceable brown shoes. Grabbing the TruthStone, she opened the door of her bedroom and looked around. She seemed to be up even before her father, something that was hard to do.

Before going to the front door, Shaeleen grabbed a muffin from the kitchen. Then she headed outside. Biting into the muffin, she wished it was sweeter. *I really do have a sweet tooth,* she realized with a smile.

It would take her a good half hour of walking to get through the city, though it wouldn't be crowded this time of day. As she walked closer to the shoreline, she noticed the early fishers already pushing off in their boats and preparing to cast their nets for the daily catch. The sun made her skin tingle, and beads of moisture formed on her brow, both letting her know it would be a warm and humid day.

Soon she came to the nobles' district. It wasn't like she wasn't supposed to be there, but she hugged the shadows anyway. It would not do for a lone girl to get caught, this early in the morning, traipsing through this part of town.

When the sun was shadowed briefly, she peered upward. It was directly behind the tallest spire of the castle, which sat on a small hill next to the shore a few blocks away. She tried to remember the way to Lady Judith's home, but she got turned around twice. Finally, she recognized the right street.

Coming to their driveway, Shaeleen noticed the gates were still closed. She growled softly. *I hadn't thought about that.* She continued walking and came around a corner of the estate. She stopped briefly to consider her options.

Suddenly, she heard, "There you are," and an older woman came up from behind her, adding, in her high-pitched voice, "Why are you dawdling around here? Get inside now."

"Inside?" Shaeleen asked as she turned around. She didn't know what this old woman was talking about. *Am I in trouble?*

The old woman clicked her tongue and smoothed down the gray bun on the top of her head. "Aren't you here to help with the party preparations today?"

Party? Shaeleen smiled at her good fortune and said, "Sure. Sure I am." Then she bowed over with pain. *Stupid lies!*

A brief look of concern crossed the old woman's face at seeing Shaeleen's obvious pain. Then she went back to her stern look. "I don't care if you are sick or not. I need the help."

The old woman led her to a back gate, through the grounds of the estate, and into a back door of the mansion. Shaeleen pushed down the pain and stood gawking again at the wondrous riches of the home.

"In here." The old woman motioned for Shaeleen to follow her again. Soon they came to a large dining room.

"Wow!" Shaeleen gasped. The room's outside wall alternated between high windows and decorated tapestries. The dark polished table must have been at least thirty feet long. And red velvet, high-backed, cushioned chairs sat around its perimeter.

"Stop gawking, and start working," the old woman said. "Lady Judith is not paying you to stand around here."

Shaeleen laughed inside. They had mistaken her for another, but this would be fun.

The old woman showed Shaeleen where all the dishes were, and Shaeleen went about the task of setting the table. But the old woman said she would check on her periodically.

Once she did, Shaeleen asked her a question: "What is the occasion, ma'am?"

"It is Lord Gregory's birthday, and Lady Judith wants a surprise dinner party for him. He is away on business this morning."

Shaeleen was surprised that, after yesterday's events, a party was still in order. She cringed inside at the mess she had made of things and then asked, "The party is still on?"

The old woman stared at her suspiciously. "Why do you ask?"

Shaeleen shrugged. She couldn't lie without feeling pain, but she could say nothing.

The old woman walked closer to her and grabbed Shaeleen's arms with both of her own hands. "What have you heard?"

"Nothing," Shaeleen tried to say but was racked with pain once again. She was able to stay standing ,though, and just had to close her eyes for a moment. Then she corrected herself by adding, "I just heard there was some trouble here yesterday."

"And where would you hear that from?" came a new voice from behind Shaeleen. It was Lady Judith's.

Shaeleen turned around and smiled, though she knew her smile was weak.

"Y-you!" Lady Judith stuttered. "What are you doing here?"

Shaeleen searched for the right words to say.

But Lady Judith didn't wait for a reply. "Alice, why did you let this troublemaker inside my home?" Lady Judith demanded, now turning her attention to the old woman.

Alice's face turned red. "I thought she was the help we'd hired for the party. There still is a party, isn't there?"

"And why wouldn't there be?" Lady Judith snapped. "I surely can't just disinvite all our important friends because of a spat, can I?"

Then Lady Judith reached her hand out, grabbed a hold of Shaeleen's arm, and pulled her away, saying, "I will have words with this one."

Shaeleen tried to think of what she could say as she was pulled into a smaller room. Lady Judith shut the door behind them, and Shaeleen looked up into her demanding eyes.

Shaeleen took a deep breath and plowed ahead, trying not to lie as she did so. "Lady Judith, I am sorry about what happened yesterday. Please don't punish my father. He is a good man and creates the best furniture in the city. Please give him another chance."

"And why should I?" Lady Judith asked.

Shaeleen searched for an answer but couldn't find one.

Lady Judith looked at her shrewdly. "How did you know about my…uh…*indiscretions* and that my husband was innocent?"

Shaeleen gulped. She couldn't tell the woman that she had a TruthStone or that she might be a TruthSeer. Shaeleen was still trying to figure out what that even meant.

"I…uh…I guess I am just good at reading people." Shaeleen braced for the pain, but it didn't come. *Curious*, she thought. Maybe she was good at reading people. She would have to think on that later.

Lady Judith squinted her eyes and pursed her lips—lips that were painted bright red. Shaeleen tried not to look away, but finally she did.

"You are right," Lady Judith said. "*Shaeleen*—isn't it?"

Shaeleen turned her face up and nodded. What was Shaeleen right about?

"Your father *is* one of the best furniture makers in the city, and it would be a waste to neglect his talents and not hire him for more work." Lady Judith smoothed her hands down over her full skirts of bright blue fabric.

Shaeleen let out a deep breath—which she hadn't realized she had been holding—and tried to smile as she bobbed her head at the woman and said, "Thank you, Lady Judith. I will go and tell him."

"Not so fast," Lady Judith said as Shaeleen began to turn away. "This favor I give does not come without a price."

"A price?" Shaeleen shifted back and forth on her feet. *What did the woman mean?*

"I want you at my party tonight," she said.

Shaeleen was confused by this.

Lady Judith continued, "I want you to tell me who is lying and who is telling the truth."

Shaeleen gasped. "I can't do that." A headache started forming at the base of her head and then spread upward.

"You *can't* or you *won't?*" Lady Judith asked, her hands on her hips, peering down like a hawk. "You do this for me, or I will destroy your father's business."

Shaeleen's heart pounded. She had never felt so afraid in her life. This woman was threatening her father's entire livelihood, his ability to take care of their family. Shaeleen had made a bigger mess of things, now, by coming back to Lady Judith's. *I should have left well enough alone.*

"Well?" Lady Judith said, waiting for her to answer.

Shaeleen felt the stone in her pocket. It was warm against her skin. She hoped it wouldn't flash green in front of Lady Judith. Then she did the only thing she could do.

"I will do as you ask." Shaeleen lowered her eyes to the ground for a moment. Then she let anger fill her, and she looked back up—her mouth tight and her eyes flashing—and said, "But you will make sure my father gets more business than he had ever thought possible. If you don't do this, then I will tell all your noble friends all your secrets."

Shaeleen's head throbbed faintly at saying that. She was pushing the truth. She didn't really know all of Lady Judith's secrets. It didn't work that way. She only knew whether people spoke the truth or not.

"Quite a bit of spunk in you, child." Lady Judith laughed out loud. "I like that in a young woman. We need more like you in Stronghaven. The men rule over too much as it is. Now, go home and at least try and find something appropriate to wear. It *is* a party for my lord husband, you know."

Shaeleen stood still for a moment, thinking.

"Off with you now!" Lady Judith waved her hand in the air. "And be back before dark."

Shaeleen said nothing more and was soon ushered out of the house, but not before she caught a glimpse of another young woman, working with the old woman in the house, the one that was supposed to have been there all along.

CHAPTER SIX

When Shaeleen arrived back home later that morning, her father demanded to know where she'd been.

Shaeleen smiled broadly. "I got your commission back for Lady Judith, and she has promised to tell all her friends about your talents."

Her father seemed at a loss for words.

But her brother, Cole, stood off to the side with a look of suspicion on his face. Pushing his dark hair out of his eyes, he walked closer to Shaeleen and their father.

"And why would she do that, Shae?" Cole asked.

Shaeleen paused to consider her words. She was getting better at not lying—or, at least, at hiding the lies among words that were technically true. "I told her how good father was and that she shouldn't punish him for what I did." *There—that didn't hurt at all.*

"And she just smiled and agreed to your reasoning?" her father asked, joining Cole in a suspicious look.

"Well," Shaeleen paused, trying to think of what to say. Then she smiled brightly. "On condition that I help her out at a party tonight for her husband."

Cole's eyes opened wide in surprise, but he stayed quiet.

Her father shook his head. "Shaeleen, I know there is something you're not telling me, but I do thank you."

Shaeleen let out a deep breath and then said, "I think you will find that she mentions you to a lot of her noble friends."

"If what you say is true, I better get to designing some new pieces." Her father left to go back to the shop.

Cole, however, walked up closer to her, grabbed Shaeleen's elbow, and led her farther back behind the shop. The day was growing warmer, and it was more humid among the grass and trees. Beads of sweat began to form on Shaeleen's brow.

"What are you up to, Shae?" Cole asked.

"Me?" Shaeleen asked, trying to look innocent. But this didn't work on her brother.

"Shae?"

As Cole stood immovable in front of her, she realized how tall he had grown lately and that his shoulders were more broad now. His face had thinned, and he was looking more like a man all the time.

"I can figure things out," Cole said. "You agreed to find out something for her about one of her noble friends, didn't you? Using your TruthStone or whatever it is."

Shaeleen was surprised at her brother's leap in logic. But that's how he always was. The Labradorite IntelligenceStone had been broken up so many times and spread throughout the kingdom of Galena in the last two hundred years that it was hard to find much in any one person. But her brother seemed to have a higher dose of Labradorite flowing through his veins than the rest of the common folk did. He also had extreme strength in and skill with the sword—a power that normally came from the kingdom of Gabor.

"She did invite me to help out at her party tonight," Shaeleen said. "That was not a lie. I just have to report to her afterward who was lying and whatnot. It's not a big deal, Cole."

"I don't think that is what the TruthStone is supposed to be used for, Shae." Cole's eyes squinted at her.

Cole and his desire to always do what was right... She was getting mad at his patronizing tone.

"How would you know what it should be used for? Have you ever had one?" Shaeleen said, deciding to tear into him. "Do you know the burden I carry or the pain I feel when others lie around me now?" She brushed sudden tears from her eyes and turned her head away.

They stood in silence for a moment.

Then Cole took a step toward her. "I'm sorry, Shae. I was being insensitive."

Shaeleen brought her head up slowly and smiled, blinking back her tears. "So, you *can* be wrong," Shaeleen teased.

"Wrong?" Cole raised his dark eyebrows. "I wasn't wrong. You shouldn't be messing with magic like this. But I should have tried to understand how you are feeling."

Shaeleen looked up at him. His light blue eyes stared back intently at her.

They had talked—numerous times in the past—about the color of their eyes and if that meant anything. Up until recently, it hadn't. But now it seemed that maybe it had been a sign to what might lie ahead.

"Then come with me tonight."

"What?" Cole seemed surprised. "How will that work?"

"I will inform Lady Judith that you are there to protect my honor in a strange home. She won't say no."

Cole scrunched up his lips, something he always did when deep in thought. "I accept. It will be interesting to see how the nobles act."

Shaeleen smiled at her brother, and he smiled back. She actually would feel a lot better with Cole there. In a room full of nobles, there was bound to be many lies—lies that would cause her pain.

* * *

Later that night, dressed in their best clothes, Shaeleen and Cole showed up early at Lady Judith's home. Shaeleen really didn't like wearing such a tight-fitting dress—cinched at the waist—but Cole looked dashing in his black trousers and blue tunic.

They announced themselves at the front gate, and then a servant met them at the front door.

"Lady Judith has informed me of your attendance tonight, Miss Shaeleen, but not that of another guest." The servant had to look up because of Cole's height.

"This is Cole, my brother, and he is here to protect my honor in a house I am not familiar with," Shaeleen said.

"This is the third time you have been in my home," came Lady Judith's voice from down the grand hall, and her footsteps echoed on the hardwood floors. A bright yellow, trumpet styled dress swirled around her as she walked—tight around her body and flaring out below her hips—and silver jewelry adorned her ears, neck, and wrists. Nobody would mistake who was in charge of this function or this home. "I would have thought by now you would feel comfortable." She stopped in front of Shaeleen and smiled wickedly. Then, turning to Cole, she ran a finger down the side of his cheek. "But he will add a fine look to the evening."

Cole blushed profusely but bowed ceremoniously to the woman. "I am pleased to be welcomed into your fine home, Lady Judith."

The woman clapped her hands in apparent joy and laughed. "Oh, Shaeleen, your brother is everything you aren't."

Cole's face turned dark.

But before he could say anything, Lady Judith waved a hand in the air and said, "I will uphold your sister's honor while she is in my home, Master Cole."

The servant then escorted Shaeleen and Cole to the ballroom. Tables were set up in the front third, and musicians practiced off in the corner, in front of a small dance floor. A chandelier with at least forty candles lit the room, with smaller lamps and chandeliers spread throughout. It was the largest room Shaeleen had ever been in—even larger than their church's chapel. Golden picture frames on the walls and artifacts on shelves shimmered while reflecting the bright candlelight.

The old woman that had put Shaeleen to work that morning approached the siblings. She frowned at Shaeleen before saying, "You two will keep the guests' glasses full. There is water, wine, and ale. No one goes thirsty tonight."

Shaeleen and Cole nodded their heads.

Soon guests began to arrive. As conversations started and Shaeleen and Cole began to make their way around the room, offering drinks on a tray, Shaeleen tuned in to snippets of the conversations around her.

A man in his forties—dressed in a blue jacket over a white, ruffled shirt—stood talking to another man a few years younger than himself. The second man sported a long mustache that drooped down at its edges.

Shaeleen had to bite her lip to keep from laughing because his mustache was kind of scraggly.

"The regent has promised me new trade routes," the first man said. "I'm going to ship goods from Gabor to Mistport, along the Myr River."

A slight headache came to Shaeleen as she refilled their glasses.

The second man frowned darkly. "That is Prince Calix's preferred route of trade. The regent doesn't have the right to do that."

"Regent Warin has consulted with Prince Basil—the young man will be king soon."

Suddenly, Shaeleen couldn't help but bend over as pain shot through her gut and up through her head. Her tray of glasses fell to the floor and shattered all around their feet.

The growing crowd quieted, all except for Lady Judith, who seemed to be by Shaeleen's side in mere moments.

"What have you done?" she whispered harshly to Shaeleen. "Are you here to embarrass me?"

Shaeleen straightened. Her face felt drained, but some of the pain had subsided. Cole ran up to put his arm around her.

"Shae, are you all right?" Cole asked. "What happened?"

Shaeleen looked at him and shook her head minutely, hoping her brother would get the hint. She couldn't explain in front of Lady Judith.

Soon a group of servants had cleaned up the mess, and then the crowd returned to their conversations.

"Nothing like that better happen again," Lady Judith warned Shaeleen in a stern voice. "Or," the woman added under her breath, "there is no deal."

Shaeleen understood what Lady Judith meant. She would have to steel her mind against the pain. She would need to learn to ignore it.

Someone on the other side of the room called for more drinks, and Cole turned to refill their glasses. Shaeleen glanced around the room for a moment. She couldn't listen to everyone. She had to focus on something. Off in a corner stood a group of men and women who seemed to be talking in conspiratorial tones, so she headed in their direction.

One woman said softly, "Prince Calix will make his move soon."

Shaeleen took her time getting drink glasses ready to bring over to the group.

A man in the group nodded and said, "He can count on my house. Prince Basil is too lenient to be king, but Prince Calix has our needs in mind. He will protect the nobles."

Shaeleen's head started pounding, so she knew Prince Calix would not protect anyone but himself. She pushed the pain aside and approached the group.

"Prince Basil will not know what happened until it's over," another man said, the oldest in the group. His gray hair was slicked back on his head, and he carried a cane with a golden handle.

Shaeleen recognized this man from descriptions she'd heard before. It was Bancroft, the minister of relations with Gabor. It was said that his ancestors hailed from the northern kingdom. Looking at the man again, Shaeleen could see strength in his body, despite his advanced age. The kingdom of Gabor had been given the Red Jasper StrengthStone at the same time Galena had been given its IntelligenceStone by King Wayland.

"Gabor will stand with Prince Calix?" asked another woman in the group, who was hanging on the arm of the first man that had spoken.

"Yes," the minister said. "Prince Calix can rely on the strength of Gabor to get him the throne of Galena."

Another lie. Shaeleen's gut turned sour this time. But she held herself straight and, during a brief silence in the conversation, poured them all fresh drinks.

Upon leaving, she heard the first man laugh and then say, "But what will we do with the regent?"

Shaeleen couldn't hear the answer. She had to get away from the lies of this group, lies that they sometimes didn't even know they were telling. But these people were openly planning to dispose of Prince Basil. She would have to tell Lady Judith about what she'd overheard.

Soon the guests were led to the tables, and then Lady Judith stood up, at the head table, with her husband, Lord Gregory, the current minister of defense under Regent Warin, the princes' uncle.

Lord Gregory was indeed a specimen of strength, and high intelligence shown from his dark eyes. He was wearing his blue military uniform, perfectly pressed and held firmly across his large body by his broad shoulders. But he didn't look happy to have everyone there for his birthday.

Once Shaeleen and Cole had walked around and filled any empty glasses, Lady Judith stood and raised her glass in the air. "I propose a toast. Today is my husband's fortieth birthday, and I couldn't be more happy."

A lie. But Shaeleen kept the pain concealed – but only barely. *I can't take much more!*

"Lord Gregory has worked tirelessly to defend our borders during the reign of our beloved regent," Lady Judith continued.

Shaeleen had taken a few steps back. She wiped beads of sweat from her forehead. Cole rapidly moved to her side.

"Are you all right?" Cole whispered as he leaned in.

"I'll be fine," Shaeleen said through gritted teeth. A battery of emotions and feelings swirled through her body. Some of what Lady Judith said next was definitely true, but some was sorely false. How could Shaeleen decipher all of it? She would have to tune out the rest of Lady Judith's words in order to maintain her own decorum.

Finally, the woman put her finishing touches on the toast and said, "So, I toast to my good husband…"

That part is true, Shaeleen thought. *He is a good man.*

"…and to our beloved regent…"Lady Judith continued.

Shaeleen's gut heaved with pain. *Lady Judith does not love the regent.*

"…and, finally, to our favorite prince, Prince Basil."

This final statement caused Shaeleen's vision to blacken as her stomach churned and her mind exploded with the implications of what she was hearing.

"I need to go," Shaeleen whispered to her brother.

Cole set down his tray of drinks and pulled her by the hand out into the kitchen. As they moved through the doorway, Shaeleen turned back and, above the raised glasses of the crowd, met Lady Judith's eyes. They sparkled with wicked betrayal—and a warning that Shaeleen better not go too far.

"Outside," she groaned to her brother, and Cole rushed her out a back door and down the walkway.

Shaeleen leaned over, with her hands on her knees, and vomited into some bushes behind the mansion. The pain in her head exploded, and she began to fall over. With the help of Cole, she sat down on the cobblestone walkway, but harder than she had intended to.

"Shae, Shae!" her brother said, sounding worried. "What happened in there?"

Shaeleen only shook her head, for she couldn't speak. Then she wrapped her hand around the stone in her dress pocket, and a green light enveloped her arm, running up to her neck, then to her head, down into her heart, and finally to her stomach. It felt cool and refreshing, washing away the pain she had felt.

Cole had scooted back a few feet but had stayed on the ground with her.

What must he be thinking?

Then noises came from the direction of the back door.

"Shae," Cole said, reaching his hand toward her glowing arm, but he stopped before he touched it. "Others are coming. You must stop."

Shaeleen didn't want to stop. The euphoria from the TruthStone was a blessing after the pain from the lies she had heard. But she knew Cole was right. If she was found glowing, who knew what trouble would ensue?

"All right," Shaeleen said to Cole, and she reluctantly let go of the stone. The green glow subsided just as three men came around the corner and past the bushes.

CHAPTER SEVEN

As Cole helped Shaeleen to stand back up, the three men gave them sly smiles, and one of them winked, a tall, skinny man, who looked like he had taken too much to drink himself.

"Having a little fun outside, I see," the man said. "Maybe you could share her a bit."

Cole was instantly in the man's face, his muscles tensed. "She is my sister, sir."

The man, half drunk, stepped back and put his hands up. "No need to get angry, young man. Just looking for some fun at this boring party."

Cole put his hand on the man's chest.

"Cole," Shaeleen said and put her hand on her brother's arm. "It's fine."

As Cole jerked his arm away and peered down at Shaeleen, the three men continued on their way.

"Your hand. It's freezing," Cole said.

Shaeleen shrugged. She couldn't tell and frankly didn't care at the moment. She was just glad the pain was gone.

Just then, a servant poked his head out the back door and beckoned them back inside to continue pouring drinks for people.

For the rest of the night, Shaeleen tried to stay away from hearing too many lies. She had heard enough minor lies to tell

Lady Judith those later on. Hopefully the woman wouldn't push for more.

Toward the end of the evening, Lady Judith pulled Shaeleen into another room. She sat down on a sturdy stuffed chair, spreading her skirts around her, and, with a glass of wine in her hand, commanded Shaeleen to tell her what she knew.

"Well, there were so many people it was hard to tell for sure," Shaeleen began and felt the stirrings of a small headache. She couldn't even lie to herself.

"Try," Lady Judith said.

"One of the men is cheating on his wife," Shaeleen said first. "He said he wasn't, but I know he was."

Lady Judith laughed. "Tell me something I don't know."

Shaeleen sifted through what she had heard. She definitely wasn't going to tell Lady Judith what she now knew about Prince Calix. She had heard something earlier that was interesting, though.

"I heard someone who works with Prince Basil say the prince is going to send someone off to bring his intended bride to him," Shaeleen said. "He also said the prince was going to Gabor, but that wasn't true."

"Yes. Continue." Lady Judith waved her hand in the air. Each finger was adorned with a jewel large enough to support Shaeleen's family for all of their lifetimes.

"Well," Shaeleen paused for a moment to gather her thoughts, "based on what wasn't said in the conversation, I think his wife may be coming from Verlyn." Lady Judith stood at hearing that news, but Shaeleen felt a small headache from what she had said.

This TruthStone is infuriating sometimes.

Shaeleen was finding that people may or may not choose to speak the truth, but then—on top of that—sometimes they thought they were speaking the truth, but it was still a lie. Those statements were the ones that were harder to decipher. The pain in her gut always came first, with a dreadful headache afterward—though the headache also came when someone, herself included, danced around the real truth.

Shaeleen was fairly certain the intended bride of Prince Basil was coming from Verlyn, but she had felt in her mind a difference between *intended bride* and *future wife*. However, she wasn't going to give Lady Judith any more information than she had to.

"And what else did you hear, my dear?" Lady Judith asked as she sat back down and motioned Shaeleen to sit on a smaller chair opposite her.

"She will be here for his seventeenth birthday," Shaeleen continued, "when the prince will announce the betrothal—and accept the crown of Galena."

Splitting headache once again. *What did I say wrong?*

Lady Judith tilted her head to the side. "Anything else?"

She seemed to be fishing to know if Shaeleen had overheard anything about Lady Judith's and her cronies' plan to betray Prince Basil. But Shaeleen wasn't going to share what she had heard about that.

"One of the ministers was telling a man who owns a large shipping company that the fish in Mistport are especially good this year. But it was a lie."

"Hmmm," Lady Judith mumbled. Then she stood and excused Shaeleen.

As Shaeleen reached the door, she turned around and blurted out, "And you don't really care for your husband—who is a good man, by the way."

"How dare you?!"

Shaeleen quickly turned and left the room before Lady Judith could yell at her. She couldn't help the small grin that formed on her face. She enjoyed goading the woman.

Going back into the ballroom, she found Cole, who seemed relieved to see her return. The number of guests had dwindled, and the few that were left were more than a little drunk.

"Let's go, Cole," Shaeleen said. "We're done here. I have kept my side of the bargain."

Cole nodded, and together they walked toward the kitchen. On the way there, they crossed paths with Lord Gregory, who eyed the two suspiciously.

"Happy birthday, sir," Shaeleen said with a curtsy. Cole joined in with a last-minute bow.

Lord Gregory looked from Shaeleen to Cole and back again. "You are the carpenter's daughter. What are you doing here?"

"I came to help your wife, as penance for not acting very nice the other day. I apologize to you also, my lord."

There, I can tell the truth and be nice.

Lord Gregory waved a hand in the air. "No need to apologize, young lady. And who is this?" Lord Gregory asked as he scrutinized Cole.

"This is my brother, Cole," Shaeleen said.

Cole extended his hand and shook Lord Gregory's with it. "My pleasure, sir."

Lord Gregory kept a hold of Cole's hand for a moment longer and seemed focused on Cole's eyes. "You are endowed with much power, young sir. I hope you intend to use it to protect the kingdom."

Cole stood straighter. "Yes, of course, sir."

"You could be a great addition to the king's council when you are older."

"I will always be willing to support the throne of Galena," Cole answered with pride in his voice and his eyes.

Then Lady Judith called from across the room, "Oh, Gregory, come bid our guests goodbye."

Lord Gregory let out a sigh and then looked embarrassed.

Before they parted ways, Shaeleen gave him a look intending to say that she understood. After taking a few steps, Shaeleen turned back around and called out, "Lord Gregory?"

The minister of defense turned.

"Guard the regent and the prince well," Shaeleen said in warning.

Lord Gregory frowned and took a step back toward Shaeleen, and she was sure he would have more questions.

"Gregory!" Lady Judith called out once again.

"Coming," Lord Gregory grunted.

That gave Shaeleen and Cole a chance to get away. Soon the two of them were out on the road leading back to their home. It was late and dark, but the warm night still brought sweat to their faces as they walked briskly toward home.

"So, what did you really learn tonight, Shaeleen?" Cole asked with a voice that brooked no argument.

Shaeleen sighed. Her brother was loyal to the crown and would not be happy with what she had to tell him.

"Prince Calix is planning on taking the throne," she said in summary.

Cole stopped walking for a moment and stared at her. "Is that what the warning to Lord Gregory was about?"

Shaeleen nodded her head.

"We must warn Prince Basil," Cole said emphatically. "He will be the next king."

Shaeleen tried to hide the headache that then hit her between the eyes, but she didn't know if she had been successful. A pattern was developing that she didn't like: every time someone mentioned Basil being the next king, she had felt pain. If not him, then who? Prince Calix? Nobody wanted that. *Well, except for Lady Judith and her greedy friends.*

"Race you home," Shaeleen said to avoid more conversation. Then she picked up her skirt in one hand and started running. Underneath the long skirt, she had on her more serviceable shoes.

Cole laughed at her and took the challenge.

Soon both of them entered their front gate—winded, tired, and laughing. That was a good relief from a long and painful day.

I'll have to find more ways to laugh, she thought, *or I will kill myself with the pain.*

CHAPTER EIGHT

The next afternoon, Shaeleen was sitting in her room, reading the journal entries by the previous TruthSeers. She held the stone in her hand, and its green light glowed around her and the book. She was trying to find information on how to limit the pain she would feel when hearing or telling a lie.

"Shaeleen!" her mother, Gleda, called out.

As Shaeleen's bedroom door began to open, Shaeleen dropped the TruthStone into her blankets as fast as she could, hoping her mother wouldn't notice.

"Shae," her mother repeated more quietly. Then she glanced over her shoulder, turned back again, and walked into the room. "What was that light?"

"There wasn't any light," Shaeleen said, forgetting not to lie. Her stomach roiled, but she continued on. "Maybe it was just the sun you saw."

Her mother cocked her head and looked at Shaeleen intently. "You have been acting strangely these last few days. You've been cooped up here in this room for hours on end. Something is going on."

Before Shaeleen could deny or affirm her mother's statements, Cole stepped up to her door and said, "Yes, Mother, there is something going on with Shae."

Shaeleen couldn't believe Cole had said something. She glared at him.

He shrugged. "She is becoming a typical, brooding, female teenager." Cole tried not to smile.

Shaeleen burst out laughing more loudly than she would have expected. The relief from him not saying anything about the TruthStone and the fact that what he'd said was true, causing her no pain, proved that her brother was quite smart.

But I am so far from being like any typical teenager!

Her mother joined them in their amusement for a moment, then turned serious. "Oh, the reason I came in here was that an errand boy just dropped a note off for you from Lady Judith." Her mother brought forth the note, which had been hidden behind her back.

Shaeleen and Cole glanced at each other. Then Shaeleen opened the note, read it, and felt the blood drain from her face. She dropped the note onto her lap.

"What did she say?" her mother asked.

Cole sat down, picked up the note, and read it aloud: "Darling Shaeleen, I invite you to join me and some of the other noble ladies for a meeting with Prince Basil. A carriage will arrive to pick you up first thing tomorrow morning. Your services are needed."

Her mother put her hands on both of Shaeleen's cheeks and gasped. "Shaeleen, what a wonderful opportunity. You must have greatly impressed Lady Judith."

Shaeleen sat in a state of shock. *Could I get out of it? Not likely.* The woman was vindictive enough to still ruin her father's business.

"I will go with her," Cole said sternly.

"Son," their mother said, "you can't go to a women's meeting with the prince."

"But—"

"Shaeleen will be fine. Obviously, Lady Judith has taken a liking to Shaeleen and now wants Shaeleen to meet her friends—and meet the prince. Oh, Shaeleen, how wonderful. I must tell your father." With that, their mother ran out of the room, leaving Shaeleen and Cole alone.

"I don't know if I can do this, Cole," Shaeleen said. "Those ladies—if they are Lady Judith's friends—all they will be doing is lying."

"But the prince is a good man."

That rang true within Shaeleen, and she smiled. "Yes, he is and..." she added, smiling for the first time since getting the note, "not bad-looking either."

"Shael!" Cole said. "Don't set your sights so high. We are children of a carpenter."

Shaeleen shrugged. She'd heard of the integrity of the prince. At least being around him wouldn't be so bad for her headaches and stomach pains.

* * *

The next morning, Shaeleen's father called out for Shaeleen from the front yard of their home.

Opening the door, Shaeleen was met by two beautiful white horses and a coachman, along with a small two-seater carriage. Shaeleen was wearing the only other adequate outfit that she owned. The layered blue dress came down just short of her shoes. But it made a nice complement to her blue eyes and a contrast to her brown hair. The fur lining the edges of the dress were slightly out of place in the warm weather—but she didn't have much to choose from. It would have to do.

The coachman held out a hand and helped her up into the carriage. Already seated in the carriage was a young woman Shaeleen had never met. The young woman rolled her eyes at Shaeleen's clothes—the best Shaeleen had, but obviously not good enough for the young woman of noble birth she now sat next to.

"Hello." Shaeleen bobbed her head to be polite.

The young woman, who looked one or two years older than Shaeleen, sat in a gown that was probably worth more than all of Shaeleen's clothes combined. Its yellow hue accented her light brown skin and large, soft brown eyes quite nicely. And her dark hair hung in ringlets past her shoulders.

"I am Shaeleen."

The young woman turned her head slowly and once again looked Shaeleen up and down. Returning her eyes to Shaeleen's face, she replied to Shaeleen's introduction, "I am Lady Clarise, the daughter of Lord Dawson, the minister of ships."

Shaeleen tried to smile—though the young woman's arrogance didn't deserve her niceties—but Shaeleen figured the young woman's rudeness was more a product of her upbringing than anything else.

"So, we're off to see Basil, then?" Shaeleen said, trying to make small talk.

Clarise gasped. "*Prince* Basil. Oh, I can see this isn't going to go well." Clarise shook her head and said, almost to herself, "Why did Lady Judith invite you, anyway?"

Shaeleen squinted her eyes at Clarise and grabbed a side handle as the carriage took off down the road. "Oh, Prince Basil. Have you met the prince before, Lady Clarise?"

Clarise sat up straighter. "Prince Basil and Prince Calix are my second cousins. I have known them since I was a child. We know each other quite well."

And the lies start. Shaeleen felt the familiar pain, in both her gut and head, but held it at bay. It must be a small lie that Clarise knew the princes quite well. Most likely they were cousins of sorts and she had met him a few times.

"I've met him once before," Shaeleen said. This brought a small pain as it was just stretching the truth: she had seen him sparring with Cole, and the prince had glanced her way. But any pain she felt was worth the look on Clarise's face.

"Oh." Clarise lifted her eyebrows, as if to question the validity of Shaeleen's statement. "I am sure he will not remember someone of your standing."

A smoldering anger was building up in Shaeleen at Clarise's attitude, but she let the anger go and stared out the window instead. Others, walking along next to them, would turn and point at the carriage, clearly wondering who the young women were. Shaeleen found she quite enjoyed the attention.

As the castle loomed closer and closer in their view, Shaeleen sat back and then closed her eyes for a moment. *I am actually going to get to see the inside of the castle!* She pushed down the butterflies and tried to maintain her decorum. She wouldn't let Clarise ruin her excitement.

Soon the coachman stopped the carriage at a great stone residence next to the castle. He escorted the two young women out of the carriage, and they walked together to the front of the three-story mansion.

Before they got to the door, two women came outside. Shaeleen sucked in her breath, for the two women were from the group that she'd heard at the party, discussing the plans of Prince Calix.

What have I gotten myself into?

Rushing out behind the two women was Lady Judith, dressed in all her finery. Shaeleen admitted to herself that Lady Judith did look radiant. Today, her dark brown hair hung loose over a dark blue gown, with a strand of pearls accentuating her neckline.

"It's about time you arrived. We're almost late," Lady Judith said as she gathered up Shaeleen and Clarise.

Shaeleen knew that statement wasn't true, but she played along with it anyway. It was a way for the woman to gain control.

"I hope you two young ladies can maintain proper decorum today in front of Prince Basil," Lady Judith said, specifically shooting her eyes at Shaeleen.

Shaeleen gave a sweet smile in return and said, "I'm sure Lady Clarise will be fine."

The two women with Lady Judith covered their mouths to stifle their laughs. But Clarise blushed and gave a menacing look at Shaeleen.

"Shaeleen," Lady Judith said as she motioned to the two women, "these are Lady Florence and Lady Bernia."

Shaeleen bobbed her head at the two women. They were not dressed as precisely as Clarise or Lady Judith, but they did hold themselves in the same snooty way.

Lady Judith continued, looking at Clarise and Shaeleen, "You two will remain silent today and are only here to observe. Clarise, this will be an opportunity for you to catch the prince's eye so he may find you a suitable suitor." Turning to Shaeleen, she said, "You are not here for a suitor, Shaeleen. I expect you will remember your place."

Shaeleen ground her teeth but nodded her head. This woman was the most vile person she had ever met.

Lady Judith motioned for the others to follow her—with Ladies Florence and Bernia behind her and then Clarise and Shaeleen, walking side by side, taking up the rear.

It was a short walk to the entrance of the castle, and Shaeleen was taken aback by all the wealth that extended into the castle grounds. A decorative water fountain—surrounded by benches, statues, and a short walkway—sat in front of the castle. Carriages drove up through the large iron gates, dropped off their guests, then circled back out again.

Then something caught Shaeleen's eye as they stood waiting in line at the gate. Someone was moving behind one of the statues to her left. She stepped out of line a few steps to see better.

"Shaeleen," Lady Judith said with a forceful whisper. "Get back in line, and quit gawking around."

Shaeleen complied, but she kept her head cocked to the side. From behind a large statue of old King Wayland himself, she saw a head poke out to the side. She stifled a laugh. *Cole! What is he doing here?*

Cole nodded to her as he moved behind another statue, closer to the group. Her brother seemed to have more skills than she had known about. Right before Lady Judith and her other companions entered through the gate, Cole struck up a conversation with a group behind theirs.

Shaeleen turned back around at hearing Lady Judith calling her name.

"What has gotten into you, child?" Lady Judith scolded. "Move along."

Clarise just smirked at Shaeleen as she stepped in front of Shaeleen and followed the three older women onto the castle grounds.

CHAPTER NINE

An hour later, the five women still were waiting to see the prince. Lady Judith seemed to be put out and continued to pace the small waiting room where they were being held. With her lips pinched together, she would look at the door, back at Shaeleen, and then frown.

What did I do? Shaeleen thought. She had been sitting in silence, absorbed in the details carved into the crown moldings and chair rails. Two small curio cabinets made of glass and cherry wood were no less exquisite. She admired the woodwork on them all. Her father would like to see these pieces, she was sure.

A servant eventually entered the room. He was an older man and seemed all serious and businesslike in his demeanor. "Please follow me," he said, directing the women. "The prince will see you momentarily."

"About time," Lady Judith said under her breath.

But the servant had heard her. He turned around with a raised eyebrow. "The prince is a busy man, my lady. He sees to the affairs of all in this land."

Shaeleen could almost see Lady Judith roll her eyes. The woman had no concern for anyone else in the land—she only thought about herself.

They stood waiting again for about a quarter of an hour, this time behind two ten-foot-high doors. The doors were of solid wood, with an ornate gold thread running through its grain. And Shaeleen had to fight the urge to touch them multiple times.

From down the hallway, Shaeleen finally heard a bit of noise and turned around. Cole stood there with another group of men. He smiled and bobbed his head to her. She smiled back. *He is checking up on me!* She took a deep breath and felt better knowing her brother was here with her.

Eventually, one of the tall doors opened, and another servant—this one younger—took a step out and informed them, "The prince and regent will see you now."

Led by Lady Judith, the five women walked into the room. Shaeleen was once again taken aback. The wealth of the tapestries, marble floors, soft velvet-covered chairs, and tall stone columns humbled Shaeleen. This castle had been the seat of power in Galena for almost two hundred years, and, even before then, it had been where King Wayland had ruled the entire continent from.

At the back of the room, there was a throne, which sat empty. The prince stood up behind an extraordinarily large table. It was polished and shone like glass. An older man stood to his right—Regent Warin, the brother of their last king and the uncle to the two princes. The regent's dark eyes were intelligent, and his expression brooked no frivolity. He had done a good job leading the kingdom the past five years and preparing the prince to rule.

"Ladies, it is a pleasure to see you," the prince said. "It is always a pleasure to meet those in our great kingdom."

Shaeleen felt no signs of duplicity or lies behind his greeting. The prince was truly impressive. She remembered him from the sparring time with her brother only days before. He was good-looking enough, growing into a man, but it was his eyes that made him who he was—they shone with extreme intelligence. Being in the royal family, Prince Basil had surely inherited more than his share of brains—the Labradorite IntelligenceStone would have taken care of that.

Lady Judith stepped forward. "Prince Basil, so nice to see you are well."

A pounding began in Shaeleen's head. So, it would be Lady Judith and not the prince that Shaeleen would have to brace against that day.

"Thank you for your concern, Lady Judith. Will you introduce the rest of your group to me?"

Lady Judith stepped to the side and motioned the rest to come forward. "These are Lady Bernia and Lady Florence—wives to Lords Ansel and Nathaniel. More loyal subjects would be hard to find."

Shaeleen cringed at the pain and had to close her eyes momentarily to keep the pain at bay. The woman's words were constant lies. When Shaeleen opened her eyes again, Lady Judith was introducing Clarise, but the prince's eyes were on Shaeleen. He cocked his head to the side, as if thinking about something. His eyes bore into hers, but she hoped her face showed no unpleasant emotion. Then he turned his attention back to Clarise.

"Lady Clarise, you are most welcome in the castle today. It is a brighter place with you in it," Prince Basil said.

Shaeleen smiled slightly, wondering if the prince was mocking Clarise. But, surprisingly, she felt no pain from his words.

Clarise blushed and curtsied to the prince. "You are as kind and wise as they say, my lord."

Prince Basil waved a hand in the air as if the comment was not needed. "I love all my people, Lady Clarise, and wish them all well." With those words, he turned back to Lady Judith with eyes that—Shaeleen noticed for the first time—were not brown but actually dark blue.

Then Prince Basil looked at Shaeleen and smiled. "And who is this lovely lady?"

Shaeleen held his gaze for a moment and then turned away. She wondered if the prince knew about her abilities.

Lady Judith snorted softly. "She is no lady, my prince, only the daughter of a carpenter. I brought her along today for the sake of charity. Even those not of noble birth should have the opportunity to meet their next king, don't you think?"

Shaeleen's stomach cramped, and it was all she could do to stay standing.

The prince came around his desk and moved closer to Shaeleen. "Are you all right, miss? You look pale."

Shaeleen was stunned by his compassion. Taking a deep breath, she nodded her head.

"Lady Judith didn't mention your name."

"Shaeleen," was all she could say.

"A lovely name," the prince said and then cocked his head again. "I think we have met. Or, at least, I have seen you before."

Shaeleen heard a small gasp from Clarise, and Lady Judith took a step closer to the prince and Shaeleen.

"I am sure you haven't met *her* before," Lady Judith said. "She is no concern of yours."

Prince Basil turned so rapidly that Shaeleen would've sworn he must have some power of speed with him—but the Garnet SpeedStone was held in Antioch. The prince's eyes flashed darkly as he looked at Lady Judith.

"My dear lady," he said through tight lips, "all my people are my concern. Those in power and nobility—such as I…and you—should understand that. It is our duty to take care of and protect all—especially the innocent that don't have the means to do so themselves."

Lady Judith's eyes tightened, and her face paled noticeably. But she kept her composure and glared back at the prince. "Isn't there some privilege of rank, some honor that should be given to us? Surely, you wouldn't have just anybody approach a king or a lord."

The prince smiled, turned around, and walked back to his desk. He glanced at Shaeleen again, as if to ask if she truly was all right. She gave him a nod, and he turned his attention back to Lady Judith.

"Your husband, Lord Gregory, is one of my most trusted advisors. His duty is to protect all in our land, as my minister of defense. *All* means everyone, Lady Judith. The beggar in the street, the fisher on the sea, those living in the forest and in the cities, the nobles, and the children of merchants." With that, he nodded his head toward Shaeleen.

Lady Judith opened her mouth to speak, but the prince cut her off by saying, "I am glad you are here today to meet with me. There is much to discuss."

"There is?" Lady Judith said, her mouth falling open. Shaeleen guessed that Lady Judith was having a hard time following the prince's line of thinking. "Well, of course there is," Lady Judith said as she stood up straighter. "We have come to discuss the planning of your engagement, my lord. If we might know who will—"

"My lady," the regent said and stepped forward, having not said a word until this time. A quick wave of his hand had cut off Lady Judith's words. "Don't presume to come in here and tell the prince what you want to know."

Lady Judith sneered at the older man. "Regent Warin, our dear prince just got done telling us that all have the same privilege in this dear land under his reign. I only humbly ask for the information of who will be his betrothed so we can begin to plan for the festivities."

Shaeleen's head pounded, and she absently put a hand to her head to squelch the pain. There were so many lies in Lady Judith's statement—*dear prince...humbly ask...plan for the festivities...* It was all a lie. Lady Judith wanted information that she could use against the prince to help his brother gain control of the kingdom.

Before the regent or the prince could respond, Lord Gregory walked through a side door and into the room. Shaeleen watched him look at his wife. He was good at hiding his feelings, but his eyes held the truth—he was disgusted with her. He moved his eyes over the rest of the group. When he saw Shaeleen standing there, he stopped in apparent surprise.

Then Lord Gregory walked over to join the prince and regent. He leaned over and whispered a few brief words to Prince Basil. The prince took a quick glance in Shaeleen's direction but, besides that, didn't say anything else.

"Ladies," Lord Gregory said, giving a quick bow, "I am sorry to have interrupted your meeting." With that, he headed back out the same door he had entered from.

"Lady Judith," the prince said, "it looks like our meeting will have to be cut short today. However, I do have an event I would like you to organize for me."

Lady Judith leaned in closer. "Yes, my prince, of course. Anything for you."

Shaeleen felt pain once again but kept her face straight. She was getting better at holding things in. She knew, however, that she would pay for it later.

"I am concerned about the growing numbers of poor in the city," Prince Basil continued. "I would like for you to organize a charity event to help raise money and bring in clothes for these people. My steward will help you find a suitable place to hold it."

Lady Judith's eyes bulged wide. Lady Bernia and Lady Florence looked taken aback as well.

"But, my lord, your betrothal?" Lady Judith said. "We should be working on that occasion," the woman sputtered.

"All in good time." Prince Basil smiled widely, almost as if enjoying Lady Judith's discomfort. "I expect that, with your extreme connections and resources, something should be organized within the next two weeks."

"Two weeks?" Lady Judith looked like she was about to faint.

"Do you not have the resources to pull that off, Lady Judith?" the regent asked. "Maybe we should find someone else to play such a vital role in the city."

Shaeleen smiled at how they were playing on the woman's own vanity to get something good done. Lady Judith was stuck, and she knew it.

Smiling sweetly, she just shook her head. "No, no," Lady Judith said. "That will be fine as long as Clarise and Shaeleen here are able to help us."

"I would appreciate seeing what Lady Clarise can do with this occasion," the prince said. "This will be great training for you." The prince turned to Clarise. "I, myself, and a few of my friends will attend as well."

Clarise blushed at the implication that maybe one of the prince's friends would be a possible suitor for her.

"But," the prince continued, "I am afraid that Lady Shaeleen will be busy. I have a few things for her to do myself."

"L-Lady Shaeleen?" Lady Judith stammered, apparently appalled that the prince had referred to Shaeleen as a *lady*.

Shaeleen was also surprised by this and raised her eyebrows at him. The prince smiled and crooked his fingers to motion her forward. Shaeleen glanced at Lady Judith, who looked livid. But there was nothing the woman could do at the moment.

"Miss Shaeleen," the prince said as he bobbed his head toward her. "I have noticed you're not feeling too well this morning. Are you well enough to join me for a few moments? I have something to ask of you."

Shaeleen nodded her head. "I am better now, my lord." She really was, for no lies had been told for the last few moments of the conversation, though she knew she still held the previous pain inside.

The prince waved his hand toward Lady Judith. "Thank you again for visiting me today, ladies. I'm so glad you are able to help me with serving the poor of the city. It means a lot to me. I will make sure Miss Shaeleen gets back home safely."

A steward was motioned to come and show the other women out. Before exiting the room, Lady Judith turned her head and shot Shaeleen daggers with her eyes.

Shaeleen let out a long breath. "That woman is insufferable," she muttered under her breath.

The prince laughed. "That is the truth, isn't it?" His intelligent eyes held on to hers. "But she is one of my people, just the same."

Shaeleen was sure his comment about the truth referred to her TruthSeer abilities. She wondered what he wanted with her.

A servant came forward at the beckoning of the prince.

"Please let Miss Shaeleen freshen up first and then show her to my smaller meeting room. Then go and fetch her brother, who is outside with the next group, and have him join us also."

Shaeleen looked from the servant to the prince. Her eyes went wide, and she couldn't find her words.

"That is your brother out there—Cole, I believe—isn't it?" The prince smiled. "I know you wouldn't lie to me."

She shook her head. *He knows. Prince Basil knows about me.* She became lightheaded and knew that she didn't have much longer until she'd become sick; this time from worry rather than lies.

The prince seemed to understand and motioned for his servant to take her to the nearest privy.

CHAPTER TEN

About fifteen minutes later, Shaeleen sat in a more private room, on the edge of the red velvet cushion of a chair. For the moment, she was all alone. After vomiting and then freshening herself up, she'd let the servant lead her into this room. He had left a few small sweet cakes on a tray, along with some juice.

At first, Shaeleen didn't feel like eating anything, but soon her curiosity got the better of her. She stood up and walked to where the tray sat on a shiny maple table, pausing to glance out of an enormous window. She pushed the long rose curtains out of the way and looked outside. The crystal waters of the Bay of Jalen were extraordinarily clear today. She took a moment to admire the view before picking up a small sweet cake.

Shaeleen had just taken a bite when the door opened. She tried to chew quickly but was caught with the bite of cake in her mouth.

Her brother walked inside with the same servant that had brought her in. At first, Cole's face was serious as his eyes darted around the room. But, seeing Shaeleen with her mouth full and the rest of the cake in her hand, the corner of his lips curled up.

"Can't stay away from the sweets, can you, dear Sister?"

Shaeleen gave him a mock glare. "You should try one. They are really, really tasty."

Cole laughed.

"The prince will see you in a few minutes," the servant said. "Make yourself comfortable."

The servant closed the door behind himself, and Cole came closer to Shaeleen. She offered him a sweet cake, but he turned it down. He continued walking the room, surveying it carefully.

"What have you done now, Shae?" He turned and looked at her seriously.

"Me?" Shaeleen said, licking the sugar off her fingers. She was tempted to take another, but she refrained. She didn't want sticky fingers to greet the prince with. "Why do you think I've done something?"

"Because you always do something," Cole said. "And, ever since you found that stone—"

"Cole!" Shaeleen said, cutting him off. "Don't talk about that." She looked around the room, feeling as if someone could be spying on them. For all she knew, someone could be.

The door opened behind them, and in walked the prince, all by himself. Shaeleen was surprised to not see any servants or guards with him.

He must have felt her questioning stare, for he asked, "Do I need protection from either of you?"

Cole bowed deeply and formally, saying, "My prince, you have nothing to fear from either of us." He stood up and glanced at Shaeleen, giving her a look to warn her not to make trouble.

"Please sit down." Prince Basil motioned to the chairs. "This is to be an informal meeting. I am among friends, aren't

I?" His smile was wide and warm, the dimple in his right cheek grabbing Shaeleen's attention.

Shaeleen sat and then looked from Cole to the prince. "I have heard nothing yet that would make me think otherwise, my lord."

Prince Basil barked out a short laugh. "My, you are a complicated woman, aren't you?"

"You have no idea," Cole mumbled. Then, after realizing what he had just done, he spoke his apology. "I'm so sorry, my prince."

"No need. I have some questions for your sister," Prince Basil said. "And it wouldn't be seemly for me to meet with her alone, would it?"

Cole nodded his head. "No, sir, it would not."

"Cole, I can see honor means a lot to you," the prince said, "so I will ask that anything we discuss here today does not go any farther than the two of you."

Cole stood up. "Of course, my prince. I am a faithful servant of Galena."

"Please sit down," Prince Basil said. Then he turned to Shaeleen. "And you, Shaeleen, will you protect the words that are said here?"

Shaeleen took a deep breath. Was the prince really this careful with his words? Or, was he trying to trick them into something? He was smart—she could tell that. But she also didn't hear any lies...yet. She decided to venture out a bit.

"As long as you are truthful," she said, "you have no worries from me."

"Shae," Cole whispered. "He is the prince."

Prince Basil smiled. "That's fine, Cole. I see that your sister is a little more loose with her tongue than you are. I find it refreshing. You have no idea how careful everyone treads around me all the time. It can get exhausting."

The prince stopped talking, seemed to grow a bit more serious, and then stood up. Shaeleen and Cole sat stiffly for a moment, awaiting his words. Then Shaeleen glanced around the room. It had a small desk, a grouping of chairs around a table, where they sat, and a bookcase full of books on a far wall. It was to this bookcase that the prince now walked. Putting a hand on a book, he glanced back at the two of them for a moment—as if deciding whether to go ahead with his actions or not.

Pulling three books out from the shelf, the prince put his hand back inside the bookcase. Then Shaeleen heard a soft click, and a portion of the case swung outward, revealing a small, two-foot-wide cupboard. It had some type of lock on it. The prince produced a key, from a chain that hung inside his shirt, and used it to open the cupboard.

Shaeleen couldn't sit still any longer. She stood up and took two steps toward the prince. But Cole reached his hand up and grabbed her arm.

"Shae, wait here."

"But I can't see what Basil is doing." Shaeleen tried to pull her arm away from her brother.

"*Prince Basil*," Cole said. "You have to call him *Prince*."

Shaeleen succeeded in pulling her arm away from Cole and then continued walking forward. She heard Cole get up and follow her over.

"Shae!" Cole said one more time, trying to get her back to her seat.

Then Prince Basil turned around. In his hand was a small, black-velvet pouch. He looked from Cole to Shaeleen and said, "Shaeleen is fine. She is drawn to it, aren't you?"

Shaeleen felt something stir inside of her. The only other time she'd felt that was when the old keeper, Melindra, had first given her the stone in the marketplace. Shaeleen found that her hand was resting on the TruthStone in her pocket. It was growing warmer as her other hand reached out toward the pouch.

Prince Basil smiled widely. "You want what is in the pouch, Shaeleen?"

Cole stepped up between the two, in a defensive posture. He glanced from Shaeleen to the prince and then back again.

Shaeleen glanced at her brother and said, "It's fine, Cole."

The prince untied the velvet pouch and put his hand inside it. Slowly, with a sly grin on his lips, he pulled his hand back out, and a dark blue light began to glow around his hand.

Cole and Shaeleen gasped.

"It's Labradorite," Shaeleen whispered. "The IntelligenceStone!"

Without thinking about it first, Shaeleen brought her hand out of her pocket, holding the TruthStone inside it. A bright green glow flew out between her fingers. The green glow grew larger and moved toward the prince. It surrounded his hand and melded with the blue light—creating a type of surreal, ethereal light of cyan hue—almost the color she had seen in the bay minutes earlier.

Shaeleen felt power course through her veins, bringing with it not just truth but intelligence, knowledge, and pure adrenaline.

"Open it!" she told the prince in a commanding voice.

Her brother, standing still next to her, gasped out loud at her audacity in commanding the prince.

But Shaeleen knew that—in this moment, in this power—somehow she was the prince's superior. It felt wrong to think that way, but it was the truth!

Prince Basil opened his hand slowly, and there in the middle sat a small, bluish stone with black cracks running through it.

"It's so small," Shaeleen said, "barely bigger than a large pea."

Prince Basil nodded, a sad look in his eyes as he glanced up at the two siblings. "It is all that is left. After two hundred years, what had started off the size of a melon—so I have heard—is almost gone now. Bits and pieces were shared with others through the years, given for bravery or bribes, for help or hurt. Its effects are now washed weakly through the blood of many in Galena."

The prince continued as he watched Cole intently, "I sense that you have more than your share. I do not know why. Maybe it is to help protect the stone Shaeleen now holds in her hand. Both of you share the lighter eyes of the people in Verlyn—maybe their blood flows through your veins more purely than through mine."

Shaeleen's fist was still closed around her stone. She gazed intently into Prince Basil's eyes and saw his unspoken request.

Then she opened her hand widely, and there on her open palm sat a priceless, egg-sized stone of Moldavite. As Shaeleen concentrated on it, the stone suddenly floated up above her hand and gradually spun around, sending its luminous green rays of power throughout the prince's private office.

"It is so much!" the prince said. "How do you stand the lies, the pain it must bring?"

"I am learning," Shaeleen admitted.

"My stone calls to you, doesn't it?" the prince asked.

Shaeleen felt tears stinging at the edges of her eyes. "It does."

"What do you mean?" Cole asked, his first words in a while. "I don't understand."

The prince held his stone out to Shaeleen.

"No. No. No." Shaeleen shook her head. "I can't take it from you. It's all you have left."

"And that's why you must take it. It is yours, as it has been promised."

"Promised?" Cole asked.

"For years, we who have held the stones in the royal families have known that one day a TruthStone would emerge and call all the other stones to it. The holder of that TruthStone would be a powerful TruthSeer—one that would hold precedence over all other stones. That day would be an awakening of the truth, a time for Wayland to be refreshed."

This is too much for me. She wiped the tears from her eyes and glanced down. The stone had settled back down into her upturned palm.

As Prince Basil moved his hand closer to hers, the cyan light around their hands brightened. With obvious difficulty and emotion, he dumped the small IntelligenceStone onto the open palm of her hand. And the TruthStone absorbed it into itself, growing slightly bigger as it did.

"Is it supposed to do that?" Cole asked.

Shaeleen turned to him and shrugged. "I don't know, Cole. I don't know about any of this." Tears flowed freely from her eyes, running down her cheeks.

The prince put an arm around Shaeleen and ushered her and Cole back to their chairs. Before sitting down, he wrapped his hand around Shaeleen's, closing her fingers back around the TruthStone. The light faded into itself, and soon the glow was gone altogether.

Prince Basil handed Shaeleen the velvet bag he still held in his other hand. "Put the stone in this. It will protect the stone from prying eyes."

Shaeleen must have looked surprised at this direction, but she did as she was bidden. Then she put the pouch into a hidden pocket in her dress.

"The pouch is protected. Keep the stone in there whenever you can," Prince Basil instructed. "There are others who will want to take it."

Shaeleen leaned her head back against the chair and closed her eyes for a moment. She could still feel the euphoria of both stones, but the power was receding now, becoming only a faint presence in the back of her mind.

After a long, quiet moment, she opened her eyes back up.

"How did you know about me?" Shaeleen asked the prince. "No one knew, except for Cole."

"As the keeper of the IntelligenceStone, I could tell you were pained by the lies. I know that Galena's own TruthSeer is with my brother and my mother in North Bay. Lately, it had become too painful for her to stay here—I do not know why. But there is only one TruthSeer per kingdom. So, when I saw you, I knew you must be the prophesied one."

Shaeleen nodded, then smiled. "What do I do now?"

The prince seemed to turn serious before continuing. "For now, I'm afraid we must keep your status a secret. But I do have a favor to ask of you—an errand for me, if you will."

Shaeleen nodded for the prince to continue.

"I need you to go to North Bay and see what my brother is up to in person."

"Sir," Cole jumped in. "Shaeleen is only a young woman. How will she defend herself? How will she know what to do?"

The prince put his right hand up to quiet Cole. "That is why you will be going with her."

Cole's eyes opened wide, but he kept his mouth closed.

Prince Basil's eyes grew dark. "My brother is stirring up trouble. I will be betrothed on my birthday and become king. But he wants to destroy me. He wants my crown, but it's not his to have."

Pain erupted in Shaeleen's gut and exploded behind her eyes, more excruciating than any she had ever felt before. She leaned over, putting her head in her hands, and tried to breathe. She tried to push the pain away, but it was too much. *The stupid TruthStone is trying to kill me.*

Both the prince and Cole jumped up from their seats and were at her side in moments.

"Shae?" Cole said.

"What's wrong?" Prince Basil asked.

"What did you say?" Cole asked, turning on the prince. "Why would your words cause her such pain?"

The prince stood up. "I didn't say anything false. I have more honor than that, Sir Cole. All I said was—"

"No," Shaeleen squeaked out. "Don't say another word."

The prince stopped and then wrung his hands while Shaeleen recovered herself. Finally, she opened up her eyes and leaned her head back against the chair again. Prince Basil poured her a glass of water. And she drank it all down in a few gulps. The headache was going away bit by bit.

"Do you need a doctor?" the prince asked.

Shaeleen shook her head. "No. It's getting better."

After a few more minutes, all three were sitting back down again. The prince had his hands under his chin and his elbows on his knees. His dark black hair reflected the lamplight from above, and Shaeleen caught a glimpse of his signet ring on his right hand.

"I am sorry," the prince said. "Surely I am. I didn't mean to cause you such pain. If I had known what I said—"

Shaeleen put her hand up. "I will think about it later. You spoke truth as you know it, but the words you spoke were not true...somehow. I don't know why. I will think about it. Only time will tell, I suppose."

"I have put you through too much today. I am once again sorry." The prince stood and went to the door, calling a servant in.

"Please escort Lady Shaeleen and Sir Cole back to their home," he said to his servant. "Take our finest carriage."

Cole and Shaeleen stood.

With one hand behind his back, Cole bowed low before the prince. "Sir, I am sorry if I have accused you of anything. That was not my intent. I was only worried for my sister."

Prince Basil extended his hand to Cole. "Sir Cole, if only every sibling could have someone as honorable as you to defend them. I've never had the privilege of having one myself. My brother and I don't see eye to eye on most things. Please take care of Shaeleen. Both of you please come back tomorrow, and we will continue our conversation then."

They finished saying their goodbyes and then followed the servant out of the castle. After a few moments, a six-horse carriage, pulled by the prince's own white horses, drove up. Once they got on their way, Shaeleen let out a deep breath.

"Quite a way you have…with stirring things up," Cole said, leaning back against the red leather seats, with his eyes closed.

Shaeleen sighed again and then pulled the curtains aside to look out. Walking next to them was Lady Judith and her cronies, Lady Bernia and Lady Florence, with Clarise walking a few steps behind them.

As Shaeleen passed, they looked over at the carriage. Then they did a double take as they saw who was inside. Shaeleen splayed her fingers at them with a wiggle as she rode on past.

CHAPTER ELEVEN

Shaeleen and Cole's family came running out of the house when the prince's elaborate carriage pulled up. Neighboring tradesfolk wandered out from their houses and shops to see who would be coming to their part of town in such a grand way.

Alva came running up to her siblings as they stepped down out of the carriage. "How did you...? What happened to...?" Alva said, but she couldn't string together a complete sentence.

"We met with Basil today," Shaeleen said as she lifted up Alva and tried to swing her around, but her sister was almost as tall as she was and it was difficult. The power of the stone had made Shaeleen feel better on the way home. "He is quite charming." She blushed thinking about his smile and the charming dimple in his right cheek.

"*Prince Basil*, Shaeleen." Cole furrowed his brows at her. "He is the prince, not just your neighborhood friend. Have some respect."

"Oh. Yes, yes. Prince Basil," Shaeleen said, not offended at her brother's usual sense of honor.

"Is he as nice as they say?" their mother asked.

Cole nodded his head. "He is as honorable and caring as the people say. A good man."

"Well, what did he want with you two?" their father asked, appearing uncomfortable with the situation.

Shaeleen didn't know what to say. How could she explain the prince's attention without talking about her newfound powers? She also couldn't lie. Then Cole saved her from doing either one.

"The prince would like the ladies to organize a charity event for the poor in the city," Cole said in a purely truthful way.

Their father turned to Cole and asked, "And how did you end up being there and meeting him? I thought you were practicing your sparring again."

Cole's face turned a slight shade of red. "I followed Shaeleen. I was worried about her," Cole admitted. "The prince saw me there and brought me in to meet with him and Shaeleen."

Shaeleen could tell that their parents had more questions, ones she and Cole wouldn't be able to answer, so she changed the subject: "How is business today, Father?"

Their father smiled. "Very well, Shaeleen. Lady Judith has kept her promise. I have other nobles asking for commissioned pieces now."

Shaeleen could feel the truthfulness and the intelligence of both stones coursing through her body. "You should hire someone to help you," she said. "The extra work you will get would more than pay for this. Also, if you buy your wood in greater bulk, you will save more money. I would buy a larger wagon also, so you can spend less time delivering your furniture."

Her father stood gaping at her. Then she realized she had just babbled on. But she had felt ideas coming to her that she hadn't thought about before—the effects of the IntelligenceStone, she was sure.

"Just some ideas," Shaeleen added and then smiled.

Her father and mother looked at Cole, who only shrugged his shoulders at them, as if to say he didn't understand either.

Then they all laughed, and her father turned back toward his shop. "Well, they are good ideas," he mumbled to himself.

Shaeleen laughed and skipped into the house. "I'm hungry, Mama. Anything sweet to eat?" After using the stones, her appetite had seemed to pick up.

Later that evening, a messenger arrived, asking for Shaeleen's and Cole's presence with the prince again the next morning. Shaeleen's parents were delighted with the interest their beloved leader had taken in their children.

A gnawing feeling grew in Shaeleen's stomach. Prince Basil had mentioned something about checking on his brother Calix, but her headache had put off any further discussion. She had the strange idea her life had now taken another turn—and would never be the same again.

* * *

The next morning, soon after their first meal, a smaller carriage rode up, and Cole and Shaeleen were escorted inside. The servant was someone new and wasn't as helpful or as friendly as the previous one. He didn't even help Shaeleen into the carriage.

The carriage took off at a high speed, and Shaeleen fell against Cole.

"What is that maniac doing up there? He's not in a race." Shaeleen held on tight, doing all she could to keep from falling over.

Pushing the curtain aside, she saw that they were heading in the opposite direction of the castle. Shaeleen pointed this out to Cole, who only surmised that the prince was meeting them somewhere else. Shaeleen guessed that could be possible, but something didn't feel right.

Sticking her head out the window, she yelled up at the driver, "Where are you taking us? This isn't the way to the castle."

"Get back inside. I'm taking you to the prince, of course."

Shaeleen immediately felt pain. "He's lying," Shaeleen said to her brother.

"How do you know?" Cole asked without thinking.

Shaeleen glared at him.

"Oh yeah," he said. "I guess you do know."

"I don't think he is Prince Basil's servant," Shaeleen deduced.

Cole put his hand on his sword, which always hung at his side. Suddenly, the carriage turned a sharp corner, and Shaeleen flew across the seat, landing on her brother. Then it grew darker outside the carriage window, and they heard a large door close as the carriage stopped.

Untangling herself from Cole, Shaeleen stood up and reached for the carriage door's handle, when the door flew open and two rough hands grabbed her.

"Hey!" Shaeleen shouted. "Let go of me."

Cole charged out with his sword already drawn. Four older and stronger men stood in front of them with their swords drawn also.

"Just try something," one of them said. "I'd like nothing more than to show you my fighting skills."

Cole turned and gave a focused look at Shaeleen. Then he turned back to the four men. He took a stance and raised his sword out in front of himself.

"Cole. No!" Shaeleen said. "You can't fight all of them."

"I won't let them hurt you, Shae."

"We won't hurt her," came a female voice from the corner of the room. "At least not too much." Out walked Lady Judith. She had a dark cloak around her with a cowl pulled up over her head.

"What is the meaning of this, Lady Judith?" Cole asked, his sword still in his hand. "The prince is waiting for us."

"*The prince is waiting for us*," Lady Judith mocked. "You must think you're so special now, don't you?" Then she turned to Shaeleen and, with spittle spraying from her lips, said, "The prince is a pathetic, weak, ignorant fool."

Shaeleen doubled over with pain. Of course that was a lie.

Lady Judith laughed and clapped her hands. "I am right," she said to one of the guards. "Lies cause her pain. Watch this."

Shaeleen tried to keep the pain inside, but the woman was so completely evil it was difficult.

Having two guards hold Shaeleen tight, Lady Judith walked up to only inches from Shaeleen's face and, with a sweet voice, spewed forth as many lies as she could: "I love the prince and the regent... I want Basil as my king... I look forward to meeting his betrothed... I am anxious to organize his charity event..."

And the lies went on and on.

Each time, Shaeleen felt as if someone had slugged her in the gut or had pounded her head against an anvil. Over and over again, the pain and agony washed over her. Then darkness started spreading across her vision, and a ringing sounded in her head. She knew she would soon pass out.

Cole screamed with a raging animal's roar and plowed into the guards. Taking one down immediately, Cole turned to face a second one. His eyes flashed with anger, and his sword flicked quicker than Shaeleen had ever seen it move before. The second guard went down, and Shaeleen felt a loosening of the guards' grips on her as they moved to help their fellow guards.

Shaeleen sank to the ground as Cole fought like a madman. Spinning through the air, jumping and dodging their strikes, he moved incredibly fast.

"Madam, we need to leave." The carriage driver pulled Lady Judith away.

"No, I will not leave without her," Lady Judith screamed, pointing at Shaeleen.

Shaeleen tried to scoot away from her, but Lady Judith kicked Shaeleen with her pointed shoes and rained more lies down on her: "Shaeleen, I am a loyal subject to the prince. You must know I would never do anything to hurt him."

Pain. The more the woman yelled and purposefully lied, the more pain exploded in Shaeleen's head.

"I love telling the truth," Lady Judith continued. "It gives me so much pleasure." Lady Judith's eyes looked crazy, and she kicked Shaeleen once again.

But the pain from these kicks was nothing compared to what Shaeleen felt inside. Shaeleen's stomach cramped, and she vomited all over the floor and onto Lady Judith's shoes. In the back recesses of her mind, Shaeleen found some modicum of joy in that.

Cole had finished immobilizing three guards, with only one guard remaining. But Shaeleen saw that Cole was tiring and that the other man had backed Cole into a corner.

"Cole!" she screamed, her voice raw after having vomited. "You can do it." And speaking the truth brought her strength. "You have trained for this. You are one of the best swordsmen in the city."

Hearing this, Cole stood taller and began to push back his opponent.

Then the servant pulled Lady Judith away once again, and this time she went with him. They ran to a nearby door of the dark warehouse they were in.

Before exiting, Lady Judith turned back to Shaeleen and said, "I'm not done with you yet, girl. Next time you will do my bidding or die."

Shaeleen smirked. "The first truths you have said today, Lady Judith." She pulled herself up to a sitting position and leaned back against a pole. "But there won't be a next time." That fact Shaeleen knew to be true.

"Finish them off!" Lady Judith yelled at the remaining guard. Then she fled the building with the carriage driver.

Shaeleen was so weak she could barely think. She watched Cole and the other guard push each other back and forth. Then Cole stumbled and fell down, his sword flying away from his hands. Shaeleen watched with dread as the guard approached her brother, who was trying to scoot away, toward his fallen sword.

She gripped the velvet pouch in her pocket and grabbed the TruthStone out, resting it on her leg. The stone awakened a power deep inside of her once again, and the now familiar green light flared forth, filling the room around her.

She couldn't bear for Cole to get hurt for her sake. The embedded IntelligenceStone brought back flashes of memory—snippets from the small book she had read parts of. Words moved through her mind at an astounding speed as she searched for the right answer. Then she found it.

Pulling strength from the stones, Shaeleen weakly held the TruthStone up in the air, as high as her comparably feeble arms could manage. Green and blue light flared around her. Then she pointed the stone toward where Cole lay on the ground. The guard was inches away, and he had raised his sword high.

"Cole, you are my protector!" Shaeleen shouted to him as loudly as she could. Power burst forth from her hand and raced toward Cole. It hit into him, almost lifting Cole off the ground.

The guard paused a moment, as if deciding whether to finish the job or run away. Cole took a deep breath and then let out a wailing sound that was part pain and part delight. The wave of light from the TruthStone wrapped itself around Cole and then swirled rapidly, coalescing on his chest.

"Shaeleen, what have you done?" Cole roared as loudly as a wild animal. Then he jumped up off the ground. Summoning his sword to his hand, it flew through the air, and the pommel landed in his palm. Turning toward the final guard, Cole pointed the sword directly at him, mere feet separating the two foes.

The guard's eyes opened wider, and he threw down his own blade, turned, and then ran.

Of the three other guards on the ground, two groaned with fear, while the third one stayed still. Cole turned as if seeing things around the room that weren't there—things only his mind could see. Gathering the sword in both hands, he raised it high in the air above his head as he now turned his body to face Shaeleen. His blue eyes had grown even more pale with the power now coursing through his veins.

What have I done to my brother?

Shaeleen got up onto her hands and knees and then pushed herself to her feet, steadying herself with one hand against a wall. Power swirled above the sword, until it filled the room.

"Cole!" Shaeleen shouted above the wind caused by this swirling power of light. She closed her hand around the TruthStone, and the light somewhat diminished. "Stop it, Cole."

His eyes seemed to come into focus. He smiled and nodded his head toward her. Then, sword still in the air, Cole spoke softly but with a force of words that Shaeleen could not deny: "Shaeleen, I am now your wizard guardian. I protect the truth and will protect your life with mine."

Tears came unbidden to her eyes as she walked with ragged steps toward her brother. She reached him and put a hand on his forearm. He looked down at her and lowered his sword from the air. The power swirled once more around the room. Then it formed into one straight line, zoomed into the tip of the sword, and traveled down the length of the sword, jolting Cole. He stumbled forward, but Shaeleen put her hands out to hold him up. Finally, the light blinked out and his arm dropped, the sword's tip touching the floor.

The room stood dark and quiet, except for the soft groaning of the men who still lay on the warehouse floor.

Shaeleen lowered her arms from Cole as he steadied himself. Cole brought forth a small flame that stood in the air between them, spreading eerie shadows around the warehouse. His eyes were even lighter for a moment—almost clear. He moved his left hand over his hair, smoothing it back down.

"Looks like we're quite the pair, aren't we?" Cole said.

Shaeleen laughed quietly. "A TruthSeer and her wizard protector! How are we going to explain this to Father and Mother?"

Cole shook his head. "And to little Alva."

"And to little Alva," she repeated.

Cole hooked his sword through his belt and then draped an arm around his sister. "Should we go and see the prince now?" He led Shaeleen toward the door.

CHAPTER TWELVE

It took Shaeleen and Cole over an hour to walk back to the right part of the city. At first, they felt weak and worried, looking around every corner for Lady Judith or any more of her guards. But, smelling the aroma of food in the air, Shaeleen begged Cole to stop for a moment in front of a small shop, where an elderly man worked at a food cart. Cole bought himself a drumstick of chicken; Shaeleen, a sweet roll.

Using the power always makes me hungry.

Cole laughed out loud.

"What?" Shaeleen asked. "What's so funny?"

"You are," Cole said. "You and your sweet tooth."

"Well, I'm hungry."

"Me too!"

Cole devoured his chicken in a few bites. And soon they began walking quicker, their strength returning as the castle loomed closer in front of them.

Right before reaching the gates, Cole turned to Shaeleen. "So, do you know what I can do?"

Shaeleen shook her head. She'd read little about a guardian's power in the journal. But a TruthSeer always had a wizard guardian.

"I'm not sure, Cole. I barely understand my powers. I guess we'll learn together."

"Hmmm." Cole appeared deep in thought. "There is something in my mind that is connected to you now. I'm not sure I welcome having you in my head."

"That could be helpful if Lady Judith tries anything again," Shaeleen said.

Cole only grunted.

Shaeleen glanced up at the castle in front of them. The stone walls were ancient, dating back to before the founding of Wayland—before the first TruthSeer or the gemstones. The castle had stood as a beacon of strength for so long out on the peninsula that many people could hardly remember its beginnings. Even the histories about the first people coming to the island were vague about the timing, though it was generally accepted that they had arrived as refugees from a land far to the east, across the sea.

Cole informed the guard who they were, and then they were escorted inside immediately.

As soon as they stepped into the castle, Prince Basil came running up to them. He looked from Shaeleen to Cole, and, seeing Cole's eyes, the prince's own widened in surprise. "I see we have more to talk about. I was worried when my carriage didn't pick you up. I have men out searching for you."

Shaeleen looked at Cole as the prince escorted them to the same room they had met in the previous day. Her brother's eyes had begun to revert back to their normal light blue—a color that was still rare in Galena—but they still held a distinct opaque quality to them.

The prince had a servant bring in drinks and a tray of meat and cheese. Then the prince invited Shaeleen and Cole to sit down. He motioned for them to take whatever food they wanted. Cole was hesitant, at first, but Shaeleen dug right in. After a moment, Cole followed suit.

The prince spoke first, looking at Cole: "I see you have found your power also?"

Cole nodded. "Seems that way. Did you know this would happen?"

"I'd hoped so." Prince Basil smiled, but it did not reach his eyes. "Though your life now will not be your own."

"My life has always belonged to the kingdom. I am yours as needed," Cole said sincerely.

Prince Basil jumped up. "No, no, Cole—you are not mine; you're hers." He pointed to Shaeleen, who had glanced up at him between bites of meat. "Her life is more important than mine. You are her guardian wizard, not mine and not the kingdom's."

"But, my lord..." Cole began but trailed off at a look from the prince that brooked no argument.

The prince walked to the window, overlooking the Bay of Jalen. Walking farther down the wall a few steps, he came to a balcony door. Putting one hand on the door handle, he motioned with his other for Shaeleen and Cole to follow him outside.

They all stood in silence for a few minutes, Shaeleen and Cole seeming to both be wondering what the prince was thinking about.

He drew them north, toward the edge of the balcony. From this position, they overlooked the Bay of Jalen.

Pointing north with his left hand, he finally spoke. "King Wayland stood here almost two hundred years ago as he was envisioning how he would set up the land he ruled. He carved it up into the five kingdoms, each named after one of his children—Galena, where we stand; Gabor, to the north; Shema and Antioch, to the west; and Althea, to the south—and he gave each of them a gemstone of power that he had received from the island of Verlyn, each stone carrying its own specific power—intelligence in Galena; strength in Gabor; Healing in Shema; speed in Antioch; and hearing in Althea."

The sun was high overhead now, and Shaeleen watched a flock of birds dive toward land in the castle's gardens. A breeze from the ocean picked up and cooled the humid sweat starting to form on her forehead.

She turned from the gardens to Prince Basil. His dark hair hung over his forehead, and his blue eyes were piercing, seeming to take in everything around him all at once. He carried his authority and intelligence well.

But what did he say the other day that had caused me so much pain? She'd tried to put part of her mind to work on that, without having to think about the exact words he had said, because she didn't want to feel the same pain again.

While lost in this thought, Shaeleen had missed a few of Prince Basil's current words. So she focused her attention back on him. He was talking about the TruthSeers now. His passion and his enthusiasm—about his kingdom and the power of the gemstones—were clear in his words.

"Along with the gemstones," he continued, "Verlyn supplied a TruthStone for each kingdom as well as a TruthSeer from Verlyn. The Truthseers were tasked with keeping each king and queen honest in their dealings with their people and with each other."

Shaeleen had read about some of this from the journal. "Then," she interrupted, "a man, pure of heart and full of honor, was chosen to be the TruthSeer's guardian wizard—the TruthSeer's protector."

The prince nodded, looking at Cole. "Yes. His power was tied to the TruthSeer's, but he had more than the power from the magic: his own honor and truth gave him power, power to see things others didn't, power to rise above all else. You see, the TruthSeer was outside of a king's or a queen's laws and rule. He or she was an entity unto themselves. And the guardian, as an extension of the TruthSeer, was not beholden to any king or queen either."

"That sounds dangerous," Cole said. "I am your loyal subject. I always have been loyal to Galena. I want to serve this land and protect our honor."

Shaeleen put her hand tenderly on Cole's arm. She had never seen him so upset before. She smiled up at him, and he took a deep breath, relaxing somewhat.

"I'm sorry," Cole said. "It's just that…well, this is all quite new for me to deal with."

Prince Basil smiled. "To all of us, my friend. Never has a TruthSeer risen that was outside of the five that were set up. Every few decades, an apprentice came along for each TruthSeer to train—someone with at least some blood from Verlyn. Then, as each TruthSeer would die, the apprentice became the new TruthSeer: an unbroken string from then until now."

"So, am I to be an apprentice, then?" Shaeleen asked, already knowing the answer deep inside of herself.

Prince Basil shook his head. "I don't believe so, Shaeleen. Plus, I don't really see you following directions from someone else that way." His smile was wide, and mischief showed in his eyes.

"Don't you know it," Cole mumbled.

Shaeleen glared at them for a moment, then laughed.

The prince continued, "There has always been a prophecy bandied around by the royals that serve as kings and queens. It is about an additional TruthSeer that would someday arise. He or she would have control over all other TruthSeers—and even over all the other stones." Prince Basil shrugged his shoulders. "No one knows for sure what the prophecy means. Even those in Verlyn argue about its meaning. Many there now lean toward keeping all magic to themselves and leaving Wayland to fend for itself."

"The keeper—when she gave me the stone—told me to gather the other stones," Shaeleen said. "I didn't know what that meant. But after yesterday, after you gave me yours, I'm beginning to understand. Also, there were others from Verlyn chasing after the keeper, trying to get back what she had given to me."

"Yes, the IntelligenceStone is already working with you," Prince Basil said in excitement. "I would expect the stones from all the kingdoms have grown quite small. The TruthSeers we've had recently haven't always used their abilities for good.

The regent—my uncle—and I have done our bests to keep us protected here in Stronghaven. But…" the prince looked Cole and then Shaeleen in the eyes, "I'm afraid the gemstones are failing and, with them, the protection they hold over the land. Fighting has broken out in Althea. Lightfort has closed themselves off from all others, my own brother seems to be aligning himself with Gabor, and Verlyn doesn't seem to want to help us at the moment."

All three stood in silence for a moment, watching some gulls land on top of the tower.

Then Cole spoke, his voice deep and thick with emotion: "I think I understand, my lord." Cole stared intently at Shaeleen, and she could see tears in his pale blue eyes. The power inside him spoke to hers. "My sister is the hope of Wayland. She is the one destined to restore the gemstones and restore peace to the land. And I must protect her in this quest. If our hopes are with her, then my life must be in her hands."

Cole took a step toward Shaeleen and took her hands in his. Tears slipped down his face as he peered into Shaeleen's eyes. She saw power, honor, and love circling within them.

Then he kneeled down in front of her and said, "I pledge myself to the truth. We are above law and kingdom, above family and friends. Where you go, I will follow. When you fight, I will be your arm. And when you feel the pain of lies and wickedness of men and women, I will comfort you and carry you. I will be of no kingdom now—a wizard without a home—until the truth is found and established once again throughout all of Wayland. Be it known, I serve the truth!"

Shaeleen's heart swelled to see such tenderness in Cole's words, and she wiped the tears from her own eyes. She looked up at the prince as her brother kept his own head lowered in front of her. The prince's own eyes also glistened.

She put her hand out for her brother to grasp and said, "I accept your pledge and your protection. We will find the truth together. Rise, Cole, and be my wizard guardian and protector."

"I will protect the truth," Cole said firmly as he rose to his feet and held his head high. Strength radiated from him, and tendrils of power flared around his shoulders and arms.

Then the prince approached Shaeleen, and, although he did not prostrate himself on the ground, he did bow his head to her. "TruthSeer, know that I have freely given you my IntelligenceStone. Remember that Galena was the first to acknowledge your power and position over all the gemstones of power. I release you from any ties of fealty to Galena. You are no longer my subject, but I am yours in all things you would command in the name of truth."

Shaeleen breathed in deeply. She couldn't believe what was happening. Only days before, she was sneaking through the marketplace on her way to see Cole practice with his sword. She shook her head slightly, trying to clear her thoughts.

Prince Basil smiled at her. "Quite a bit to take in, I imagine."

Shaeleen laughed and tried to wipe the tears from her eyes. "You have no idea."

The three moved back into the castle, inside the smaller meeting room.

"And the errand you had for us, my lord?" Cole asked.

Prince Basil looked deep in thought. "I cannot command or compel you now..." He paused. "But I would ask that you still go to North Bay and find out what my brother's intentions are. Find the truth of the matter."

Shaeleen brushed a stray strand of her brown hair out of her eyes and nodded. She too felt the need to go to North Bay. Every time she thought of Prince Basil ruling Galena, sharp pains enveloped her. She needed to find out what that meant. *What is Calix up to?*

The prince's mouth went tight. "Be careful, though. My brother has a way of manipulating others. My mother is there, and so is Galena's TruthSeer. But he holds something over them. I know he is planning on coming here and trying to take my throne."

Pain!

Cole's blade came free in a flash, and he took a step toward the prince.

"Cole, no!" Shaeleen shouted.

Prince Basil stepped back and put his hands up, to show he'd meant no harm. Then Cole's eyes focused back on both of them, and he lowered the sword.

"I am sorry," Cole apologized. "I saw Shae in pain, and my instincts took over. I meant no offense, Prince."

The prince nodded his head. "None taken, my friend. You are learning your duties still."

"Talk no more of the throne, my lord." Shaeleen shook the pain off. "There are truths there needing to be discovered."

"Well, I don't know if Calix will help clear things up," Prince Basil said. "But brace yourself for his lies."

"Thank you for everything, Prince Basil," Shaeleen said. "I would ask you to keep these things quiet for now. I think we will travel in disguise for the time being."

"I understand," Prince Basil said. "But soon you will have to declare yourself. All need to know the truth."

"Aye, the truth," Shaeleen mumbled, "such a fickle master."

CHAPTER THIRTEEN

Three days after their meeting with the prince, Shaeleen stood next to Cole on the deck of a huge sailing ship and waved goodbye to their parents and little sister as they faded into the distance, eventually disappearing from sight amongst the crowded docks.

Shaeleen's brown hair, tied back behind her neck with a small ribbon, flapped around the back of her head as the ocean breeze became stronger. The sailors worked feverishly, hoisting the main sail.

"Do you think they'll be all right?" Shaeleen asked Cole.

He nodded his head and then pushed his dark bangs off his forehead. "I think they were torn between worry, for us leaving home for the first time, and excitement, from being asked by the prince himself to allow us to leave."

They'd spent the last two days secretly preparing items to take on their journey northward. Then Prince Basil had surprised all of them by showing up at their home the previous evening, to inform and to ask their parents for the help of Shaeleen and Cole.

"They were surprised to see Prince Basil show up at our front door, weren't they?" Shaeleen laughed and then took a deep breath of sea air. Summer was fast approaching, but it was cooler out on the water. Bright blue sky was intermixed with morning clouds. And the iridescent waves lapped gently against the ship as the sailors worked around Shaeleen and Cole.

"Prince Basil didn't need to do that," Cole said.

"I know," Shaeleen agreed. "But he did." She turned momentarily sullen. "I just hope that, in the end, we can help him."

Cole stiffened a bit. "Shaeleen, it's your job to find the truth. As much as I like Prince Basil, we serve the truth now and no one else."

Shaeleen leaned over the rail in silence and stared hard at the water rushing up against the ship as they picked up speed. When she did speak again, her voice was almost lost on the wind: "But what will the truth do to me?"

Cole patted Shaeleen's back. "You are not alone here, TruthSeer. I'm your brother and your wizard guardian."

"Cole!" Shaeleen stood up straight and glanced around. "You can't say that. I'm not a TruthSeer yet."

Cole raised his brows at her. "I don't think there will be an official ceremony naming you thus."

Shaeleen frowned. "Remember: we go in under different identities here. No one knows who I am…or, for that matter, who you are either."

"I know. I just wish I knew better what I am and what I can do. I wish I had someone to teach me." Cole ran his fingers through his hair.

"Don't I know it." Shaeleen smiled. "I guess all we've got is each other for now."

A few sailors walked over by them. Then one of them spoke to Shaeleen. "Miss, you might want to go down below now. The waves will be a bit choppy as we head out farther into the sea. Once we tack back into the Bay of Jalen and go on to North Bay, the waters will be calmer."

Shaeleen nodded her head and beckoned Cole to follow her. The sailors were under the assumption that she was a rich merchant's daughter, being escorted by her cousin to meet a possible suitor in North Bay.

Soon they joined the other passengers in the mess deck below, where food was now being served. Shaeleen had counted about twenty-five other people on the large ship. It regularly took passengers up and down the east coast and had most likely begun its current journey by picking up passengers in South Bay, in Althea, over two weeks ago. Then it may have stopped in Mistport, in Antioch, before anchoring in Stronghaven. It would now continue up to North Bay and then on to Riverton, in Gabor, before it would turn back and bring other passengers in the opposite direction. From what Shaeleen had heard from her father, this was a very lucrative business. Another ship took passengers around the north and the west sides of the island.

Shaeleen and Cole sat off in a corner at a table by themselves. A simple meal of bread and fruits was being served. Most in the room seemed to be of noble birth, which was understandable, based on the price of their fares.

Shaeleen put a piece of melon in her mouth and glanced around the room, trying to ignore the snippets of conversations, which could cause her pain. Off to the other side, she spied a quick motion and noticed a boy around age twelve or so bump into the back of a man. After offering his apologies, the lad moved off to another corner and bent over, looking at something in his hand. *How had he moved so quick?*

Shaeleen nudged Cole's arm with her elbow and then pointed at the boy. He pulled a green cap off his messy, blond hair and stuffed something into it. Then he put the cap back on before continuing his way around the room. His clothes were older, but fashionable, with a white shirt under a thick, green coat. These sat above black trousers that came just below his knees, showing green hose and black shoes to finish off the outfit. It was quite a dapper look for one so young.

They watched the boy walk by the table of a noble family engaged in conversation. Suddenly, the boy stood a few feet away, by an empty table.

"Hey, did you see that?" Shaeleen asked her brother. "What was that?"

"The boy took a package from that table." Cole stood up abruptly, his face dark and his lips held tight. "That boy's a thief."

Cole took a step toward the boy. But Shaeleen stood up next to Cole and put her hand on his forearm, saying, "Don't cause a scene, Cole. It's not our business."

"What he's doing is not right, Shae."

Shaeleen rolled her eyes at her honorable brother but inside took joy at his sense of right and truth. She just shrugged as she watched Cole stride forward with singular purpose. In the blink of an eye, he was next to the boy—faster than Shaeleen thought should have been possible for Cole.

A few others in the room had now turned their heads to look at Cole. Their surprise showed that they didn't know where he had come from, and small whispers ensued around them. Cole put his hand on the boy's shoulder, and the boy froze and looked up at Cole. His light green eyes grew wide, but, to Shaeleen's amazement, the boy didn't try to run.

Cole held his other hand out in front of him and said, "Give me the package."

"What package, sir?" the boy said. His accent was not from Galena but maybe from Antioch, if Shaeleen had to guess.

"In your hand. The one you took from these good people." Cole pointed at the table next to them. The nobles there had turned their heads and were taking in the exchange with interest.

"Mother, my package is gone!" said a young woman at the table. "The necklace we just purchased in Stronghaven."

Cole raised his eyebrows at the boy and reached behind him to look for the package in his hands. The boy spun around and brought out both his hands in front of himself, with nothing in them.

"You must be mistaken, sir," the boy said with a small smirk. "I have nothing here."

Cole took a deep breath and turned the boy around. "Where is it?"

The boy turned around in a swift, swirling motion and bent down under the table next to the nobles. When he came back up, the small package was in his hand. He offered it back to the young woman.

"It must have fallen off your table, miss. I'm glad I found it for you."

The young woman took it and turned back to her parents, chattering about its contents. The rest of the room soon lost interest in the exchange, but Cole kept a hand on the boy's shoulder and directed him over to the table where Shaeleen stood.

He motioned for the boy to sit down with them and said, "I know what you did."

The boy raised his brows at Cole, grabbed a piece of bread, and stuffed it in his mouth. After chewing it and swallowing it down, he smiled. "Thanks for the food." He began to stand up, but Cole shoved him gently back down.

"Leave him alone, Cole," Shaeleen said. "Can't you tell he's just a street urchin who slipped on board to get some food?"

"I'm not a street urchin," the boy said, his eyes flashing at them.

Shaeleen didn't feel any pain, and she gave a look to Cole that he immediately understood.

"Then who are you?" Cole asked. "And no lies. She will know." He pointed to Shaeleen.

"My name is Orin. My father works on this ship."

Cole looked at Shaeleen, who nodded back. The boy was telling the truth.

"And, did you take that package?" Cole asked, looking down menacingly at the boy.

"No," Orin said defensively.

Shaeleen felt a sickening of her stomach with the force of Orin's words. "You are not telling the truth, Orin."

"Yes, I am," he said again.

This time Shaeleen almost doubled over, but she tried to remember what she had learned about pushing the pain away.

"What's wrong with her?" Orin asked Cole. "She looks sick."

Shaeleen shook her head at Cole to have him not say anything.

Cole seemed to struggle for the right words to say. "If I see you steal again, you will face punishment by the law, Orin," Cole said. "You understand?"

"Only if you see me steal," Orin said with a smirk.

Quick as lightning, Cole lifted the cap off the boy's head and turned it upside down on the table. A few trinkets and some money fell out.

For the first time, Orin looked afraid. "How...?" was all Orin could say.

Cole laughed and turned to Shaeleen. "Shae, he's got speed."

Shaeleen frowned, not quite understanding Cole.

"He's from Antioch and must have inherited some of the powers of the Garnet SpeedStone," Cole said, keeping his voice low. "And I *saw him*."

Orin tried to grab back his stuff, but Cole moved faster. Shaeleen was surprised. *This must be one of the powers he inherited as my guardian wizard.*

"But how?" Orin asked, looking more fearful now. "You're not from Antioch. I can tell by your eyes and hair."

Cole didn't answer Orin's question but instead looked back at Shaeleen with understanding in his eyes. Turning back to the boy, he shoved the hat at him and kept the rest of the items out.

"What are you going to do with those?" Orin asked.

"Give them back to their rightful owners," Cole said.

Orin sat back in his chair with a loud huff. "That's not fair."

"Fair?" Cole said. "You stole these from their proper owners."

"I only take what they don't need. It's boring on the ship. It helps to pass the time."

"And what do you do with all the items you steal, Orin?" Shaeleen asked, hoping he wouldn't lie.

The boy thought a moment, looked into Shaeleen's eyes, and then stated, "I give them to others that don't have much. Some use them to buy food."

Shaeleen felt compassion for what the boy had done. "You aren't keeping them for yourself?"

"No." Orin's head turned down in embarrassment. "I only steal to help others, miss. I'm not a bad person."

Shaeleen felt surprisingly well after his statements, for she had expected lies. She nodded to Cole. "You can go now, Orin." Shaeleen wanted to talk to her brother alone.

Orin stood up and gave a short bow to Shaeleen.

"I'll be watching you, Orin," Cole said as he also stood up, to watch the boy move out of the room. When Cole sat back down, he shook his head and said, "That boy has no honor."

"But he isn't keeping the items for himself, Cole," Shaeleen said. "He is doing something that is good."

"The ends don't justify the means, Shae." Cole opened his arms out to the side. "That would give everyone the right to make up their own rules and laws. But there has to be order and stability."

"Cole, settle down. He's only a boy, and the world is not always black and white—right or wrong."

Cole grunted and absently popped a grape into his mouth.

"Do you know how fast you moved toward Orin?" Shaeleen said in a quiet voice, leaning closer to her brother.

Cole nodded. "I just thought about what I wanted to do— get to that boy as quickly as I could. I felt a small stirring inside. Then I was there. Do you think anyone else noticed?"

"Some noticed that you seemed to come from nowhere, but I don't think they thought anything else about it."

Just then, Shaeleen had to grab onto the table with both hands as the ship rocked to the side. Others in the room gasped out loud, and one woman fell to the floor.

Before Shaeleen could say anything, Cole was at the woman's side, helping her up.

"Are you all right, my lady?" he asked.

The woman seemed slightly shaken up, but she nodded her head. "Yes, yes, I am quite fine now. Thank you, young man."

Cole waited until the woman was back in her seat and then walked back to Shaeleen.

"Cole, you can't keep doing that." Shaeleen looked around the room. Off to one side sat a lone figure in a dark cloak, his head bowed. A hood covered his head, but he had the build of a man. Then he slowly brought his head up and stared hard at Cole.

"I can't help it, Shae," Cole said.

"Well, you have to," Shaeleen snapped back harder than she'd intended. "Others are noticing."

Cole looked in the direction that Shaeleen had just been looking moments before, but there was no one there now.

"There was a man there," Shaeleen said. "He was staring at you as if he knew what you'd done. His eyes were light, like ours, Cole, and he had power in them. I'm not sure who he is."

Cole nodded. "We need to be more careful. You are right. I'm going to our room. I need to rest." He stood up and then turned and surveyed the stolen items on the table. "Can you give these back to their owners?"

Shaeleen let out a deep sigh. "Yes, Cole. I will." *Sometimes his sense of honor and right go far beyond reason.*

As she went around the room to find the owners of the items, Shaeleen thought about why she didn't feel bad about the boy's stealing. *Why did that not hurt me? Is there a difference between what is true and what could be right?*

With that thought, she finished up in the mess deck and then went to join her brother in their shared room.

CHAPTER FOURTEEN

It took Shaeleen and Cole a few days to reach North Bay, a typical seaport. Nestled in the corner of the Bay of Jalen, the city was on the border of the kingdoms of Galena and Gabor. And, as such, there were abundant soldiers in town on both sides of the border. Historically, there had been some bad blood between the two kingdoms. But, of late, things were quiet—almost too quiet. The soldiers seemed restless, and bar fights broke out constantly.

Even though they now stood on dry land, Shaeleen still felt like she was moving back and forth. She was glad she didn't get sick on the ship—besides during the lies she'd heard. They had seen Orin a few other times, but he had seemed to purposefully avoid them—especially with the looks Cole gave him.

Today, the sun was warm and the air was thick with moisture from the sea. Shaeleen wiped her brow and motioned Cole toward the shade of a nearby building. The buildings here were different than the ones in Stronghaven. They were newer, for the most part, the port having grown in size over the last ten years or so. White was the predominate color here. And most of the buildings stood about three stories tall, with shops on the bottom and living quarters on top.

"So, Shae, what's first?" Cole asked.

Shaeleen thought for a moment, pulling on the power of the IntelligenceStone to order her thoughts. "We need to find out where Prince Calix resides."

Cole nodded his head. "Well, let's find an inn first. We will need a place to stay for at least a few days. I wonder what part of town is the best. Where would a lady of your stature stay?"

"The prince's quarter is where you want to be, my lady," piped up a younger voice. Orin was peering around the corner.

"Ah, Orin." Shaeleen smiled. Then she squinted her eyes at him, wondering if they'd said anything that shouldn't have been overheard. "How long have you been there?"

"Long enough to know I can help you." Orin looked from Shaeleen to Cole. "At least, if your *guard* here will allow it," he said, emphasizing *guard* in a way that made Shaeleen know that Orin knew more than he was letting on.

Shaeleen glanced at Cole. "Well?"

Cole nodded at her, showing that she was in charge. Then he spoke to Orin. "You must follow my rules. I guard the lady here and won't abide any stealing, lying, or cheating."

"Is he always this way?" Orin asked Shaeleen.

She laughed. "Oh, yes, Orin. He is very serious about protecting me and living up to his code of honor. I wouldn't push him if I were you."

"I will require some payment up front," Orin said.

Cole opened his mouth to push back, but Shaeleen put her hand in the air and waved it in a brisk motion, saying, "Pay the boy, Cole. I have a feeling he will be useful."

Cole growled softly and reached toward his pocket to pay Orin. Before he could do so, Orin proceeded to take a small pouch out of his own pocket and hand it sheepishly over to Cole.

"No hard feelings, sir."

Cole's eyes went wide, and his face turned red.

Shaeleen stifled a laugh behind her hand.

"How did you...?" Cole asked. "That's my pouch. Were you not going to tell me?"

"I did tell you...well, I gave it back to you, anyway," Orin said, his cap hiding his eyes. "Isn't that the honorable thing to do?"

"Why, you little..." Cole said as he stepped toward Orin, moving mere feet in the blink of an eye. But, when he reached the spot where Orin had been, the boy still stood a few feet away. Cole ground his teeth and jumped again, appearing at the boy's side before Shaeleen could even figure out what was going on. Again, Orin still stood a few feet away from Cole.

Shaeleen watched in wonderment as both of them used the power of the SpeedStone. Cole was turning red, and Orin had a big grin on his young, freckled face. Suddenly, Cole reached out his hand and, without touching him, knocked Orin to the ground. With two strides, Cole stood over the boy.

"Don't ever play games with me again, boy."

"Cole, Cole!" Shaeleen raced to her brother's side. "What has got into you? What did you do?"

"I don't know, Shae," Cole whispered in embarrassment, out of Orin's hearing. "I don't know how to control my new powers."

Quietly, Orin stood up on shaky feet, staring at Cole. He gave a small nod of respect. "Sir, I apologize for provoking you. I can tell you are much more than you seem."

Shaeleen ground her teeth in frustration. If Cole continued to use his newfound powers in public, rumors would start to spread.

"Let's go, you two." Shaeleen crooked her finger at both of them. "No more bickering. Orin, you will act honorably with us or you will leave my employ immediately. Cole, you need to watch yourself and don't let a mere boy goad you. I thought you had more sense than that. I am here on important business and can't have this type of distraction."

Both Cole and Orin looked ashamed, and they mumbled their apologies to Shaeleen.

"Well then," Shaeleen continued. "Orin, show us the way to the prince's quarter."

Cole shoved a few pieces of luggage into Orin's hands. "It would not do for Lady Shaeleen to carry her own luggage."

Orin glared at him but took the luggage anyway. He struggled under its weight, but Shaeleen could tell that Orin would never admit it.

After walking a few blocks away from the docks, they turned onto a larger street big enough for two carriages to pass each other. The street was made of smooth stone, with walkways on either side. The buildings here were still predominately white, but the awnings were colorful, with each shop showcasing its name in bright lettering.

The fishy smells of the docks had faded behind them and was replaced here with something new and wonderful. Shaeleen stopped without warning and moved her head around, her nose in the air.

"What is she doing?" Orin asked Cole.

Cole grinned. "Looking for something sweet, I would assume. It's her vice."

Shaeleen turned to the two. "I can smell something so delicious. Cinnamon and sugar…" She proceeded across the street and down two shops.

When Shaeleen entered the bakery, the smell of sweet cinnamon bread filled the air. Shaeleen rushed to the counter and looked at all the cakes, pies, and breads they had for sale. Her stomach rumbled, and the portly man behind the counter laughed.

"You sound hungry, miss," the man said, wiping some stray flour off his arm. "If you don't mind me saying, we have the best sweet cinnamon bread in all of North Bay."

Shaeleen had heard similar boasts before, but this time she felt the stirrings of truth. She motioned for Cole to play his part as her guard and protector. He stepped forward and opened his pouch of money. He sent a quick glare at Orin, as if to say, *Stay away from my things.*

"Three of your finest please, sir," Cole said, removing a silver coin from the pouch.

The man brought out three of the largest sweet rolls Shaeleen had ever seen. Her mouth was watering just by having to wait the few precious moments for Cole to finish the transaction.

Soon they sat themselves down at a small table outside the store. Shaeleen was oblivious to anything else as she devoured the tasty treat. But, suddenly, she felt more than saw Cole stiffen, and then Orin, who was sitting beside her, gazed intently down the street.

"We're being followed, miss," Orin said.

Shaeleen looked at Cole. "He is correct, Shae. A man in a long, dark cloak lags behind us a few shops and looks in our direction."

With the pretense of using a cloth to wipe some stray crumbs off her face, Shaeleen turned slightly in her seat. She tried not to show her surprise but turned around slowly.

"It's the man from the ship," Shaeleen said in a whisper. "I'm sure of it."

"Why would someone be following you?" Orin asked. "Aren't you here to meet a suitor?"

Without having to give a lie, she ignored the boy's question and only asked one of her own: "How far until the inn, Orin?"

"Another block," Orin said. "Not far at all, but..."

"Just show us the way." Cole motioned them all to stand, and then they began to walk forward.

"I'm going to go into this shop," Cole said as he stopped in front of a leatherworker's shop. "I need a new belt and scabbard for my sword."

Shaeleen rubbed her forehead. Cole was lying. But she didn't want Orin to know, so Shaeleen nodded and motioned for Orin to stay with her. She knew Cole was going to try and get closer to the man that was following them. It was a smart thing to do, but she still worried about her brother.

"I will meet you at the inn," Cole said, his eyes telling Shaeleen to be careful.

Shaeleen took Orin's empty hand in hers, and they continued down the street. Out of the corner of her eye, she saw Orin redden from the tips of his fingers to the ends of his ears. She smiled and pulled him along faster.

Before getting too deep in the crowd, she glanced back and saw the man again. He was just passing the store Cole had gone into. The man's eyes scanned over the area.

"Hurry, Orin," Shaeleen prodded. "That man is still following us."

Orin moved out in front and pulled Shaeleen along.

Soon they came to the front of a five-story building. It was twice as wide as any other building on the street. It had a set of double doors on each end of the building and a generous porch connecting them together.

Shaeleen took just a moment to smooth out her skirts and pat down her hair. It was still back in a ponytail from being on the ship. Climbing the steps, she turned back around before entering the inn. The man was nowhere to be seen. She hoped Cole was all right, but a feeling of worry began to form inside of her as they walked inside.

Stepping up to the counter, she asked for a room with two beds. The middle-aged woman with graying hair nodded, grabbed a key from a hook, and directed them to the stairs.

"Is it only you two, my lady?" the woman said, looking a little confused.

"Oh, no," Shaeleen said. "My guard is coming soon, just picking up a few items. This is my nephew. I'm supposed to keep him out of trouble. They will share a bed."

Shaeleen pushed a hand into her stomach and took a deep breath to regain control after saying these lies. She felt the pain begin to spread from her temples outward, but she willed it back inside for the moment.

"Young boys do have a way of getting into trouble, don't they?" The woman laughed and led them to their room.

Once inside the room, Shaeleen walked to a window overlooking the front street they had just entered from. Putting her head out the window as far as she could, she glanced down the street in the direction they had come from. She saw the tall, dark-cloaked man. But, instead of following them, he had found Cole and now had him by the arm and was escorting him behind another building.

"Cole!" Shaeleen yelled out loud. Without telling Orin what was going on, she ran out of the room and down the stairs. She stood for a moment on the inn's porch, looking down the street. Then Orin caught up to her.

"What's the matter, miss?"

"I saw that man take my brother," Shaeleen said. "I need to help Cole."

"Your brother?" Orin asked, appearing confused. "I thought he was your guard."

Shaeleen ignored the question and took off at a run, not noticing or really caring if Orin kept up with her or not. She could not let Cole get hurt. He wasn't trained yet at being her guardian wizard.

CHAPTER FIFTEEN

Shaeleen stood at the opening of a small alley that wound its way between two white stone buildings, and then she yelled out for her brother, "Cole! Cole!"

A few people walking down her side of the street behind her glanced her way, but they only dismissed her as a young woman looking for her friend. Orin stood next to her, looking up and down the street.

Then they both trotted farther into the alleyway. Shaeleen tried a few doors on the sides of the two buildings. One was locked, another led to an old empty room, but the third was the laundry area for a family.

"Have you seen my brother?" Shaeleen asked the family inside. "He is tall, with shaggy dark hair, and was being chased by a man in a dark cloak."

The woman in the laundry room looked at a girl then back to Shaeleen and shook her head.

Shaeleen bent over in pain. "You're not telling me the truth." She stood back up with difficulty.

A younger girl ran up to the woman and hid behind her skirts. The woman looked behind herself and then back at Shaeleen and sighed.

"Please, he might be in trouble," Shaeleen pleaded.

The woman took a step forward. "He has eyes like yours?"

Shaeleen nodded.

"Like the prince's wizard," the woman said. It was not a question, and Shaeleen knew it for the truth.

The woman pointed down the alleyway—in the direction Shaeleen and Orin had been heading earlier. "He ran by here a few minutes ago," the woman said and began shuffling Shaeleen and Orin back out of the door. "Please leave us alone. We don't want any trouble with your kind."

"*Our kind?*" Shaeleen asked. "What are you talking about?"

The woman began to push the door closed.

"I'm from Galena, from Stronghaven," Shaeleen said as the woman finished closing the door on them. Shaeleen didn't know what to think of the woman's attitude. Their eyes had not caused that much trouble before.

"She thought you were from Verlyn," Orin said.

Shaeleen wanted to ask him more about that, but first she needed to find her brother.

Running out of the alleyway, she began shouting for her brother again. Her heart was beating fast, and her breathing was coming harder. *Where could they have gone? Would the man in the black cloak hurt Cole?* Tears formed at the edges of her eyes, but she brushed them away angrily. Crying would solve nothing at the moment. She needed to find Cole.

More crowds moved around the busy street now, either coming or going to the nearby shops of the merchant district. The shops' colorful awnings made it hard for Shaeleen to see far. She stood on her tippy toes and looked right and left, trying to see over the crowds—it didn't help much. Off to the right, at the end of the road, was a much larger building than any other she had seen so far in the city.

"What is that building?" she asked Orin, who had seemed to know his way around the city earlier.

"The prince's mansion—or *palace*, as he calls it."

"Could that man have taken Cole there?" Shaeleen asked out loud, but more to herself. She didn't think so. The prince couldn't have known they were here.

Suddenly, Shaeleen remembered something. Besides being her brother, Cole was her guardian wizard. She should know where he was. Closing her eyes, she thought about him hard. A flicker of life came to the corner of her mind. It was moving— but what direction? She thought harder and then felt a power flare up inside of her. Cole was moving north—toward the prince's mansion.

"Shae!" Orin said suddenly. "You're glowing!"

Shaeleen opened her eyes to find nearby strangers gawking and pointing at her. She looked down and found that she held the TruthStone inside her fist. The green glow must have been even brighter moments before. Now it was beginning to fade, but not before onlookers had stopped and stared.

"Oh no!" Shaeleen realized what she had done. She obviously had not drawn on the IntelligenceStone when she had thought about using her powers—it was hard to get used to having access to all the powers she now had.

"She's got a stone of power," shouted a young boy to his mother.

Then others joined in, saying, "That girl has magic!"

So much for coming into the city unnoticed.

Orin grabbed her hand and pulled her quickly back the way they had just come. The alleyway blurred around her as they sped back down its length in a matter of moments. Shaeleen groaned at the sensation of Orin's use of speed and then at the realization they were moving farther away from Cole. But she had to get away from those who had seen her use magic.

Back at the street where their inn was, they stopped and looked behind them. Shaeleen breathed a sigh of relief when she didn't see anyone following them. They tried to walk unnoticed back to their room, though Shaeleen thought for sure her beating heart would give them away. Once in the room, she collapsed onto her back on one of the beds, closing her eyes for a moment. The connection with her brother was still there.

Opening her eyes, she found Orin standing in front of her with a questioning look on his face.

"Miss Shaeleen, what was that back there?"

"It was nothing, Orin," Shaeleen said. "Don't worry about it."

A slight pounding began behind her eyes. "Stupid stone," she said softly.

"What did you say?" Orin asked.

"Nothing, Orin." The pain roared louder in her ears. Then she sat up and said angrily, "All right. It is something, Orin. I do have magic. There—are you happy now?"

Orin backed up a step, but didn't look very happy.

But Shaeleen's headache was dissipating, and so she didn't feel overly bad for the outburst. It was better than being sick.

After a few silent moments, Shaeleen noticed Orin's face. It was twisted up as if he was thinking about something.

"That's how you did it," Orin blurted out. "That's how you caught me on the ship. You could tell when I was telling the truth or a lie."

All Shaeleen could do was nod her head.

"You have magic just like me!" Orin grinned with a toothy smile. "You and your brother can do things. What else can you do?"

Shaeleen smiled at the boy's enthusiasm, but she wasn't ready to tell him all. "I can't tell you, Orin—it's for your protection."

Orin's grin turned to a pout. "I can protect myself. I can run faster than anyone I know."

"I know you can, and just now, I am grateful for that," Shaeleen said. "I will tell you, though, that I am here on a special mission from Basil. But first I need to find my brother. Will you help me?" Shaeleen felt she could trust the boy. Oh, he was mischievous, but she sensed he was a good person.

Orin's grin returned. "You bet I will...but, will your brother get mad at me again? He's scary when he's mad."

Shaeleen laughed. "Cole scares you? Cole is the least scary person I know. He would never hurt you."

"But he did threaten me and knocked me to the ground." Orin sat down on the other bed with a frown.

"He is very loyal to his principles, Orin. It's what drives him." Shaeleen stood up. "Anyway, I know where he is."

"Where?"

"At the prince's mansion."

Orin's eyes lit up. "I've always wanted to go there. But how do we get in?"

Shaeleen shook her head. "I don't know yet, but we need to get closer."

* * *

Finally, Shaeleen and Orin stood at a corner behind the back of the prince's mansion. They had waited until late in the day, after the sun had set. It had been hard for Shaeleen to do so, but it would be easier to slip inside unnoticed in the dark. Servants seemed to routinely go in and out of a back door. As people came and went, Shaeleen began to listen to their conversations for any clues of what to do next.

"The prince returned today," said a young male servant carrying in an armful of food. A young woman walked next to him, her arms equally full. "I heard he was in Gabor."

"Is there going to be a war, Elden?" the young woman said.

Elden shook his head. "I don't know, Marni. He seems obsessed with taking the crown. I've heard that he talks about the kingdom belonging to him."

Shaeleen found that she felt no pain from this. *That is odd.* Prince Basil would be crowned the next king on his birthday— in less than two months. She tried to walk closer to the pair before they would enter the back door to the mansion.

"I don't think he would make a good king," Marni said. "His temper…"

Elden nodded his head. "I don't like him either, but this is our job. Mama needs our help since she's been sick."

They opened the door to the mansion and stepped inside.

"I hear the TruthSeer is in the dungeon," Marni whispered, "and that she chose to come on her own."

"Don't listen to rumors, Marni," Elden said as the door closed behind them.

Orin looked up at Shaeleen. "What does all that mean?"

Shaeleen shook her head. "I'm not sure. But it doesn't sound good. First, though, we need to find my brother."

Moving back behind a small copse of trees, Shaeleen reached out with her mind. Then she turned her eyes upward. "Up there." She pointed. "Cole is on the third floor."

Orin's gaze followed Shaeleen's over to a white trellis that ran up the side of the building and next to an upper room's window.

Shaeleen smiled. "Do you think it will hold us?"

Orin looked back at her. "It will hold me, at least."

"You're not going in there without me," Shaeleen said and began walking toward the corner of the building. "That's my brother in there."

Orin sighed. "All right."

They reached the trellis, and Orin began climbing first. Ivy had grown up it and had wrapped itself around the painted wooden trellis, but Orin seemed to find handholds as he climbed higher. Shaeleen stood looking up at him as he neared the third floor. He reached over and jiggled the window, eventually pushing it open.

"What's up there?" Shaeleen whispered as she put her right foot on the bottom of the trellis and began climbing.

"It's too dark to tell," Orin said, putting one leg through the opening.

Shaeleen heard a grunt, then a scuffle, then silence.

"Orin, Orin?" she whispered, climbing up more quickly. Her foot slipped on the ivy, and she grabbed on hard with both hands. One foot dangled below her, and then the trellis gave a groan. *I'm almost there.*

A few more steps up, and she put her hand over the window's ledge. An arm reached out and grabbed a hold of her arm. She screamed, and her feet slipped. The arm above her became two arms.

"Let me help you inside," came a deep voice as the second hand grabbed her other arm and pulled her up, into the room, and onto the floor.

Shaeleen rolled over and gazed into the face of the man from the ship. The man that had been chasing them. The man that had taken her brother. The man with pale blue eyes like theirs. *A man who has power!*

CHAPTER SIXTEEN

Shaeleen and Orin were tied up in the corner of a dark room. With only some stray light from lamps outside the building, she saw that the only things in the dusty room were a few shelves with scattered items and a table with three chairs—nothing of importance.

Then the man that had captured them came into view and stood over the two and glared. His hood still covered most of his head, but Shaeleen saw wisps of gray hair coming out its sides. This was definitely the same man from the ship.

"What have you done with my brother?" Shaeleen asked as she tried to put on a brave face.

The man laughed, but there was no humor in it. "Your *brother*? Ahh, so that's who he is to you. It was hard to tell on the ship. If you would like to know, he is meeting with the prince right now. The prince has taken an interest in your brother, it seems."

"In my brother?" Shaeleen was confused. All along, Shaeleen had thought this man had been after her. "What would he want with my brother?"

"Come now—*Shaeleen*, isn't it?" The man stood over her, obviously taking delight in scaring her and Orin. "You must know what your brother is."

"*Is?*" Shaeleen asked, stalling for time while she tried to figure out what to do. "He is just an ordinary man."

The pain roared through her gut. She shut her eyes, to try and steady herself, but it was all she could do to keep from falling over.

When she opened her eyes, the man in front of them tilted his head at her as if trying to figure something out. Then he shook his head and paced a few steps.

Shaeleen stole a quick glance over at Orin. He was trying to loosen the ropes around his hands. She would have to keep the man busy.

"I think you know he is more than that," the man said. "He is a wizard—and an untrained one at that. But we can't have a wizard traipsing around the kingdom on his own."

Her brother wasn't on his own. *He has me—although I am as untrained as he is.*

Orin coughed and looked up with wide eyes. He moved his gaze from the man to Shaeleen and back to the man again.

The man laughed. "Oh, your little friend here didn't know that, did he?"

"A wizard?" Orin shook his head. "You're crazy. Wizards don't just pop up from nowhere these days."

"Ah, you are correct, young sir. Wizards only come forth when there is a need to protect something or someone."

Shaeleen could feel the TruthStone in her pocket. With all the energy she possessed, she willed it to be safe in the pouch Prince Basil had given her. She couldn't let this man know what Cole was really guarding.

The man continued, "That is what the prince is trying to find out."

"And, if Calix doesn't find out anything?" Shaeleen asked. "Then what?"

"Oh, Prince Calix will find out something. He has his ways."

Shaeleen felt her face drain of color. She couldn't let Cole be tortured.

"Anyway," the man continued, "we now have you… That should provide sufficient leverage for your brother's cooperation." The man turned and started to cough. It took him a few moments to get his coughing under control.

He didn't sound very well.

Shaeleen opened her mouth to reply to his threats, but before she could, suddenly Orin was between the two of them. He bent over and rammed his head into the man's gut. This attack caught the stranger by surprise, and he fell backward. Orin grabbed a knife at the man's waist, and, before Shaeleen could wonder what was happening, she felt the ropes being cut off her wrists.

The man stood up and waved a hand in the air. A current of wind gusted forth and pushed Orin to the ground. Orin tried to use his speed to get away, but the man seemed to move almost just as fast—both were blurs to Shaeleen's eyes. Trails of color streamed through the dark room as they moved after each other. And, while the two were chasing each other around the room, Shaeleen moved closer to one of the small chairs.

Then Orin stumbled, and the man grabbed his arm and pinned him to the wall. Shaeleen flipped her foot around the chair leg and kicked it up into the air. Catching the seat in her hands, she flung the chair at the back of the man. This diversion caused the man to release Orin's hands. In only a second, Orin was on the other side of the room, standing next to Shaeleen.

"Enough!" the man roared, bringing his hands together.

A bright purple glow erupted around him. *The power of the stones.* In the sudden flash, Shaeleen saw the lightness of his eyes and the power coursing through them. The man's muscles bulged, and he flung out his wrists at them. The power engulfed Shaeleen and Orin and pushed them up against the wall.

Shaeleen began to dig inside for her own power. She had used it before. The power of truth combined with intelligence could possibly allow them to escape. Before she could gather it, however, Orin yelled out, pushing against his bonds.

"It seems your brother is not the only one with some gemstone power," the man said, his face red and his breathing hard. "Little Orin here has some speed."

A noise sounded out in the hallway, and the man turned his head slightly.

As the man did so, Orin turned to Shaeleen and whispered, "Don't use whatever magic you have, Shaeleen."

"You're right." Shaeleen nodded, feeling both truth and intelligence flow through her. "I need to wait until the right time."

The man turned back toward them and waved his hands. The power that bound them pushed them forward now, toward the door. "It's time for you two to see the prince now. We'll see if your brother needs some additional incentive."

He pushed them with his power into the hall in front of himself. Then the man led them down a long corridor. A few servants flitted by, but one look at this captor's hardened face sent them running down the hall.

Soon Shaeleen and Cole came to a door with two guards in front.

The man motioned for the guards to open the door.

One of them stepped forward and said, "The prince is still in session. He left word not to be interrupted."

"I am his wizard, boy, and am always allowed in," the man said.

"*His wizard?*" Shaeleen said softly to herself as she began to put things together. She felt the power of the IntelligenceStone flow through her, giving her knowledge. This was the kingdom of Galena's one wizard—the guardian wizard of their TruthSeer.

A TruthSeer must be close by if her wizard is here. Rumors had her in the dungeon, but that didn't make sense.

"Don't listen to him," Orin blurted out.

The man pulled the power tighter around both of them. Shaeleen could hardly breathe, and Orin's face turned red. "Quiet, you two!" The man put his hand to the door and pushed it open with little effort as the guards stood off to the side, grumbling.

The wizard pulled Orin and Shaeleen into the room behind him. Shaeleen glanced around. The room was more ornate than Prince Basil's study in Stronghaven. Gold-lined mahogany frames held giant pieces of artwork, antiquities from around Wayland sat on shelves, and heavily cushioned chairs sat in the corner around a small table—which held delicacies of food.

On the chairs themselves sat the prince and Cole. Both stood abruptly at the intrusion.

"Shaeleen!" Cole ran to Shaeleen's side. "What did they do to you? And Orin?" Cole turned back around. "Prince Calix, what is the meaning of this?"

Prince Calix took three long strides and stood in front of the new group. His hair was dark and curled a touch at the edges, and his face was paler than Prince Basil's, but the other features were similar enough to be uncanny. He wore a dark blue cape over a light blue shirt and dark trousers. A gold ring glittered on his right hand—the signet of a prince.

"Yes, Faegon," the prince said, looking hard at the man that had brought them in. "What is the meaning of this?"

"They were caught sneaking in, and then they attacked me, Prince," Faegon said.

Prince Calix laughed. "They attacked you—the mighty Faegon, ancient wizard of Galena—this young lady and small boy?"

Orin growled at being called *small*, but Shaeleen silenced him with a look.

"The boy has the power of speed, Sire," Faegon said, clearly not enjoying being put down by the prince.

A small gasp ensued from the back of the room. Shaeleen turned toward it. A servant boy had been standing so still there that she hadn't noticed him before.

Prince Calix whirled around and walked with deliberate steps to the boy. Without hesitating, the prince backhanded him across the face. "I told you that you are never to speak in this room, Poe."

Tears welled up in the eyes of the boy, but he said nothing. A large, red mark with the outlines of the prince's fingers reddened his face.

Shaeleen sucked in a deep breath. *This man is dangerous. Basil obviously received all the genes for compassion.*

The prince turned around and glared at her. "Do you have a problem with the way I discipline my servants, miss?"

Cole glared at her as if silently willing her to not say anything. But she couldn't lie. "I think there are better ways to teach your servants."

The prince pinched his lips tight, his face turning red. "How dare you tell me how to treat servants in my own kingdom."

"It's not your kingdom," Shaeleen said forcefully. "It belongs to your older brother."

As these words tumbled out, pain roared through her entire body. Shaeleen had never felt such agony before, and her body instinctively tried to bend over on its own. But the power of Faegon still held her tight. Then she retched on the floor in front of them.

"Shaeleen?" Cole rushed to her side. "Let her go!" he ordered Faegon.

Faegon looked at Prince Calix for confirmation, and the prince nodded his head. A puzzled look fell over his face.

Released from Faegon's power, Shaeleen fell, but Cole caught her before she could hit the ground. Orin, who had also been released, grabbed Shaeleen's other side, and together Orin and Cole lowered her softly to the ground, away from the vomit.

Shaeleen closed her eyes for a moment to try and push the pain back inside. When she opened them, the prince was still staring at her.

"Curious," he said with a thoughtful look. Then, turning to Faegon, he said, "Take them to the guest quarters."

"But, sir." Faegon's face barely held his anger in. "They are dangerous."

"Nonsense." Prince Calix waved a hand in the air. "Put guards on their doors, and magically seal it, if you wish. Cole hardly understands his powers, and this boy is just a renegade with a bit of Garnet in his blood. The girl, well…" He paused and studied Shaeleen again, tilting his head in a way that reminded her of Basil. "She may need some additional looking after."

"My lord?" Cole asked. "She just needs rest and some food."

Prince Calix nodded, smiling at Cole. "Of course, my young wizard. Anything for your sister. I am sorry this happened. After you have her settled, please come back. I would like to finish our conversation about how you can serve me and the throne of Galena."

Shaeleen stood up on her own, but Cole and Orin still walked at her sides. *What did the prince mean?* She looked at her brother, who shook his head at her questioning eyes. This time she did stay quiet and let Faegon lead them to go to the guest quarters.

As they left the room, Shaeleen heard the prince tell the guards to clean up the vomit, then report to him for punishment. They'd had orders not to let anyone enter and would bear responsibility for their actions.

At their suite of rooms, Faegon closed the door behind them. Orin and Cole led Shaeleen to a golden couch, and she lay down on it and closed her eyes for just a bit.

She had felt truth and lies around Prince Calix. An increasingly uncomfortable thought began to grow in her mind. She pushed these incomplete thoughts away for the moment. She didn't want to face what it all meant—at least, not right now. She was very tired and needed to rest.

CHAPTER SEVENTEEN

U pon awakening after a brief rest, Shaeleen noticed her brother was not in the room. Orin told her Cole had gone back to meet with the prince and the wizard Faegon. She was worried that her brother was being manipulated by Prince Calix.

A note had been left for them, inviting Shaeleen, Cole, and Orin to attend dinner with the prince that evening.

A small basin in the corner of the room allowed them to clean up as best they could. Shaeleen stared at herself in a small mirror and tried to smooth her hair down. Her skin was pale, and her eyes were puffy and tired. It had only been that morning when they'd left the ship—and the day was still not over.

Taking a deep breath and clearing her mind, she approached the door with Orin in tow. A guard escorted them to the dining hall. Although Shaeleen had thought it would be a private affair, around the room sat at least ten small tables, with groups of two to four people at each. As her eyes flicked in quick succession over each one, Shaeleen was surprised at the presence of Lord Bancroft, Galena's minister of relations with Gabor. She hoped he wouldn't recognize her from Lord Gregory's birthday party.

In the back corner, two women sat talking with heads close to each other. Both wore exquisite gowns, making Shaeleen grateful they hadn't forced something nice on her to wear. One of the women had dark, shoulder-length hair, curling lightly at the shoulders, while the other's hair was gray, slightly covering her ears.

As if feeling Shaeleen's attention on them, both women glanced up at her at the same time. Shaeleen let out a small gasp. The dark-haired one was the queen mother—mother to Basil and Calix—still a striking beauty, with smooth skin and intelligent eyes. The other woman looked directly into Shaeleen's eyes, and Shaeleen felt the world spin faintly.

"Shae!" Orin held on to her arm. "You feeling all right?"

Shaeleen broke eye contact with the other woman and turned her head to Orin. "Yes, yes, I am fine." Though her stomach began to sour.

Shaeleen flicked her eyes back to the older woman for a brief moment, but the woman had turned back to her conversation with the queen mother. Shaeleen was still sure the woman was the TruthSeer of Galena, a woman who had served the two prior kings and, by the haunted look in her eyes, had gone through numerous bouts of pain.

Is that how I will end up?

She cursed the keeper who had given her the TruthStone, although, upon thinking about it, her hand had crept into her pocket and felt the weight of it there.

Still scanning the room, she spied Cole at another table, in conversation with Faegon. They were laughing, and Cole seemed relaxed. He looked over and beckoned Shaeleen and Orin to their table.

"I don't like that man, Faegon," Orin grumbled.

"Because he was faster than you?" Shaeleen teased him.

Orin reddened. "Not just that."

"I know what you mean."

Shaeleen nodded her head as she wound her way through the tables. The men and women seated there stared hard at her and Orin, obviously trying to figure out who they were.

"I don't like him either," she admitted. "I wonder why he's here with Prince Calix, rather than in Stronghold with Prince Basil."

Shaeleen and Orin sat themselves at the table with Cole and Faegon.

Faegon gave them a slight nod, but he said nothing. He was younger than the TruthSeer he served, but not by much. The look in his eyes seemed to hold a lifetime of knowledge and experience.

Orin glared at the older man as if, by doing so, he could scare the wizard away.

Cole leaned over to Shaeleen and whispered, "Faegon has been telling me about my powers, Shae." His eyes glowed bright with joy.

Shaeleen leaned back. "Be careful, Cole. I don't like him."

"But he is the kingdom's wizard. He serves Galena."

With her lips close to Cole's ears, Shaeleen said, "I'm not sure if he serves Galena or Calix."

"*Prince* Calix, Shae. He is a prince of Galena." Cole's eyes darkened. "Serving one is serving the other."

Shaeleen shook her head at her brother's need for honor and protocol. "Just be careful," she whispered. "Remember our mission."

"Our mission is to find out the truth, Shaeleen."

That it was. And what was the truth here, in Prince Calix's dining room? Once again Shaeleen's eyes roamed the room. Off to one side, she spied two other guests that had been at Lord Gregory's party—friends of Lady Judith, she was sure. Seeing them heightened her sense of danger. *Why have I been invited to this dinner?*

Double doors opened on one end, and Prince Calix strutted in. His dark cape swirled around him. Gold jewelry adorned his neck, wrists, and fingers, sparkling brightly in the candlelit room. His eyes surveyed the room then settled on Shaeleen. A small smile formed on his slightly downturned lips. Shaeleen turned away from his attention.

The prince seated himself at the table with his mother and the TruthSeer.

"That is Erlinda with the queen mother, Queen Raisa," Faegon offered.

Shaeleen turned to the wizard, surprised at his sharing this information.

"It is no secret, young lady. She is our TruthSeer, the one and only TruthSeer of Galena. I have served her for over forty years," Faegon said.

Shaeleen braced for the pain—as Erlinda was not the only TruthSeer in Galena at the moment—but the pain never came. Faegon gave her a surprised look, as if he had been testing her.

The lack of pain must have been because of the way Faegon had worded his statement. Unknown to him, Shaeleen was not a TruthSeer of Galena, but of all of Wayland. And, for the time being, Shaeleen willed that secret to stay hidden. But, with a glance over at the prince's table, she caught TruthSeer

Erlinda's eyes and knew that at least one other person in the room knew who she was—or, at least, suspected her abilities.

Soon servants came into the candlelit room, carrying plates of wonderful-smelling food: roasted meats, steamed vegetables, and bowls of clam chowder, a seafood dish that North Bay was famous for. The sounds of silverware clicking and of a slight laugh from the back of the room were the only sounds Shaeleen heard as the dining experience began.

Shaeleen was enjoying her first real meal of the day. She took a deep breath and reveled in the aroma of the feast.

"This is horrible!" Prince Calix shouted moments later. He stood up with his bowl of soup in hand and threw it against a wall. Shaeleen jumped up at the sound. The rest of the room went quiet. The servants froze in place. And then Shaeleen found that she was the only guest standing. The prince glared directly at her, his face contorted in anger.

Cole reached his hand over to Shaeleen's arm and tried to pull her down, but she stayed standing.

"Do you have a problem, Miss Shaeleen?" the prince said, directing his attention to her. The rest of the room looked back and forth between the two, the servants looking relieved that the prince's attention was not on them.

"No." She shook her head. "You just startled me, that's all."

"And do you agree with my assessment of the soup?" Prince Calix asked, his tone defensive—as if daring her to disagree with him.

Shaeleen happened to glance at the TruthSeer and caught her eye. The woman gave a slight shake of her head, as if telling

Shaeleen to not disagree with the prince. But the soup, in fact, was very tasty—one of the more creamy clam chowders she'd ever eaten. Using her new intelligence, scenes of varying outcomes quickly played out in her mind, and she chose a course that she hoped would let reason prevail in the room.

"It's only soup, my lord," Shaeleen said, trying to soften the occasion. "The age of the clams, where they were harvested, and the spices used will understandably result in varying degrees of taste in any given batch and for each person tasting it."

The prince seemed taken aback by her answer, but his face softened somewhat.

Shaeleen let out a deep breath and smiled in return. She had reached the man's senses and thwarted a difficult situation.

Turning to the nearest servant, Prince Calix said, "Tell the cook who prepared the soup to leave my home. He will be blacklisted in all of North Bay. And get someone out here to clean up the mess. I hope the roasted pork has been prepared more to my liking."

Shaeleen covered a gasp from her mouth, and this time did sit down.

Faegon glared at her and shook his head in a condescending way. "You should not have spoken to him that way."

"What way?" Shaeleen looked into the old wizard's eyes. "I just pointed out the obvious to him."

"Don't you think he already knew what you told him?"

Shaeleen opened her mouth to retort and then closed it again.

"Shaeleen, he is the prince," Cole whispered to her. "Have some respect."

"I don't care if he's a prince," Orin said to the table. "He is rude. The poor cook doesn't deserve to be fired from his job. Prince Calix is a bully."

Both Faegon and Cole shushed the boy, but not before a few others at nearby tables had overheard his comments. Luckily, the prince hadn't heard.

The meal proceeded without any other interruptions or tantrums from the prince. The food was actually quite good, and Shaeleen enjoyed it immensely.

During a break in conversation between Cole and Faegon, Shaeleen turned to Faegon and said, "So, what are all these people doing here?"

Faegon raised his eyebrows and glanced around the room before answering, "They are friends of the prince."

Shaeleen rolled her eyes at him. "I'm not that gullible, Faegon. There is no way Calix has this many friends."

"Shae," Cole whispered loudly in her direction.

How can two brothers be so different? She thought about the excitement and compassion in Basil's eyes when he had thought about his people.

"Well, it's true," Shaeleen continued. "His brother, Basil, is adored by *his* subjects. But these people only hang around Calix because they want something." Shaeleen scanned the room shrewdly and then turned back to Faegon. "What does Calix have to give them?"

Faegon frowned at her. "Why do I have the feeling you're more than just the sister of a random wizard?" He placed his hands under his chin and leaned forward, mere inches from Shaeleen's face.

It took all she had to not back away. But she had to find out what was going on here, so she kept her eyes fixed on Faegon without flinching.

He finally growled, "You are an exasperating woman!"

Orin stifled a laugh, and Shaeleen gave him a stern look to be quiet. Turning her attention back to Faegon, she brought forth some of the power of the TruthStone and repeated her question. "What do they want from him?"

Faegon flinched and moved back a few inches. His whiskers seemed to twitch of their own volition, and his face reddened. "They want power, Shaeleen. Power that only a prince...or a king can give them."

Now it was Shaeleen's turn to flinch, but there was no pain. But the implications were almost worse than if there had been pain. It meant Faegon was telling the truth. *Stars! That's what this is all about; Prince Calix wants the throne.*

Faegon sat back and folded his arms, looking smug once again, now that Shaeleen's power had receded. "Not that it's any concern of yours," Faegon said. "I'm not even really sure why you are here, in fact. You were traveling under different identities on the ship—why was that?"

"And why were you on the ship, Faegon? What were you doing in Stronghold?"

Faegon laughed and spread his arms out to his sides. "My dear, I am the wizard of Galena. I can go anywhere I please."

"Then why do you stay here, with Prince Calix, rather than with Basil, the crown prince?"

Prince Calix stood up, and Shaeleen didn't receive her answer from Faegon. The prince looked over the entire group with a sneer and then growled, "The women may leave the room now. I have things to discuss with my supporters."

The first to stand was the prince's mother, Queen Raisa. She nodded her head toward Shaeleen, motioning for her to follow.

"Take Orin with you," Faegon said. "This is not a place for a little boy."

"I am not little," Orin said, his lips pouting.

Shaeleen gave Cole a questioning glance.

"I'm fine," Cole said.

"A young wizard might be valuable," Faegon said.

"Just be careful, Cole," Shaeleen offered.

Upon exiting the room, Shaeleen caught the prince's eyes one last time. They reflected a hungry desire for power. She needed to get back soon and warn Prince Basil about what his brother's intentions were. She would know more about his specific plans when Cole returned from the meeting.

CHAPTER EIGHTEEN

Glancing around the next room they entered, Shaeleen was amazed and impressed by the grandeur of Prince Calix's mansion in North Bay—artifacts from neighboring kingdoms, rich tapestries, and exquisite furniture filled the room. The queen mother ushered Shaeleen and Orin into the farthest part of the room away from the dozen or so other women.

Orin pulled on Shaeleen's sleeve and whispered up to her, "I don't like this."

A small smile tugged at the corners of Shaeleen's mouth. This room definitely was not going to be an exciting place for a boy.

"Young man," Queen Raisa turned to Orin, "I can tell you're not very comfortable here. Maybe you would like to sit on the balcony. I will have some desserts brought out for you. The views of the sea and the stars at this time of night are quite amazing."

Orin looked relieved.

"I have two sons of my own," Queen Raisa added, her bright lips parting into a wide smile. "I understand."

Erlinda leaned over and whispered something into Queen Raisa's ear. The queen mother raised her eyebrows in apparent surprise before turning back to Orin and saying, "But I must ask that you honor my accommodations and not wander around." Her dark eyes bore directly into Orin.

Orin took a step back, and his cheeks colored. He and Shaeleen both knew to what Queen Raisa was referring to—his ability of speed. He nodded to her, and she had a servant bring him out to the balcony.

Shaeleen studied the rest of the women in the room— wives of men important to the prince's cause, no doubt. She took a step toward a group of them. With her abilities, she was sure she could find out more information to bring back to Prince Basil.

But Queen Raisa put a hand out and took hold of Shaeleen's arm, the grip a little too tight. Shaeleen turned and frowned.

"I can't have you wandering around here on your own," Queen Raisa said.

Shaeleen gave her a questioning look but said nothing.

"I wouldn't want you to be in pain," Queen Raisa added.

That caught Shaeleen by surprise, and it must have shown on her face.

Queen Raisa pulled Shaeleen back into the far corner of the room. Erlinda followed behind them, silently watching the room as they sat in a group of chairs in a small alcove, away from listening ears.

Shaeleen's eyes swept the room once more. Burgundy, overstuffed chairs and couches sat in small groupings around polished cherry wood tables. The ornate designs on the legs and edges of the tables' wood were impressive. And a few glass-encased cabinets sat against a far wall, with artifacts from around the five kingdoms of Wayland.

She could smell the sweet desserts that had been brought out to Orin, which made her turn her head that way. Queen Raisa smiled and motioned for a servant to bring a plate of desserts over to the three of them. Shaeleen nodded her thanks and, with a small napkin, took a small, icing-covered cookie and then bit into it. It was wonderfully delicious. *I really must commend the cook.*

During this entire time, Queen Raisa and Erlinda had not said a word. But Shaeleen was beginning to put things together.

"Why are you here, Queen Mother?" Shaeleen asked after finishing her cookie.

Queen Raisa's eyebrows rose in surprise. She smoothed back a dark strand of her coiffed hair. "What do you mean?" Queen Raisa asked.

"Why are you here with Calix instead of in the capital with Basil?"

"Ahh." Queen Raisa nodded her head. "Well, after my husband, the king, passed away five years ago, I couldn't stand being in the city any longer."

Shaeleen felt a small twinge of pain in her gut: not enough to suggest a total lie but enough to cause suspicion at Queen Raisa's words.

"I would think you would want to be there," Shaeleen said, "to support your son and the regent."

Queen Raisa's eyes flicked to Erlinda then back to Shaeleen. "The regent is a good man. He does not need my help."

Shaeleen was growing frustrated. She glanced around the room again. A group of women stood talking together across the room. One woman seemed to be different than the others. Strength showed from her posture, and her long, blond hair, rather than feminizing her, strengthened her. Both beautiful and strong.

"That's Commander Kerr's wife, Brigitte," Queen Raisa said.

Shaeleen turned with a questioning look.

"The commander of Gabor's army," Queen Raisa added.

What is going on here? Shaeleen could tell Queen Raisa had tiptoed around her questions. The queen was obviously used to having Erlinda—the kingdom's TruthSeer—around. Then an idea occurred to Shaeleen, and she turned to Erlinda.

"TruthSeer, what is your take on what is going on here?" Shaeleen asked, her mind jumping steps ahead of where they were.

Erlinda actually jumped in her seat. Her short, graying hair bobbed around her neck. Her eyes held deep-seated pain and crackled with small strands of power. As she peered at Shaeleen, Shaeleen's entire soul was bared for the TruthSeer.

Using her own power, Shaeleen cut Erlinda's intruding mind off from her own.

Erlinda swayed a bit before saying, "I have served Galena for many years—through two kings—and now…" Erlinda stopped as if surprised that she had been about to say something.

Shaeleen smiled and pushed forward. "Go on. What were you saying?"

Erlinda looked at Queen Raisa and then back to Shaeleen. "Nothing," she said and shook her head.

Pain crept into Shaeleen's mind. *A definite lie.* She tried not to wince, but Queen Raisa seemed to notice.

Shaeleen had had enough of their games. "Erlinda, why are you and your wizard here in North Bay with Calix instead of in Stronghold, helping Basil and the regent?" Shaeleen winced inside as she thought about her brother chastising her for being informal with the princes' names.

Erlinda's face twisted in pain. She squirmed uncomfortably in her seat and looked over at Queen Raisa.

"A TruthSeer owes no deference to any man or woman," Shaeleen said. "Why do you keep looking at Queen Raisa before you answer me?"

"Enough questions!" Queen Raisa said, raising her voice loud enough that others in the room stopped talking and glanced over. She waved her hand in their direction to return them to their own conversations.

Then Queen Raisa lowered her voice and faced Shaeleen as she said, "I don't know who you are or even why you are here. Faegon thought your brother important, and you travel with another of abilities..." She turned her head to the balcony, where Orin seemed to be in conversation with a serving girl. "But I suspect it is you who is the important one here. Who are you?"

"I am Shaeleen, the oldest daughter of a carpenter of some renown in Stronghaven," was all Shaeleen said. It was true enough to not set off any pain, but only barely.

"And, Shaeleen, the carpenter's daughter, why are you here in North Bay?" Queen Raisa continued.

How can I answer that without giving myself away? Instead, she reiterated her earlier question of the queen mother: "I have asked you the same, and yet, you have not answered me."

Queen Raisa's face reddened, and her lips tightened. She was obviously not used to being talked to in this manner. Instead of answering, she turned this time to Erlinda, with a questioning look in her eyes, as if awaiting an answer.

Erlinda nodded her head once, and Queen Raisa laid her head back against the cushion of the chair and closed her eyes for a brief moment. When she opened them again, they held a determined look. Then she stood and motioned for Shaeleen and Erlinda to follow her out onto the balcony. Chasing away the serving girl from Orin's side, the queen closed the glass double doors and walked to the edge of the balcony.

Orin gave Shaeleen a questioning look.

She only shrugged in response. She didn't know what was going on. But, apparently, some internal battle tore at the queen mother, who stood staring out toward the sea. The moon lit up the tips of waves and the outlines of sailing ships in the harbor. Lights seemed sprinkled across the darkness down in the town. And faint voices traveled through the air, the conversations too far away to hear.

Queen Raisa turned, her dress flaring out around her as she did. With two long steps, she stood in front of Shaeleen. She was taller than Shaeleen—most women were—and Shaeleen shrank back a step from the queen mother's presence.

"Show it to me!" Queen Raisa demanded.

Shaeleen spread her arms out to her sides. "Show you what?"

"The stone," Erlinda whispered from Shaeleen's right side. "Show us the TruthStone, child. You must have one."

Shaeleen bristled for a moment at being called a child, but, compared to Erlinda, everyone must seem so. Standing silently, she sensed more than saw Orin take a step closer to her on her left. She looked at him, and his eyes told her that with a signal he could whisk them out of the castle. But Shaeleen couldn't leave Cole. Her brother was too timid in circumstances like these. She hoped he was being treated better than she was.

Queen Raisa still stood in front of her, awaiting an answer to her demand. "I have lived with a TruthSeer for years, Shaeleen. I know one when I see one."

Shaeleen let out a long-held breath. She couldn't see any good way out of this one. She could lie and then drop to the floor in pain, or she could show them what they wanted to see.

"Every few generations, a new TruthSeer is born," Erlinda said. "I am getting old and have been awaiting an apprentice for years."

Shaeleen almost laughed out loud. *So that's what they thought?* She could play along with that for now—she hoped—without too much pain.

"I can't show you the stone," Shaeleen said, followed with a deep breath in and out. "It isn't time."

Both Queen Raisa and Erlinda seemed to relax, grim smiles coming to their faces.

"So, you do admit you are a TruthSeer?" Queen Raisa asked.

Shaeleen nodded. "Well, one that needs training, as you have said." That was true at least.

Goodness, it is exhausting to tell the truth all the time!

"And Cole is your wizard?" Erlinda said.

"Well, he's not a very good one yet," Shaeleen said, trying to lighten the mood and turn the attention away from the stone weighing down both her heart and her pocket.

"Give him time," Erlinda said with the first smile that Shaeleen had seen from the old woman. "They need more time than we do to learn their own powers."

"So, I know why you are here now," Queen Raisa said to Shaeleen.

Shaeleen only nodded. Apparently, Queen Raisa supposed her to be seeking out the TruthSeer. Shaeleen did and said nothing to persuade her otherwise.

"But why are you here, Queen Mother?" Shaeleen pushed one more time. She felt the answer to that question would help her to know what to do next.

Queen Raisa looked at Orin, then Erlinda, then back to Shaeleen. She stood for a moment, ringing her hands as if deciding what to say and do herself.

"I need you to take Erlinda away from here," Queen Raisa finally said.

"W-what?" Shaeleen said, stumbling on her words in surprise. "What do you mean?"

"There is too much pain for her here," Queen Raisa continued. "I can't stand to see her suffer any longer."

"Queen Mother," Erlinda said, "there is no need for that. I am fine."

"You are not fine, Erlinda. You have aged these past few years, and I now see constant pain in your eyes. You should not be required to keep these lies any longer."

Shaeleen tried to follow what was being said. She pulled upon the power of the tiny IntelligenceStone held within her TruthStone, for help. Then she became aware of Queen Raisa, Erlinda, and Orin staring at her.

"How?" Queen Raisa half whispered.

"You're glowing again," Orin said from her side.

"Why did you leave Stronghaven, Erlinda?" Shaeleen asked as she turned to the TruthSeer. "What lies are you keeping?"

Erlinda's eyes filled with tears, and she put a hand on a nearby chair to steady herself.

"I…uh…I…" Erlinda said.

"Tell me the truth!" Shaeleen said, pulling on a significant amount of her power, making her voice a demand that couldn't be disobeyed.

Erlinda bent over in a gruesome pain that Shaeleen understood all too well. Queen Raisa moved to Erlinda's side and lowered the TruthSeer into the chair.

"You're hurting her, Shaeleen!" Queen Raisa said, her voice pleading for Shaeleen to stop.

"Then tell me: what lie is so big that it causes her so much pain and has both of you in North Bay rather than in Stronghaven, with the crown prince?"

Queen Raisa kneeled down next to Erlinda and held the TruthSeer's hand. Looking up at Shaeleen, the queen mother's eyes filled with tears that began to spill down her cheeks, dripping off her chin. She took a few deep breaths and tried to gain control.

"Prince Basil is not the true crown prince," Queen Raisa drew out her answer slowly. Then, with one last sob, she blurted out, "Prince Calix is the oldest son."

Shaeleen had braced herself for pain, but none came. *Nothing.* It was as she had recently suspected. But, to hear it voiced was different. She now knew with certainty the truthfulness of the words. Plopping down on the chair Orin had been sitting in earlier, she tried to comprehend what this news meant to her mission.

Orin paced to the railing and back more than once.

"Orin, stop it!" Shaeleen said.

Orin turned to her, his eyes wide.

"I'm sorry," she said. "Sit down. I can't think with your pacing."

"What are we going to do?" Orin asked Shaeleen.

"You're going to take Erlinda away from here," Queen Raisa said, now standing up by Erlinda's chair.

Anger suddenly filled Shaeleen, and she stood and took two steps toward Queen Raisa. "How could you do this?" she demanded. "How could you keep this secret all these years? What have you done to the kingdom, Raisa?"

"To protect the crown, my husband and I decided to lie to protect the rightful heir to the throne while the boys were younger. It was never intended to go on this long."

"Then why?" Shaeleen asked.

"Why?" Queen Raisa raised her voice, and she wiped new tears away for her eyes. "Have you seen my son Calix? Have you seen the type of person he has become?" Queen Raisa shook with anger, and pain filled her eyes. "I hate myself for saying this. But, would you want Prince Calix as your king?"

Shaeleen now understood.

The queen stood there: once so proud and regal, now looking shaken and vulnerable. Her voice was barely audible as she added, "I kept hoping he would change or, worse yet, that something might happen that would make Basil the oldest surviving heir."

CHAPTER NINETEEN

Early the next morning Shaeleen, Orin, and Erlinda crossed over the border into the kingdom of Gabor. With Orin's speed, the border crossing caused them little difficulty. He sped across twice, taking Shaeleen and then Erlinda with him.

Shaeleen wanted more than anything to confide in Cole and to get his opinion on the matter. But the queen mother had insisted on Shaeleen and Orin getting Erlinda away from the prince's presence as soon as possible. Shaeleen knew that, in reality, she didn't have to follow any order from the queen mother—or anyone else, for that matter.

But, with thoughts of Prince Calix and Prince Basil in her head and the implications of their birth order, she had decided to help. She would get Erlinda away, return in the morning for Cole, and then they would catch the next ship back to Stronghaven.

Now they were standing off to the side of a road, watching early morning travelers and merchants making their way between North Bay to Portsmouth, a small seaside town on the border with Gabor.

"Now what?" Orin asked. "I'm hungry."

Shaeleen laughed. "That doesn't surprise me."

"This way." Erlinda motioned. "I know a good inn out of the way of prying eyes."

"I need to get back," Shaeleen said. "I need to talk to my brother. He will be worried."

"The queen mother will tell him privately that you were asked to help me and that you will be back soon," Erlinda said.

Shaeleen felt nervous being in a foreign kingdom, especially without Cole nearby. Her eyes scanned the shops around them. Most were still closed in this early morning hour. The streets were not as well taken care of here as in Galena. There were piles of garbage that made her nose twitch, and the few people she did see seemed resigned to their poor fates.

Shaeleen frowned again at the memory of having to leave her brother behind.

"Let's eat first," Orin pleaded. "I'm starving."

Shaeleen laughed. With Orin's speed, a few minutes for a meal would not hurt.

Soon they arrived at an inn on the southeast side of town. A slight breeze was blowing in off the bay, and gulls were beginning to scavenge for food. They sat down at a table in the corner of an outside patio. Just then, a heaping plate of hotcakes, sausages, and melon was brought out.

The young serving woman bowed her head to Erlinda. "Compliments of the house, ma'am."

After their server had walked away, Shaeleen turned to Erlinda with a questioning look on her face.

Erlinda smiled and seemed to relax for the first time since Shaeleen had met her. "Being one of only a handful of TruthSeers in Wayland does give me some notoriety and a few privileges now and again."

Orin filled his plate and began to shove the food into his mouth.

"Breathe between bites, Orin," Shaeleen scolded with a laugh. "It's not going anywhere."

Orin looked up and said with a full mouth, "But we might be."

Shaeleen nodded her head in understanding. Life had been moving quickly lately. She put some food on her own plate but began looking around after her first bite.

"Need something?" Erlinda asked.

"She's looking for something sweet, I would bet," Orin said between bites. His plate was almost clean already.

Shaeleen blushed, but Erlinda waved over the serving girl. "Please bring some sweet rolls for my friend here."

The serving girl returned in a few moments with steaming sweet rolls, their frosting dripping off their sides. Shaeleen picked one up carefully so as to not burn her fingers. She took a small bite. Sucking in a puff of air to cool her mouth, she grinned.

"Wonderful!"

Erlinda and Orin laughed.

The three ate in relative silence for a few moments, enjoying the food and the cool morning air. Toward the end of their meal, they heard the sound of many footsteps coming down the road from the small port just to the south. Turning their heads, they saw troops coming down the street.

"Seems like a lot of men, this close to the border." Shaeleen frowned.

Erlinda nodded her head. "I fear it is part of the prince's new alliance.

"Calix?"

"That boy is going to bring war to our land." Erlinda pursed her lips.

"Not if I can help it," Shaeleen said without further thought.

Erlinda tilted hear head at Shaeleen. "What are you not telling me?"

Orin stopped eating and glanced at Shaeleen. She shook her head at him to not say anything.

"Aah," Erlinda said. "You are learning that, if you have to lie, it is better to not say anything at all." Her face flushed, and then she sat back and smiled. "Well, I guess that's part of the training. Though, I don't like you keeping secrets from me."

"I will tell you when the time is right," Shaeleen said.

And that was the truth. *Let Erlinda keep thinking that I am an apprentice.* She did need to learn. The power had been thrust onto her so quickly that she'd hardly had time to know how to use it. It came instinctively at times, but being able to understand her abilities would make planning out things much easier.

"I understand," Erlinda said. "Now, if you will excuse me, I'm going to see what is going on with those troops."

After Erlinda left, Shaeleen turned to Orin and sighed deeply. "I need to go to the capital of Gabor, but I'm sure your father is worried about you."

"I thought we were going back to get Cole," Orin said.

Thoughts raced through Shaeleen's mind. She could feel the connection to her brother, who was just southwest of where they were. She really could use the help of his abilities. But, as soon as she'd seen the soldiers from Gabor, she'd realized she needed to get to the capital of Gabor soon. Another stone awaited her there.

Seeing her expression, Orin's face lit up. "I can get us to Riverton. I've been there before." He grabbed another sausage and then frowned.

"What's wrong?" Shaeleen asked.

"It's the last one." Orin's face fell.

Shaeleen laughed and then covered her mouth to stifle the sound. After getting her fit of laughter under control, she put her hand on Orin's arm. "There's still plenty of melon."

Orin screwed up his face. "I don't like melon."

"Well, then you will just have to wait until the midday meal. Now, about your father, Orin. Won't he be missing you?"

"I sent him a note that I was engaged in important business for the princes of Galena and would meet him later. If I don't see him in Riverton, we will meet up again in Stronghaven."

Shaeleen sighed. "Sometimes I don't know about you, Orin. You're too young to just be running around on your own. When I was thirteen, I barely left the merchants' quarter."

Orin looked down for a moment, and his face scrunched up as if he were deciding what to say. "With my…uh…*abilities*, he's used to it," Orin said.

"No more stealing, Orin." Shaeleen waggled a finger at him.

Looking around the patio first, Orin then leaned in closer to her and said, "Then you don't want to see the note I took from the TruthSeer?"

"Orin!" Shaeleen said too loudly. Then she moved in closer herself. "You can't do that!"

"She's coming back soon." Orin waved his hand toward the inn. "Do you want to know what it says or not? It's from Queen Raisa."

Shaeleen turned around, looking for Erlinda. *Of course I want to know what it says.* She stuck her hand out in front of her. "Give it to me."

Orin proceeded to pull a small paper out of an inside pocket and shoved it into her outstretched hand.

Shaeleen took the paper and began to read it to herself.

TruthSeer, keep an eye on the young woman and her friend. I suspect she is not all she pretends to be. Keep her out of Galena. Things here are too volatile for another TruthSeer. The truth must not get to Basil, until the time is right for him to act. Go in peace, and play your part well.

Shaeleen glanced back up at Orin. "Did you read it?"

Orin nodded his head. "What do you think? Can we trust the queen mother or the TruthSeer now?"

"I don't know. Queen Raisa seemed legitimately sorry to have held the secret for so long, and she clearly doesn't think Calix is ready to rule. But..."

"But?" Orin asked. Then he looked around the patio. It was getting more crowded.

"The law is firm in all of the kingdoms of Wayland. The oldest heir gets the crown, either when the parent passes away or if already dead, when he or she turns seventeen."

"How old are the princes of Galena?"

"They turn seventeen in less than two months. On that day, the oldest heir becomes king and they announce his engagement to marry."

"Wow!" Orin sat back, with amazement on his face. "That's not very long from now."

Shaeleen sat back in exasperation. "Stupid stone!"

"Don't ever say that!" Erlinda said from behind her, making Shaeleen almost jump out of her chair. "Don't ever blame the stone. It is a privilege you've been given, young lady. TruthSeers have served the kingdoms of Wayland ever since King Wayland was given the stones of power from Verlyn, as a gift for his lifetime of service."

Shaeleen noticed Orin scrambling to get the letter back into his pocket, so she kept Erlinda's attention on herself with a question: "And, do you serve the kingdoms, oh great TruthSeer?"

Before she knew what had happened, Shaeleen felt her face sting from the slap of Erlinda's hand.

"Hold your tongue, girl," Erlinda chastised. "You're a babe, with barely any knowledge of what you speak. How dare you question my loyalties."

Shaeleen stood up and glared down on the old TruthSeer. Power gathered around her, and she let it shine forth this time.

"Shae!" Orin tried to warn her, but she put him in his place with a look.

Power crackled across her fingers. "Erlinda," she said, purposefully leaving off her title, "I want an honest answer. Do you serve the queen mother, Prince Basil, or Prince Calix?"

Erlinda stood, staring up at Shaeleen with a surprised but determined look on her face. Erlinda was clearly weighing her options.

Shaeleen was tired of playing these games and of having others treat her like a little girl. She so wanted to pull the large Moldavite TruthStone from her pocket and tell Erlinda who she really was. But instead Shaeleen reached out and put her hand on Erlinda's arm. Power raced from her fingertips up Erlinda's sleeve.

For a brief moment, she saw inside Erlinda's mind and knew she had the power to force an answer from the old TruthSeer. But before Shaeleen could do anything, Erlinda pulled her arm away with a jerk and took a step back from Shaeleen.

"Shae!" Orin reached out toward Shaeleen. But before touching her, he pulled back his own hand. "You're making a scene."

Shaeleen glanced around. Patrons from the inn as well as a few soldiers at the back of the marching line were watching their confrontation. *So much for staying inconspicuous.* They needed to get away, but Shaeleen needed an answer first.

Turning back to Erlinda, she glared at the woman. "Who do you serve?"

Erlinda let out a deep breath. "I serve the kingdom of Galena, as have all the TruthSeers of our land before me." She then sank back down into her chair.

Shaeleen released the power. She plopped back down into her own chair in thought. Erlinda had indeed spoken the truth. But that truth hid a multitude of meanings. A showdown was imminent between Prince Basil and Prince Calix. Prince Calix, as the oldest, was the legitimate ruler but might destroy the kingdom, while Prince Basil was beloved of his people but was not the legal heir.

"The way of truth is not always the best way, is it?" Shaeleen whispered.

Erlinda nodded her head slowly, her face looking older and more tired now. "That is one of the first lessons you must learn."

"And that is what causes us so much pain," Shaeleen said.

Then Orin pointed toward the troops, and Shaeleen and Erlinda turned. A man was marching back toward them with stern looking men walking by his sides.

"The captain," Erlinda stated and motioned for Shaeleen and Orin to stand and follow her back inside the inn. As they went, Erlinda motioned Orin ahead of them and then turned to Shaeleen and caught her attention. "Don't ever try to force the truth from me again, Shaeleen. Your strength has amazing potential—more than I have ever heard of—and I don't dare to think right now what that means. But you must learn to control yourself, or you could get us all killed."

Shaeleen wanted to defend herself with a rebuttal, but she knew Erlinda was right. She had lost control of herself, and she barely knew how to control her power or what the extent of it was. So, all she did was nod to Erlinda as they continued through the inn.

Erlinda nodded to the innkeeper, and he smiled back at her as he moved to the front of the inn to confront the entering captain and his men.

The three moved through the kitchens and out a back door. Orin took the lead and directed them down a few backstreets and then down to the docks of Portsmouth.

Shaeleen glanced around. Compared to Stronghaven and even North Bay, this could hardly be considered a port at all. It was nothing more than a long dock with a few smaller ships tied up, located at the mouth of the river, where it fed into the Bay of Jalen.

Orin stuck his hand out toward Shaeleen and Erlinda. "I need some money to secure us a ship."

Erlinda appeared confused. "With the young man's speed, you could be across the border and back to your brother sooner."

Shaeleen smiled and tucked her long hair behind her ears. "We're going to Riverton, TruthSeer."

"Riverton? What for?"

The power of the IntelligenceStone flowed through Shaeleen, and she knew immediately what she must do. "To see the queen of Gabor."

Once again, thoughts of moving farther away from Cole gave her some concern. But, right now, he really could serve and protect her best by keeping an eye on Prince Calix and his wizard, Faegon. And she would be back soon.

Erlinda brought a hand to her forehead and winced. "You're going to try my patience, aren't you?"

"Me?" Shaeleen mocked with an innocent look on her face. "Now, give Orin some money. We need to leave fast, before the troops detain us."

CHAPTER TWENTY

The three travelers quickly secured passage on a small trading ship traveling from Portsmouth to Riverton, the capital of Gabor. The day was warm for spring, and an easterly wind blew against them, making the going seem awfully slow to Shaeleen. She stood on the port side of the boat, watching the southern border of Gabor pass by, and rethought her decision to leave Cole behind.

Ever since he had received his wizard powers, he had been changing. He was more quick to react and less careful, and Shaeleen was afraid that he would fall into some kind of trouble. She hadn't even shared her information about Calix and Basil with Cole, for it was not something to just leave lying around in a note.

Orin came up next to her, and she shoved worries about Cole to the back of her mind. *He will have to learn to fend for himself,* she surmised.

"Not a bad boat," Orin said. "Of course, it's not as large of a ship as I am used to sailing on."

Shaeleen pointed to the shore. "More trees here than near Stronghaven. I can hardly see anything through the forest."

"I spent some time in the foothills of Great Mountain Divide when I was growing up," Orin offered. "My mother's family lived in a small village among the trees between there and Mistport. Stronghaven seems far too open to me."

Shaeleen chuckled. "Grew up there, huh? I didn't know you were full grown yet."

"Hey!" Orin punched her on the arm harmlessly and straightened his back. "I'm growing taller every day."

"And faster," Shaeleen said in a lower voice. She looked around to make sure no one was listening. "How did you first discover your power?"

"It was about three years ago," Orin said, "just after my tenth birthday. My friend's older brother was picking on us. He was trying to take some food from me, and I was getting frustrated. When he tried to grab me again, I just moved— faster than I'd ever done so before. In only a moment, I was behind him." Orin smiled as if reliving the scene in his mind now. A few gulls landed on the bow of the ship, up ahead of them, and squawked as if telling the humans to leave.

"What did you do then?" Shaeleen asked.

"I ran as fast as I could back home. I couldn't believe how quickly I got there, but I was really tired. My friend showed up sometime later and asked me how I'd gotten away. At the time, I didn't understand what had really happened. But, over time, I've learned to use the power better."

"Hmmm," Shaeleen muttered under her breath. "These kinds of powers among the common people, like you and me, was never meant to be. The powers were given by King Wayland to his children to be used in ruling and protecting the land."

Orin looked away as if avoiding any more conversation on the subject. "I won't give it up."

"Something is changing in Wayland, Orin."

"And you are at the center of this change, I suppose?" Orin laughed at her.

Shaeleen turned to face Orin squarely and opened her mouth for a quick retort. But, just then, Erlinda came walking toward them on the deck. Erlinda's steps were not as sure-footed as Shaeleen's and Orin's. Shaeleen gave Orin one last look and then moved to help Erlinda to the railing.

"Thank you, Shaeleen," Erlinda said as she grabbed the rail with both hands. "I've never liked traveling on the sea."

"But you've lived for years in Stronghaven with the king," Shaeleen pointed out.

"Yes, but I did not grow up there. I was raised farther inland, closer to the Myr River," Erlinda said, holding the rail tighter as the ship lurched to the right. "The river is much smoother than the sea."

* * *

Late in the afternoon, before the evening meal, Shaeleen was resting in a bunk when there was a yell up on the deck. Shaeleen went up to see what was happening. Off their starboard side were three giant warships, heading westward. A man in uniform leaned over the side of the first ship, hailing the boat that Shaeleen and her companions were traveling on.

"Prepare to be boarded!" the man yelled out.

Has word gotten out about our escape? Shaeleen shook her head. It was a Gaborian warship. *They wouldn't be looking for the three of us, would they?* She ran back down the short set of stairs.

Once she had warned Erlinda and Orin of possible trouble, the three sat in a room quietly, hoping it was just a routine inspection. All seemed fine for a few minutes, but then they heard loud footsteps coming down the stairs. Shaeleen moved Erlinda off to a far corner and told Orin to behave.

Soon their door burst open, and three men came in: two soldiers and another man of higher rank. The man's crisp, red uniform and commanding presence made Shaeleen take a step back. He stood almost a foot taller than her, and he came up and stood in her face.

"What is your name and purpose for being on this ship?" the man said with no preamble or courtesy.

Shaeleen's heart leaped with fear, but she tried to control her voice as she said, "My name is Shaeleen, and I am traveling to Riverton."

"For what purpose?" the man asked, looking even more menacing, if possible. His hair was dark and short, but his goatee was spotted with gray. And his strength was apparent through the way his uniform fit.

Without thinking, she said, "To see a friend." The words were clearly a bold lie, and she couldn't help but bend over in pain.

One of the other soldiers moved to her side and grabbed her arms, lifting her back up. "What is wrong with you?" the soldier said. "Don't you know who you are speaking with?"

Shaeleen certainly didn't know the man that had asked the questions, but she knew she couldn't afford to lie to him again—at least, not such a strong lie.

"What is your friend's name?" came the next question from the man.

Orin moved up next to Shaeleen and touched the side of her arm. She knew what he meant to do. He could whisk her out of there—but where would they go? They were on the water.

Before Shaeleen could answer the man, Erlinda stepped forward out of the dark corner. Shaeleen winced. The woman was going to give them away, she was sure.

The man standing before Shaeleen took a step back in surprise. "TruthSeer." He bowed his head slightly at Erlinda.

"Commander Kerr," Erlinda said.

"Commander Kerr, what are you doing here?" Shaeleen said before thinking—once again.

The soldier next to Shaeleen slapped her on the mouth and said, "You do not speak so to the battle commander of Gabor."

"Commander Kerr!" Erlinda stepped forward. "Kindly control your thugs."

The soldier gave the old TruthSeer a murderous look.

But the commander put his hand out toward the soldier. "Retreat, soldier. You two may wait outside the door."

The two soldiers obediently left and closed the door behind them. Then Erlinda walked over to Shaeleen and handed her a cloth to wipe the blood off her mouth.

"Since when do we go about hitting young girls, Commander?" Erlinda pulled herself up to her full height, which was still much shorter than the commander's.

"Times are stressful, TruthSeer," Commander Kerr said. "You of all people should know that."

Shaeleen gave Erlinda a sideways look. It appeared that the two knew each other. And the man's wife had been at the dinner with Prince Calix the previous evening.

"How is Queen Victoria?" Erlinda asked.

The commander paled, and his eyes opened wide. Shaeleen knew the next words out of his mouth were likely to be false, so she braced herself.

"The queen is fine and rules Gabor well, of course," Commander Kerr said with an almost memorized cadence.

Shaeleen felt the pain in her head rather than her gut this time, which seemed easier to control. She winced only briefly and saw the old TruthSeer sway slightly. Erlinda recovered quickly and didn't debate the commander's words.

"Why are you here, TruthSeer? And who are these two?" The commander turned and gave a hard look at Shaeleen and Orin.

"I am on my way to see the queen and her TruthSeer. It's been a long time since I've seen Justyn."

As the commander watched Erlinda carefully, Shaeleen noticed that Erlinda had answered without any lies.

"And these two young ones are accompanying me," Erlinda continued. "I'm not as young as I once was, and I need help."

"I'm afraid you won't be able to go to Riverton right now, TruthSeer," Commander Kerr said. "It's not safe there."

Shaeleen noticed how his demand was also worded without any lies. *Safe for whom? Them, the people of Gabor, or the queen?*

"You have no authority over her," Shaeleen said, for she knew they had to get to Riverton. The closer they got, the stronger the Red Jasper StrengthStone pulled to her, as the IntelligenceStone in Galena had done.

The commander shrugged. "Authority or not, I am sure Prince Calix would like his TruthSeer at his side when I meet with him."

As the commander moved toward the door, Shaeleen reached out in desperation and grabbed his arm, pulling forth the power of the TruthStone. It raced through her body and mind, filling her with strength and determination. The commander tried to pull away, but somehow Shaeleen held on to him.

"Why are you going to meet with Prince Calix?" Shaeleen asked, using her power to force him to answer.

She could see him struggling under her command. The power of strength flowing through his veins fought with all its might, but Shaeleen dug deeper and opened up a well of power that she hardly knew existed.

"Tell me!" Shaeleen's voice roared through the room, and a wind rushed out of her, almost knocking over the commander. The TruthStone ruled all other stones.

The commander's tongue was loosed, but he fought every word as he said, "To – form – an – alliance – to – give – Prince Calix – the – throne – of – Gabor."

"Why?" Shaeleen held his arm in her small hand and forced another answer. She could feel his muscles rippling under her fingers, from him trying to get away.

"The...TruthSeer...told...me...to," Commander Kerr said through gritted teeth. Then, with one last burst of strength, he pulled away from her and fell against the door.

The TruthSeer! What TruthSeer?

With the contact gone, the power Shaeleen held retreated back into the stone, and she crumpled in weakness to the floor.

"What have you done, child?" Erlinda said. "You can't force someone's mind like that. You could kill them."

"Shae, Shae!" Orin kneeled down next to her.

She tried to stay conscious, but she was so weak. Out of squinting eyes, she saw Commander Kerr give her the most murderous look she had ever seen in her life. He took a deep breath and opened the door.

"Take them!" the commander barked out. "All three of them."

Into the room came a dozen soldiers, swords out in front of them. The strength of the Red Jasper stone filled them all.

Shaeleen looked up into the eyes of Orin and nodded to him. He knew what she meant. He grabbed her hand and pulled on the power of the orange Garnet SpeedStone that flowed through his own blood.

They had to get away!

CHAPTER TWENTY-ONE

Shaeleen felt Orin's hold on her hand. Then everyone else in the room seemed to freeze around them as Orin worked his way across the room. It was crowded, and each time they tried to move, they would bump into one of the soldiers, and that would take them out of the speed. Then Orin would pull them back in. This constant changing of speed was confusing and disorienting.

Cries of dismay filled the room between the barking demands of Commander Kerr to "catch and hold them." Once, a soldier reached his enormous hands around Shaeleen's throat, and she felt herself getting dizzy, but Orin pulled them away again. However, the soldier came with them. His surprise allowed her to get out of his grasp. With the little strength she had, she hit him in the gut. But it did no good. Then Orin stopped speeding, and the soldier fell away.

They were almost to the door when she saw Erlinda standing there, her mouth agape at what was happening.

"Should we take her too?" Orin asked.

Shaeleen shook her head. The old TruthSeer had slowed their journey down too much. And Shaeleen was fairly certain the commander wouldn't hurt Erlinda.

In the brief moment they had conversed, the commander himself had moved to block them. Due to his strength, he was also faster than most men. He grabbed Orin, holding his shoulder. Orin tried to pull away with his powers of speed, but the strength of the commander held on to him.

Shaeleen wished that Cole could have been with them. Maybe it had been a mistake to leave him.

But she couldn't let them be caught. Shaeleen pulled once more on the strength of the TruthStone. The small IntelligenceStone of Labradorite gave her the knowledge of how to use her powers better. Somehow, by touching Orin and the commander, she as a holder of the TruthStone was able to pull upon their powers of speed and strength temporarily. The only powers she was missing at the moment were healing and hearing.

With four powers at her disposal, she brought her hands out in front of her and formed a ball of blue power, crackling in its intensity as it grew bigger and bigger. Then she slammed the ball of power into the commander with all the force she had, shards of the power flying out into all the soldiers in the room. The power had been immense, but the aftereffect was also vast.

Shaeleen screamed out in pain and then said, "Now, Orin!"

Orin pulled them through the door, up the stairs, and onto the deck of the ship in the blink of an eye. They stopped at the stern, where the warship had docked against theirs. Shaeleen fell against the railing with gasping breaths. She raised a finger and pointed to the warship.

Orin understood and, pulling her back up, they sped through the air, landing on the battle commander's warship. Most of the soldiers from the warship had followed the commander onto the boat Shaeleen had been on. But there were still a few soldiers standing here with the crew. Their eyes opened wide, and their swords flew out of their scabbards as Shaeleen and Orin appeared, almost as if out of nowhere, landing on the deck of their ship.

Shaeleen could barely stand, but she could still think. Thoughts flew with such clarity and intensity through her mind that she could hardly keep up with them. She pointed to the stern of the warship, and Orin took them there, leaving the soldiers and crew behind them. The shore was not too far away from this side of the ship.

Tied up at the back of the commander's ship was a small rowboat. Shaeleen and Orin jumped into it, and Orin, who was used to working on ships, pulled the rope that allowed the small rowboat to drop onto the water. Arrows from above were loosed around them. One stuck into the wood right by Shaeleen's leg.

"Row, Orin, row!" Shaeleen yelled out as she fought to keep herself upright.

Orin must have been tired and almost ready to collapse himself, but he pulled himself up with a determined look and grabbed the oars. Just as he began to row furiously, an arrow sailed through the air from above and stuck into Orin's shoulder.

"Owww!" Orin howled in pain and faltered in his rowing.

"Keep going, Orin. You can do it!" Shaeleen encouraged him between ragged breaths. She felt so weak. Then the power left her—all of it. There wasn't any left, and blackness began to close in around her vision.

Orin grunted and tried to pull the arrow out, but couldn't do it himself.

"To the shore," she whispered, and before she blacked out entirely, she watched in amazement as Orin's arms – even the one with the arrow in it, began spinning terribly fast. She reached a hand back, against the side of the boat, to keep from falling out. Salty water sprayed over her face as she slumped down lower.

Succumbing to the darkness, she hoped Orin was fast enough—then everything went silent.

* * *

"Shae, Shae!"

Shaeleen could hear a faraway voice calling her name.

"Shae, Shae!" the voice said, getting louder, and her mind started to clear up. "Shae, wake up. I can't go any farther."

Orin! It was Orin's voice calling to her. Suddenly, she remembered what had happened, and she slowly opened her eyes. She found herself lying on the ground. She brought up a hand to shield her vision from the fading light. Putting her other hand down by her side, she felt the small grains of sand beneath her.

"Shae," Orin said, sitting down next to her. "My power is gone and I can't move my arm."

Shaeleen noticed the stub of the arrow still sticking out of his shoulder, blood mixed with water dribbled down from it.

In response to her glance Orin turned and looked at his own shoulder. "I broke it off, but can't get it out. I'm so tired Shae, but we have to get farther inland. They may send someone after us."

Shaeleen sat up and blinked a few times. The light did not seem so bright now; in fact, she could see that the sun would set soon and darkness would fall quick up against the trees.

"I don't know what to do about the arrow, Orin," It was her fault he was hurt. "I'm so sorry. We need to get you help."

Orin's clothes were soaked, and sand clung to him everywhere. His blond hair was plastered against his head, and beside the arrow wound she could see a scrape on the side of his face. He looked exhausted, but he still wore a big smile.

"Why are you smiling?"

"Did you see how fast I rowed?"

Shaeleen shook her head and grinned. "I was out of it most of the time. But you did get us away from them."

"I sure did."

"How long have we been here?" Shaeleen asked as they both stood up. Shaeleen wobbled for a moment, still weak from the experience. Off in the distance, she could see the three warships and the smaller trading ship they had been on, sitting on the water. They seemed to be still anchored farther out and had not moved. "How long have I been out?"

"I dragged you out of the rowboat maybe half an hour ago. You wouldn't wake up, and I didn't have any more strength or speed to get you farther. I'm sorry."

"Sorry?" Shaeleen put her hand on Orin's arm. "You saved us!"

Orin flinched at Shaeleen's touch and looked at her hand, but he didn't pull away.

Shaeleen looked down in shame. She knew what he must be thinking. "I'm sorry about what I did back there with the commander. But I panicked and couldn't think of anything else to do. I had to know his intentions."

Orin watched her for a moment, appearing older and more serious than a boy his age should have to be. "Just promise me that you won't ever do that to me."

"Oh, Orin!" Shaeleen moved closer to him and tenderly touched his good shoulder. "I would never hurt you."

When she stepped back away, she noticed Orin's cheeks had reddened, and she let out a small laugh. Orin scowled and tried not to look at her. She had embarrassed him with her tenderness.

"That was crazy!" Orin finally said. "I can't believe the power you had, Shae. What are you really?"

Ahh, the question that seems to plague me.

"I don't really know for sure." Shaeleen shrugged, having spoken the truth. What was she? And, what was she really meant to do or become? "But your power, Orin. You are powerful—more so, I would guess, than most in Antioch."

Orin shrugged then laughed again. "It was fun, though!"

"You have a wicked sense of fun for one so young. Now, we need to find help. I don't know how long either one of us can stay on our feet." As the two of them began walking inland and into the forest, the light disappeared, the forest became darker, and Shaeleen grew worried.

CHAPTER TWENTY-TWO

A n hour after sunset, they could barely see the outlines of the forest around them, and the ancient pines blocked any light from the moon or stars. The forest itself held an earthy smell that Shaeleen found different from what she was used to smelling on the coast of Galena. It was not altogether unpleasant. But they were miserable in their wet clothes in the constant humidity and both were stumbling along – Orin more so. His face was flushed and he walked slower and slower as the night drew on.

Shaeleen thought she saw a flicker of light off to her right. She put her arm out in front of Orin to stop him. He tumbled into her and fell to the ground. She bent down to help him back up.

"I can't Shae," he mumbled.

Shaeleen gathered any remaining strength she still had and lifted him to his feet. Orin was shorter than her, but didn't weigh much less. She helped him toward the light she had seen. Soft voices floated through the thick trees as they approached, and they could hear an occasional laugh.

As they moved closer, Shaeleen could see a group of people huddled around a small fire. The people sat on logs and makeshift chairs and seemed to be eating and drinking.

Orin collapsed in her arms and his weight made both of them fall to the ground just inside the small clearing. The group around the fire jumped up. Two men came at them with swords in hand. Shaeleen put her hand up in the air.

"Please help us," she begged.

"They're just children, Harold," said an older woman standing up by the fire. "Put the swords away and help them over here."

Harold grumbled and motioned for the other man, about twenty years younger than himself, to do as the older woman had said. The entire group had the dusty brown look of people from Gabor.

Harold helped Shaeleen to the fire and the other man picked up Orin and brought him over and laid him on the ground. Orin's eyes flickered back open.

The woman beckoned to Shaeleen and Orin. "You poor souls. You're all wet and hurt." She was a small woman, even shorter than Shaeleen. Her hair was gray and was held up in a bun, and her clothes were simple but serviceable. A younger woman and a small child stood by her side.

"Please help Orin," Shaeleen begged, looking at each of them.

Harold knelt down and looked at Orin's shoulder. With a shake of his head and a whistle he looked back up at the group. "This is going to hurt."

"Just do it." Orin said.

Harold took a knife from his belt and held it over the coals of the fire for a moment, then he brought it back toward Orin's shoulder. Shaeleen sat down next to him and grabbed Orin's other hand.

The man reached up and cut Orin's skin around the arrow, the knife sliding effortlessly through his flesh. Orin flinched and held onto Shaeleen's hand tighter, but didn't say anything.

In short order, Harold had pulled out the arrow, the younger man had given him some salve and a cloth and quickly they put it on his shoulder, tying the cloth tight.

Orin swooned to the side and his eyes closed for a moment. Shaeleen helped him back up to a sitting position and he opened his eyes back up.

"Thank you," Orin said to the two men.

They nodded and everyone settled back down around the fire, either sitting on the ground or logs.

"My name is Genevieve," the older woman said. "Harold is my husband, and Aaron is our son. His wife is Marianne, and their young son, our first grandchild, is Tad." She had said her grandson's name with a sense of pride.

Shaeleen smiled at each in turn. "My name is Shaeleen, and this is Orin."

At Shaeleen's introductions, Orin's stomach rumbled.

Genevieve laughed. "Aaah, young boys. Always hungry." She dished out some stew in two bowls and, grabbing a chunk of bread, gave both Shaeleen and Orin a portion.

Harold and Aaron still stood off to one side. Both had strong builds and dark hair, though Harold's hair was speckled with gray. He also sported a beard and a mustache, while Aaron was clean-shaven. Aaron had a broad stature, and muscles bulged under his shirt.

Definitely a portion of the StrengthStone in these two, Shaeleen thought.

Both men continued to look out into the forest with wary expressions.

"Come back over here, you two," Genevieve ordered. "There's nothing else back in those woods." Turning to Shaeleen and Orin, she asked, "Is there? You all alone?"

"It's just us, ma'am," Shaeleen said.

"And caught in the sea, I would guess, by the looks of you." Genevieve

Shaeleen knew the woman wanted to know more about them, but she'd had the good graces not to push it. By the previous conversation, the family obviously thought Shaeleen and Orin were brother and sister. Shaeleen knew she would have to tell them something. And she would have to tread carefully. She took a few deep breaths and braced herself for pain.

"Our ship was traveling from Portsmouth to Riverton, when some men boarded us from a larger ship," Shaeleen said carefully, not telling any lies.

Then Marianne spoke her first words: "Pirates. Filthy things."

Shaeleen didn't contradict her and held back the small pain from the inferred lie.

"Pirates are bad, miss," Orin said, swallowing down his last bite of bread.

Shaeleen knew he was trying to tell the truth as much as possible while avoiding the real story. She smiled over at him to continue.

"We barely escaped over the side," Orin continued. "Then landed on the shore all alone."

"And your parents?" Harold asked, still glancing back at the forest. He didn't appear convinced that this wasn't a trap of some sort.

"Our parents were not with us," Shaeleen said with truthfulness.

"Such a shame," Genevieve said.

For the first time, Shaeleen took time to look at the wagon with its team of horses, standing off to the side of the group.

Genevieve noticed Shaeleen's gaze. "We are traveling merchants," she said. "My husband carves figures out of wood, and we sell them in the villages. Would you like to see one?"

Harold scowled at his wife, but she waved him off and walked to the wagon. She returned a few moments later with a small figure. Bringing it into the light, she handed it to Shaeleen.

She took it reverently and ran her hands over it. It was a carving of an eagle. The detail of the wings was exquisite. "It's beautiful."

Harold smiled for the first time.

"And to make it out of walnut. That must be difficult." Shaeleen marveled at the piece. "But it will last a long time."

Harold opened his eyes wider. "You seem to know your woods, young lady."

"Oh yes, my father is a carpenter," Shaeleen said with a broad smile. "He makes large furniture pieces. But your carvings are so intricate. It really is amazing. And the stain brings out the grain in just the right places."

Genevieve frowned. "You said your father is a carpenter?"

"Yes…" Shaeleen wondered if she had said something wrong.

"*Is* or *was*?" Genevieve asked with some suspicion.

Then Shaeleen realized they had assumed their parents were with them and had been taken by the pirates.

Orin jumped in to save her. "We do hope our parents are safe and we will see them again."

Shaeleen was really amazed at how deftly Orin had gotten used to saying things without lying.

Genevieve relaxed, and Harold stood and brought back a few other pieces for Shaeleen to look at. He became more relaxed as he talked about his craft. Shaeleen was delighted to share her knowledge of wood with him. It did make her miss her family, though. She thought about her younger sister and her mother also. But thinking about her brother, Cole, brought a frown to her face.

"What's wrong, Shaeleen?" Marianne asked, moving over closer to her. She held her young son in her arms. His eyes were closing, and he was just about asleep.

"Just thinking of my family," Shaeleen said. She wondered what Cole was doing and how he was getting along without her. She had no doubt he could protect himself physically; however, he was not a very social person and was quiet around others. "I hope they're each all right."

Marianne leaned over and put an arm around Shaeleen, giving her a small hug. The sudden gesture of kindness brought tears to Shaeleen's eyes. She reached her hand up onto Marianne's arm. The physical contact brought a sense of Marianne's mind to her own. These were good people.

"Thank you," Shaeleen said after a deep breath.

"You two look exhausted," Genevieve said. "Aaron, grab them some blankets. They can sleep under the wagon tonight."

Moments later, Shaeleen climbed under the wagon and closed her eyes. Orin lay next to her on the ground. She could feel the heat from his fever still and worried about him. She was so exhausted. The food had restored some measure of strength to her body, but she knew it would be several days before she was feeling like herself—whatever that was anymore.

I have changed. No. The stone has changed me. With those last thoughts, Shaeleen drifted off to sleep.

* * *

The next morning, Shaeleen discovered that Harold and his family would be making their way to Riverton, hoping to arrive for a popular summer festival the next week. Orin's fever was still dangerously high and he barely stayed awake. She herself still felt weary to her bones and didn't know how they would make it on the road.

"Why don't you two stay with us a few days," offered Genevieve. "Orin can stay in the wagon, but I'm afraid there isn't enough room for you," she said to Shaeleen.

Shaeleen nodded. "I can walk." Though she wondered if she really could.

The day passed by almost like a dream. Shaeleen's mind and body was numb from walking. All she could think about was putting one foot in front of the other. She would periodically check on Orin, but he slept most of the day away. Upon inspecting his wound that night, it was pink, but didn't look infected.

"You are healing quickly," Harold said to Orin that night around the fire. "Must be your age."

Shaeleen gave Orin a questioning look, but he just shrugged his shoulders – then winced. Shaeleen wondered if his power of speed had something to do with the quick healing. She knew so little about the use of the power of the stones.

The next two days were similar to the first, though each day, Shaeleen's stamina increased, and Orin's wound grew better. By the fourth day Orin joined her on the road. His fever had broken and he looked remarkably well.

Taking a coastal road eastward, the family with Shaeleen and Orin passed several other people on the road. Some of which Harold and Genevieve seemed to know.

Later that day, a few hours before sunset, they stopped at a small town and set up their wagon in the town square as they had done on previous days. Aaron helped Harold bring out his goods, displaying them on a blanket on the ground. A few townspeople appeared, but not as many as Shaeleen had seen in previous towns.

Orin grew bored and became antsy after lying down for so many days. He wandered around the town as any young boy would and bought some new clothes for himself and Shaeleen—at least, Shaeleen hoped he had purchased them and not stolen them.

It was a typical small town, though smaller than Shaeleen was used to back home. A single street was lined with a dozen or so small shops and a few inns for travelers on their way to and from Riverton, along the southern coast of Gabor. The houses further off the main street were well kept, with flowers blooming in window boxes and small vegetable gardens just starting to show spring growth.

"How's your shoulder?" Shaeleen asked, noticing that Orin still favored it slightly.

"Better." Orin moved his arm around. "But still can't lift my arm all the way up."

Shaeleen took a quick look at the wound; it was almost completely healed over. She wished she had the power to heal—but the pink Azeztulite HealingStone resided in Shema and she didn't know when she would get there.

"Another day or two and we'll both have our full energy back," Shaeleen said with a smile. "Then we need to get on to Riverton quickly. I'm anxious to get back to Cole."

Orin gave her the clothes he had purchased for her and then headed back out into town. Shaeleen stayed behind the wagon with Marianne and her child. The little boy was just learning to crawl and entertained them with his squeals and small discoveries. Shaeleen wondered how their lives could be so simple and removed from the dangers lurking in the world. She found herself feeling envious. It was a nice reprieve, but one that Shaeleen knew couldn't last long.

Later, she heard the footsteps of a group of people enter the town square on the other side of the wagon, where the carvings were being sold. A few voices were raised, and she grew concerned. She walked around the side of the wagon.

Aaron stood facing the largest man in a five-man group—*the power of the StrengthStone has definitely spread throughout the kingdom of Gabor.*

Harold moved out to join them. "What seems to be the trouble here?"

Aaron turned to his father. "These men are asking for protection money, Father."

"Protection from what?" Harold asked.

The largest man stepped forward. "There are bandits around here. We will help to protect you from them."

Shaeleen felt her stomach lurch, and she grabbed onto the side of the wagon. The noise caused a few men to look her way. Seeing only a simple young woman, they turned their attention back to Harold and the largest man.

"What about the local sheriff or constable?"

"We are the law here," the man said.

Another pain racked Shaeleen—this time in her head. The statement held a notion of truth, but the undertones certainly didn't feel right. Shaking her head, she resumed listening to the conversation.

"I won't pay protection money for something that should already be protected by the law," Harold stated. "This town has always been safe for traveling merchants."

One of the five men moved his foot and kicked one of the carvings. "Ooops," he said. "My mistake. I guess I'm just clumsy."

Aaron moved over in front of the carvings. "You did that on purpose. You owe us for that piece." He put out his hand for payment.

The largest man stepped closer to Harold and said, "If you pay up, I'll be nice and deduct the price of that piece from the payment."

But another bout of pain let Shaeleen know he wouldn't keep his end of the bargain.

Suddenly, Orin was at her side.

She jumped. "Don't do that."

Orin was breathing hard. "The city leaders are being held in the town jail, Shae." He saw the five men threatening Harold and his family. "Those men are bandits trying to take control of the town."

Shaeleen nodded. Then she moved back behind the wagon for a moment. She found Genevieve, Marianne, and the little boy and told the women to get inside the wagon. They'd heard the raised voices, so they agreed to do so.

"Orin, I want you to go and free the city leaders," Shaeleen said. "Can you do that?"

"Of course I can do that." Orin grinned but then furrowed his brow at her. "But should we get involved here? You're always telling *me* to not use my power so often."

Shaeleen scowled at his words. "This is the right thing to do. The town needs to know the truth. Please just speed in and unlock the lock. They will do the rest, I hope."

Orin laughed. "Sounds fun. I was bored anyway."

After Orin left, Shaeleen walked toward the bandits. They were in the process of threatening Harold again when she walked up.

"Shaeleen, get back in the wagon!" Harold ordered her. "This is men's business."

"Seems like it is the town's business, Harold." Shaeleen stood up as tall as she could—which, unfortunately, was still a foot shorter than most of the men there. *Why couldn't I be taller?*

One of the men moved closer to her, but she paid him no attention.

"These men are lying, Harold," she continued. "They are not offering protection. They are the bandits themselves and will take your money and your goods."

Shaeleen noticed that a group of townspeople had begun to gather around the fringes of the town square.

The oversized bandit leader glared at her. "You don't know what you're talking about. I'm the law here. What does a young girl know anyway?"

Shaeleen gritted her teeth against the pain from his lies, but she pushed forward nevertheless. "Do you deny that you have jailed the rightful leaders of this town?"

The eyes of all five popped in surprise. She could tell they wondered how she could have known that. Harold looked at her and tilted his head, as if asking if she had spoken the truth.

"Yes," Shaeleen said. "These bandits have put the leaders of this town in jail and now try to steal from you and all of its citizens."

Someone in the back of the crowd yelled out a curse of anger toward the bandits.

"She doesn't know what she's saying," the bandit leader said.

"Oh, I assure you that I know the truth of everything, sir," Shaeleen said.

The townspeople moved in closer. A few of the bandits looked around nervously.

Then one of them spoke softly, but Shaeleen still heard him. "You said this would be easy, Joss," the bandit said to the leader.

Joss pulled his sword and pointed it at Harold. "Pay up now, or I will kill your wife."

One of the bandits must have somehow sneaked around to the back, for he now brought out Genevieve.

Shaeleen couldn't tell if Joss would indeed kill Genevieve or not. Shaeleen's head ached, and she felt a small twinge of pain in her gut. *It must mean he hasn't decided yet.* But this was still a dangerous situation.

"Now pay up!" Joss yelled at Harold.

"Shae! Shae!" Orin's voice called from behind her.

With the crowd's attention on Joss, Harold, and Genevieve, Shaeleen took a few steps back toward the wagon, and Orin came around the corner.

"The constable and mayor and their men will be here soon," Orin said.

"But it may not be soon enough," Shaeleen mused out loud. "Orin, when I signal to you, I want you to take that large man's sword and then knock down the man holding Genevieve."

Orin opened his eyes wider at her and nodded.

Shaeleen walked back into the crowd, putting on the bravest face she could, and stopped in front of Joss. He glared at her while still pointing his sword at Harold.

"Leave now!" Shaeleen ordered Joss, her heart pounding so hard she thought the whole town could have heard it. She had been struck with this sudden idea, which might or might not work.

"Get away from here!" Joss yelled at her.

"You must think the strength of the Red Jasper stone only flows through those who look strong," Shaeleen said, loud enough that all had heard. With that, she brought her hand up toward his hand—the one holding the sword—and, with a brief hand signal to Orin to throw the sword to the ground, proceeded to grab the man's hand.

The sword flew through the air and landed on the ground. To the crowd, it had appeared as if Shaeleen had done this.

Joss stood with his mouth open wide, apparently not knowing what to say.

Then Shaeleen moved toward the man holding Genevieve and, with a quick nod to Orin, pushed a hand against that man's body. At the same time, Orin came speeding in, pushed the man himself, and then disappeared back behind the wagon.

The man fell to the ground, to everyone's surprise.

The crowd cheered.

But Joss began taking a few steps back. "She—she's a witch," was all he could say.

And then the crowd laughed.

All five bandits were backing away, out of the growing crowd, when the town leaders rode up on their horses. The bandits tried to get away, but, with a sudden blur that only Shaeleen knew the cause of, each bandit tripped and fell to the ground. This brought hysterical laughter and claps from the townspeople.

All of a sudden, Orin stood next to Shaeleen with a big grin on his face. "A little extra fun."

Shaeleen nodded her head a few times and clapped her hands. "Well done, Orin. How are you feeling?"

"Hungry."

Shaeleen laughed but continued to give him a questioning look.

Orin took a deep breath and then put a hand out against the wagon to steady himself. "And quite tired." He admitted.

"You still need rest," Shaeleen said as they walked over to join Harold and his family.

Harold leaned over and said to Shaeleen, "I don't know how you did that, but I am grateful." Then he stood with his arm around his wife.

Shaeleen smiled and felt good inside. She had used her powers for something good—*This is what my powers should be used for—to help others.*

Then the townspeople surged over to examine Harold's goods.

"Looks like you have some new customers," Shaeleen said.

Harold beamed, and then he and Aaron went out to meet them. In the next hour, many of their carvings were purchased.

Later that night, their group camped off the road in a clearing just east of the town. After a warm meal, they settled in for the night. Shaeleen fell asleep in moments, with a smile on her face.

CHAPTER TWENTY-THREE

For the next two days, Harold and his group stopped again at two more towns on their way to Riverton. His carvings had sold well, but he still held back a few crates to sell at the fair in the capital city.

Orin seemed to be able to move his arm fully now, and both him and Shaeleen seemed to be back to full strength. Orin was anxious to move quicker, and earlier that day had offered Shaeleen the use of his speed again, but, being on foreign soil, they needed to be extremely careful about the use of their powers.

They were now approaching Riverton. The sun had set an hour before, and the city gates glowed with a faint pink in the last gleam of twilight. So they decided to stop and stay at an inn on the outskirts of town and enter the next day.

Shaeleen was looking forward to a good bath, a more comfortable bed, and a different meal than stew or soup. *Then I'll be ready to meet the queen.*

After bringing the horses into the stable, the group of travelers entered the common room for a meal. Tonight's special was pork roast, steamed vegetables, and freshly baked rye bread. They ate their fill and then sat for a time, enjoying two men and a woman playing the lute and singing.

Soon the crowd in the room grew larger, and then a few couples stood up to dance.

Harold and Genevieve stood up to join in. But Aaron and Marianne excused themselves and their baby to go to their room, leaving Shaeleen and Orin all alone at the table.

Shaeleen's nose twitched as she smelled something sweet, and she looked around.

"What's wrong?" Orin leaned over to ask.

"Nothing is *wrong*." Shaeleen smiled and took a deep breath with her nose in the air.

Orin laughed heartily. "Must be something sweet. How do you do it?"

"My nose has a special ability." Shaeleen grinned and turned her head toward the kitchen. "There is no sweet cake or roll that can hide from me. I'll be right back."

Shaeleen stood up and wound her way through the crowd. Coming to the door of the kitchen, she peeked inside and caught the eye of one of the younger cooks. The woman smiled as if knowing what she wanted.

"Looking for something sweet, young lady?"

Shaeleen smiled. "Oh yes, please. Two, please."

Taking two large rolls off a steaming tray and putting them on a plate, the young cook put a dab of sugared frosting on each and then handed them to Shaeleen.

Shaeleen took a deep breath and giggled. Putting her finger on one roll, she tried to take off a small piece, but she yelped in pain instead.

"Wait a few minutes, sweetie." The cook laughed. "They're barely out of the oven."

Shaeleen was turning to go, when a young man dressed in some type of official uniform came through the back door. He carried a rolled up piece of paper with him and seemed determined to get through the kitchen. Shaeleen started to leave the kitchen herself just as the young man passed her. The uniformed man frowned at her and then continued on his way. After walking a few feet, he turned back around and stared hard at her.

Shaeleen sensed something was not right and ducked behind a large man. The young man shook his head, as if trying to think of something, then continued to the front of the room, where the owner was greeting people. Shaeleen watched the young man unroll the paper he held and tack it up on a board just inside the front door.

Shaeleen was curious, so she made her way over, trying not to be seen by the young man. Popping a bite of sweet roll in her mouth, she squinted to see what was on the sign. She was so surprised that she dropped the sweet rolls onto the floor, turned around, and pushed her way through the crowd. Before she had even reached her table, she was calling out Orin's name.

"Orin! Orin!" Shaeleen said, finally pulling his attention away from the music. "We have to leave now!"

"What?" Orin scrunched up his face at her as if she were crazy.

"We're wanted," Shaeleen explained. "A soldier showed up with a 'Wanted' poster. Your face and mine are on it—or at least a fairly good likeness. We are to be apprehended at once. And it's signed by Commander Kerr."

Behind them were raised voices that caught her attention. Walking toward them was the owner, accompanied by the young man who had put up the sign. Both looked intently in their direction.

"Now, Orin," Shaeleen demanded, her hair moving around her head as she turned back toward him. "Get us out of here! Now!"

Orin grabbed a hold of Shaeleen's hand and pulled upon his power of speed. Once again, Shaeleen noticed everything around them freeze in position as she and Orin moved in a quick blur between the tables and through the crowd, then out the front door.

Once they were out of the inn, Orin dropped his power, and they stood there breathing hard for a moment.

Orin's face went dark. "I guess Commander Kerr didn't like us escaping."

"No, he didn't," Shaeleen said. "And now, word of it has reached the capital. I need to speak to the queen as soon as possible."

"It's too late tonight," Orin said. "Unless…?"

Shaeleen knew what he must be thinking. With his speed ability, they could be inside the city in less than half an hour, she guessed. *But then what?* They would still have to wait until morning to see the queen.

Shaeleen's hands were in fists, and she glanced up and down the street. "We can hide until morning. It will be easier to hide out here and then blend in with the crowds entering the city tomorrow."

She led them around the side of the building. But, as they turned the corner, large, meaty hands grabbed them from behind. Cuffs were placed on their wrists immediately.

"It doesn't matter how fast you are or what you might do to us if you could touch us." The man laughed. "We have you now."

Orin pulled against his cuffs and then shook his head at Shaeleen. "I can't get away, Shae. They're too strong."

Her own cuffs had gloves attached so she couldn't touch anyone with her bare hands to force the truth from them. *Compliments of Commander Kerr.*

The man that held them and two other soldiers standing to his side were three of the largest men Shaeleen had ever seen. Their necks were as thick as oxen's. Their muscles bulged through their shirts, and their veins popped out as their muscles flexed with power of the StrengthStone.

She struggled but couldn't do anything about it.

"Seems you kids must have done something really bad, to make the commander so angry," said one of the men, his hair longer than the others.

"Put them in the wagon, Ned," the third man said. He appeared to be in charge.

A few minutes later, the wagon began rolling its way eastward, toward the city gates. Ned and the one in charge sat up front, driving the horses, and the third with a scowl on his hardened face, sat inside the wagon with Shaeleen and Orin.

Orin continued to try to pull on his cuffs. And, once, Shaeleen could have sworn she saw his body shake a bit with a modicum of speed. But nothing else happened, and she shook her head at him to stop.

She knew she couldn't touch anyone, but she wondered if her powers still worked upon hearing a truth or a lie. So she started up a conversation with the men.

"Where are you taking us?" Shaeleen asked the man closest to them.

"Does it matter?" Ned asked from up front.

"It does to me," Shaeleen responded, and the men laughed.

"Have any of you ever even met Commander Kerr? Seems as if you're most likely far below him," Shaeleen said, goading them.

The two drivers laughed and waved their hands at her to dismiss her statement.

But the third soldier gritted his teeth and then said, "We are strong soldiers, and Commander Kerr needs strong soldiers."

"Then why were you left behind, when the rest have gone to North Bay?" Shaeleen asked, trying to get more information from them.

The man's cheeks turned red. "He trusts us to keep things running smoothly around here. He told me so personally..."

Shaeleen's stomach lurched. So, she knew now that the handcuffs did not bind her powers. After that, she didn't even listen to the man as he blathered on about how important he was.

"Tucker," said the man in charge, "shut up. Don't let the girl goad you on."

Tucker growled but then closed his mouth.

* * *

Two hours later, Shaeleen looked up as they were taken out of the wagon and saw that they were at an entrance to the castle at Riverton. She gulped and put a hand to her breast to slow her beating heart. *This was not the way I had planned on coming to the castle.*

As the soldiers took her and Orin out of the wagon, Shaeleen continued to look up at the tall, imposing structure. It was made of dark stone blocks, stood at least four stories tall and was built more like a fortress than the castle at Stronghaven had been. The dark stone, Shaeleen knew, was from Mount Orelia to the northwest. Smaller buildings were next to the castle, intermixed with gardens, trees, and small ponds. The beauty of the grounds was a stark contrast to the castle itself.

"I demand to see the queen," Shaeleen said.

The men laughed, and the one in charge said, "No one demands to see the queen, especially dangerous children like you two."

"I'm not a child," Orin tried to pull away, but the shackles held and one of the guards pushed him forward.

They were led to a back door, past a guard, and down a long hallway, until they came to stairs leading downward.

Orin turned to Shaeleen and with a large smile said, "They don't look that big."

Shaeleen caught on. He was trying to make the guards angry so as to try and get a chance to escape. "They say the biggest men from Gabor are the dumbest ones," Shaeleen said to delay them. If they could get out of the guard's grasp they could possibly hide behind one of the smaller buildings. They had spent enough time on the road already and needed to get to the queen then back to Cole in Galena. "Something about their strength taking the place of their brains."

Shaeleen's head snapped to the side, and she yelped in surprise. The sting left by one of Tucker's large, meaty hands suggested that his slap had surely made an imprint on her face. *We are in bigger trouble than I thought.*

"Keep quiet!" the man said. "We have no orders about what shape to deliver you in."

Soon they approached another guard, who opened a door leading into the prison section of the castle. "This is disgusting." She pulled against Ned, who was holding her arms. The floors were filthy, and her nose crinkled at the rotten smell. "Let me out of here. We haven't done anything wrong." She tried to think, but everything was happening so fast it was hard to concentrate.

The prison guard sat one lone torch in the wall, sending dark shadows across the area. No other prisoners were there, and the cells looked like they hadn't been used in years. A rat ran across the floor in front of them and Shaeleen yelped out in disgust. Both she and Orin were shoved into separate cells, the bars closing tightly behind them. Each cell was barely wider or longer than her own barely five foot body. Bars covered three walls of each cell, with the stone wall of the castle in back.

As the men left, one of them spoke to the guard. "The TruthSeer will be here in the morning."

The TruthSeer! Normally, one that instilled fear in criminals, she was sure. But to Shaeleen, that was the best news she'd heard all day. *The TruthSeer will see the truth and set us free.*

"Orin," Shaeleen called him over to her cell. He took a few steps and looked through the bars at her. "Are you all right?"

Orin clenched his teeth. "As good as can be expected after being grabbed, shackled, and tossed into a prison. I don't like not having my powers."

Shaeleen had to agree with him. Even in the short time she had possessed the TruthStone, she realized the addictive nature of holding magical powers.

"You do have a plan, don't you?" Orin drew her out of her musings.

She shrugged her shoulders, "When the TruthSeer comes, hopefully he will let us go. Let's get some rest for now." They both moved away from the bars and found their own corners to sit down against. Sometime during the night she fell into a restless sleep.

CHAPTER TWENTY-FOUR

The next morning, Shaeleen heard a commotion outside of the prison doors. She stood up with difficulty, stiff from sitting on the filthy floor. The shackles had remained on her wrists in front of her. She brought them up, trying to rub her eyes and to smooth down her messy nest of hair. Then she walked the three steps to the cell door.

A guard opened the outside door and strode into their prison area. Behind him came two other guards, with a middle-aged man behind them. This last man was dressed in the royal red robes of Gabor and had a smug look on his full face.

Looking sideways, she noticed Orin was also standing at his cell door. He tried to put on a brave face, but Shaeleen could tell he was losing hope. As the man approached the cells with obvious arrogance, it seemed to Shaeleen as if his beady eyes took in everything around him. Settling his gaze on her, he gave no indication that he recognized her for anything besides a young woman. She surely didn't want to prove otherwise.

With that one look, a sudden thought flickered through her mind, and Shaeleen had to stop herself from taking a step back. The man's eyes had been darker than they should be—especially for one who held the magic of a TruthSeer—so, *This man is dangerous.*

Then he proceeded over to Orin's cell. "So, this is the young man causing our great commander so much trouble," he said, his voice nasal and whiney. "Doesn't look like much to me."

The guards laughed.

Orin sneered at the man. "And you don't look like much of a TruthSeer either. Looks can be deceiving, I guess."

The TruthSeer's eyes squinted, hardly allowing a slit to look through over his fleshy cheeks.

Then one of the guards reached his fist through the bars and tried to grab Orin, saying, "Have some respect for Erwin, Gabor's TruthSeer."

"*Erwin?* There was an Erwin in our town once," Orin mused. "The townspeople said the name meant *boar* or *friend of boars*. Judging by your size, I can see that."

One of the guards by the outer door tried to hold back a snicker. Shaeleen realized Orin was trying to take Erwin's attention off of her: to make her appear less threatening than Orin. However, Erlinda hadn't mentioned a man named Erwin being the TruthSeer—it should have been Justyn. *What is going on here?*

"Do you have magic, boy?" the TruthSeer said all of a sudden.

Orin smiled as if this was what he had been waiting for. "No," he said plainly and untruthfully.

Shaeleen felt the pain of the lie in her gut and turned away to hide her reaction. She heard a gasp from Erwin and his breathing quicken. He, too, had been affected by the lie, but his control was better than hers—he had likely been a TruthSeer for longer than Shaeleen had been alive.

"Liar," the TruthSeer said.

"I never lie," Orin said with a smirk, and Shaeleen turned back around.

The TruthSeer took a few steps back away from the cells and sucked in a deep breath. But he still hadn't noticed Shaeleen's pain.

"Orin, stop," Shaeleen said to her young friend. "He knows."

Orin turned to her. "I know he does. That's why I'm doing it, to hurt him."

"Others might be hurt also," she warned him, without admitting openly who she was. She hoped that Orin would understand her meaning.

He did. His eyes apologized to her.

Shaeleen's TruthStone still remained in the pouch Prince Basil had given her, inside her pocket. The pouch guarded it from others knowing about it. She couldn't touch the stone with shackles on her wrists, but she could still feel the power within herself.

"Sir," Shaeleen called to the TruthSeer, "I need to see the queen."

Erwin turned his head and stared hard at Shaeleen. Then he turned back to Orin.

"Guards, gag the boy. He is not allowed to speak. If he can't tell the truth, he won't say anything at all."

Two guards moved into Orin's cell. With much difficulty and squirming from Orin, they finally put a gag on his mouth and tied his hands down farther so he couldn't reach his mouth with them.

Then Erwin came over to Shaeleen's cell. "I also heard rumors of you, child."

"I need to talk to Queen Victoria," Shaeleen reiterated and tried to stand taller in front of the TruthSeer. "There is trouble in our two kingdoms that she needs to be made aware of."

"Oh, please tell me," Erwin said, mocking her.

Shaeleen felt the power of the IntelligenceStone, and a question popped into her mind. "Are you the queen's TruthSeer?"

One of the guards said from behind Erwin, "Of course he is a TruthSeer."

Shaeleen felt no lie told there, but Erwin had yet to answer her specific question.

"I am, as the guard says, a TruthSeer," Erwin said, but beads of sweat began forming on his brow.

"But, are you the *queen's* TruthSeer?" Shaeleen said more forcefully this time. She was being prompted by the IntelligenceStone to ask the question in that exact way.

Erwin squirmed under her gaze. "Of course I am the queen's TruthSeer!" he said, his voice pitched high. As soon as these words were out of his mouth, they both knew the lie that had flown from his lips.

Shaeleen leaned over for a moment and tried to control the pain. When she leaned up again, Erwin stood staring at her with wide eyes.

"You are not the queen's TruthSeer but only an apprentice to him. The queen's real TruthSeer is Justyn," Shaeleen said. "I need to warn him and Queen Victoria of Commander Kerr's intentions."

Erwin waved the guards back toward the door out of earshot. Then he leaned in closer to the bars of Shaeleen's cell. "And what do you know of the great commander's plans?"

"He is a traitor," Shaeleen said.

"What do you know of traitors?" Spittle flew from Erwin's fleshy lips. "The commander is a great man, who will save us all."

Shaeleen stepped back, for she would have sworn that a tendril of what looked like black fog had swirled around the man's hand for a moment. But, in the darkness of the cell, it was difficult to tell.

"Save you from what?" she asked Erwin, who she now knew could be manipulated through his anger.

"From the queen," Erwin said. "She is old and does nothing for our kingdom. Gabor is mostly a desolate kingdom of lava and desert, except for here, on the coast. We need more resources. But the queen has lost her strength. She only sits around, in her old age, as if waiting for some miracle to happen—for someone to come and save us all."

Shaeleen felt the truth of everything he had said, but then a bone-chilling revelation startled her. *She is waiting for me.* This revelation came to her so suddenly that she mumbled it out loud.

"What are you mumbling about?" Erwin asked. "Commander Kerr sees our plight and will be the one to save us."

"A TruthSeer is to save and protect the kingdom, not help destroy it."

"Well, maybe destruction is needed to save it," Erwin said. Then, as if realizing he had said too much, he stepped back, away from the bars.

"Guards," he yelled out. "These two are to be held until the commander returns. They are liars and a danger to our kingdom."

"No!" Shaeleen yelled louder. "I demand to see the queen and *her* TruthSeer." But the guards ignored her and followed Erwin out of the room; the thick, oak door closing behind them. Shaeleen yelled out loud in frustration.

Orin squirmed in the cell next to hers, trying to say something, but the gag remained covering his mouth. "The system has become corrupted," she said aloud to both herself and Orin. "Originally, the stones were given as a gift to serve each kingdom. Now, the strength of each stone seems to have been depleted as favors were given out over time. The rulers of each kingdom do not hold enough of their own stone anymore."

Orin walked back closer to the bars.

"Orin, kneel down," Shaeleen said.

He gave her a confused look but did as she requested. She then reached her cuffed hands through the bars a few inches and with the tips of her gloved fingers grabbed a corner of the gag and pulled it off.

Orin turned his head and rubbed his shoulder against his mouth as if to wipe away the filth of the cloth. "Thanks."

Shaeleen nodded to him and continued on her former train of thought. "The rulers of the past thought that, by giving away parts of their stones, they would secure those who were loyal to them. But now, those powers flow randomly through the blood of each land. Look at you, Orin. You are powerful with speed, but you hold no stone yourself. I would guess that the king of your land only holds a small portion of the original stone anymore, just like the IntelligenceStone I received from Basil."

A small stream of light poked its way through a barred window high up in the wall of her cell. Shaeleen hadn't noticed this before and wondered how a window to the outside could exist in a prison's dungeon, deep below the castle fortress.

Dust in the room reflected the light in this small stream as it made its way down to a spot on the floor, in the middle of her small cell. Shaeleen took a step into the light and basked in its warmth.

"But there is always hope," she continued. "The light of truth will prevail in the end." Shaeleen then lowered herself to the ground, and let the small stream of light surround her.

The two sat in silence for a moment.

Then Orin brought their minds back to reality as he said, "But how do we get out of here, Shae? You can't do anything while locked in a prison cell in the dungeon of the castle in Riverton."

Shaeleen took a deep breath peered up at the window and let the light settle on her face as she closed her eyes. And she dug deeply into her power.

Shaeleen felt the TruthStone weighing heavy in her pocket along with the small IntelligenceStone. She knew she hadn't always lived a life of telling the truth. But she was slowly learning that truth was the light that powered the kingdoms and the world around them.

Shaeleen concentrated her thoughts on the small light streaming down upon her and, at the same time, brought up her power of truth. In this moment of clarity and purpose, she connected the two—light and truth—and felt peace grow inside of her. The truth then rose upon the light as if following the light up and out of the room. With her eyes still closed, she used that light to focus her thoughts.

Shaeleen's perspective began to change. She was no longer in the prison cell, but was now looking down onto the castle of Riverton itself. She could now see that the dungeon prison they were in had been built into the wall of a cliff that rose up from the seashore below and that the small window had been carved out through the cliff.

Using her power of truth, she floated on the light that came from the sun and covered the capital of Gabor. She expanded her view and now could see the Bay of Jalen to the south and the sea to the east. She flew within the light over the city. Riverton was almost as large as Stronghaven, though not as well kept. She could see buildings crumbling in certain quarters and the poor already begging in the streets at this time of the morning.

Maybe Erwin had had a point—the queen did seem to be letting the kingdom go. But that didn't make it right to abandon her. And it didn't mean that Commander Kerr was a better option.

Basking in the light, she continued westward, over the city, until she came to the inn they'd eaten at the previous night. She grabbed hold of a ray of light with her mind and flew down it into the inn's dining room. She saw Harold, Genevieve, Aaron, and Marianne with her son on her lap. They sat having breakfast at a long table. It seemed darker the farther she went into the room, and then Shaeleen's own vision clouded and dimmed. She felt the connection with her power weakening.

Shaeleen caught snippets of the family's conversation—it was about her and Orin. She smiled at their concern. A speck of light from a window rested on Genevieve's hand as she rested it on the table. Shaeleen used that speck for her focus. Through the light, she touched it and showed Genevieve the truth of what had happened. As Genevieve gasped and looked around the room, her hand was pulled away from the light.

Shaeleen felt Orin calling to her in the cell inside the castle dungeon. She could tell her body was weak and tired. She moved back through the light to a nearby window and then back outside again.

Her thinking dimmed, and she felt so very tired. Flying as fast as she could, she made her way back over the city in the blink of an eye, following the light. She spied the small window in the cliffside. The sunlight no longer shown directly through it, but she pushed toward it nonetheless. As she approached the shadows over the cliff, she struggled to stay alert. Then, as she left the light, her powers diminished and she could barely stay conscious.

"Shae!" Orin yelled out. "Wake up!"

Orin's voice focused her for one final moment, and then she fell over on the floor in the dungeon cell. After a moment, reality slowly came back to her. She opened her eyes and blinked a few times in the darkness, the window now only a small, dim shape far above their heads.

"What were you doing?" Orin said, panic filling his voice. He stood at the bars with his face pressed against them.

Shaeleen forced herself to sit back up. Her eyes were heavy, and she needed to sleep.

"I went for help, Orin."

"What are you talking about, Shae?" Orin took a few steps back. Then he came to the bars again. "This place is making you crazy."

"No." Shaeleen smiled and then put a hand to her head. She was so tired. "*It* brought clarity to me. The light, Orin. Truth and light go together."

"Guards!" Orin yelled out. "Shaeleen needs help."

"Orin," Shaeleen said, bringing his attention back to her. "I am fine. I just need to rest, that's all." She scooted back to a corner of the cell and laid her head against the black stone wall. Its surface was cool, which helped to settle her mind.

"Shae?" Orin pleaded once again.

"Don't worry, Orin," Shaeleen whispered. "Get some rest. Help is on the way."

Shaeleen closed her eyes and fell into a deep sleep.

CHAPTER TWENTY-FIVE

Although food and a fresh chamber pot had been brought to Shaeleen and Orin a few times a day over the next two days, Shaeleen still found herself anticipating their next meal. Always three guards had come—one entering their cells while the other two stood guard at the door. But the light from the small window high in the wall was the only indication they had of what time of day it was now.

Their meals had each consisted of a few pieces of fruit, a piece of bread, and a cup of water. Even though it wasn't much, Shaeleen still listened carefully for the key to turn in the outer door.

Finally, the usual three people came in. A guard came into her cell, and, as usual, Shaeleen stayed in the back corner and didn't give him much notice. "Shaeleen," the guard whispered. Shaeleen whipped her head up and found herself looking into the beautiful, dark eyes of Aaron. Her heart leapt, and she called out to Orin.

Then one of the guards at the door said, "Genevieve felt you were in trouble, and after what you did for us, we had to try and help." It was Harold.

Shaeleen turned from Aaron to Harold and then to the other guard. The third man pulled out a set of keys and unlocked their two cells.

"I'm Marianne's brother, Shem," the man said. "These two vouched for you—and, from what I heard, you made the commander quite angry, and...well...I don't like the commander very much. He has overstepped his bounds. I am loyal to the queen."

"And that is who I need to see," Shaeleen said. "But first, is there any way you can unlock these?" She held her hands out in front of her.

Shem shook his head. "Sorry, I was only able to get keys for the cells. I cannot unlock either of your shackles."

"It'll actually be easier this way," Harold spoke up.

Shaeleen was confused. "How is being in shackles easier?"

"We will escort you out of here," Aaron said, continuing his father's explanation. "And, with the shackles still on, there won't be any questions."

"But we have to hurry." Shem motioned them out of the cells. Marianne's brother was tall, strong, and good-looking. His dark hair contrasted nicely with his bronzed skin. As he reached his hand out to pull Shaeleen along, she suddenly became aware of how horrible she must look. *And smell.* She could hardly stand this. *What I wouldn't do for a change of clothes and a chance to freshen up.*

Shaeleen tensed up as they met the first guard directly outside of the prison door. This would be their first test.

"Orders are to keep the prisoners here," the guard said as he put his arm out to stop the group.

"Orders have changed," Shem said with a voice of authority. "You know how that is?"

The other guard nodded his head in understanding.

"Just doing my duty," Shem continued. "Was told to bring them to the TruthSeer. He'll find the truth from these scum."

Shem pushed Shaeleen and Orin forward, while Aaron and Harold followed from behind. The guard seemed convinced and waved them on.

After winding through a few hallways and up a flight of stairs, Shem directed them to a doorway at the end of a dark hallway.

As soon as they all entered, Genevieve and Marianne came up to Shaeleen and Orin and gave them hugs, though Orin didn't seem very comfortable with it.

"Glad to see you are safe," Genevieve said to Shaeleen. "You did send me a message, didn't you?"

"Yes," Shaeleen said. "I'd hoped you would understand."

"I don't know how you did it or who you really are, child," Genevieve said, "but we owed you. Now, let's see what we can do to get you out of here."

Shaeleen shook her head. "I have to speak to the queen first."

"Shae!" Orin said. "It's too dangerous here."

Harold cleared his throat. "Look, Shaeleen. You helped us out and so we helped you. I'm sure you think you have a good reason to see Queen Victoria, but she doesn't see people anymore."

Shaeleen took a deep breath. She didn't travel all this way, just to be stopped now. "I know it sounds trite, but the fates of our kingdoms depend on it. I must see her."

Shaeleen watched Harold sigh and look at his wife. Genevieve walked over to a small basin of water and dipped a cloth in it. "Well, let's see if we can clean you two up a bit. Then we'll see what we can do."

Marianne grabbed a comb and headed over to Orin.

"Ouch!" he yelled out once she started combing through his dirty mop. "That hurts."

"Stay still," Marianne said. "Don't you ever comb this hair?"

Orin just grunted in response and Shaeleen chuckled. *Boys!*

"Better do what she says, son," Harold said. "She's as stubborn as her mother."

Genevieve glared at him, but then a small smile formed on her mouth, and she laughed.

A quarter of an hour later, Shaeleen and Orin were a bit more cleaned up. Nothing could be done about the clothes, with the shackles on their hands, but at least their faces were better.

Shaeleen turned to Shem. "You are stationed here in the castle?"

Shem nodded in the affirmative, and a plan began to form in Shaeleen's mind

"Is what Harold said true?" Shaeleen asked. "Does the queen not see visitors?" she asked.

"Very rarely, miss," Shem answered. "Lately, it's been the TruthSeer's apprentice that handles most of the royal business."

"Erwin!" spat Shaeleen.

"I see you've met the man." Shem grimaced. "He's an arrogant pig."

That he is. "What about TruthSeer Justyn or the royal heir?" Shaeleen continued, working on her plan.

Footsteps were heard in the hallway outside the room, and everyone went quiet for a moment. Shem waited until the sounds were gone then stuck his head out the door.

"Guards are heading to the dungeon," Shem said. "They must know you've escaped. They will be looking for us."

Shaeleen groaned. They wouldn't have much time. She turned to Orin with a questioning look. Could he speed them out of there?

"I can't," he mumbled, surmising what her questioning look meant. "I can't access my power with these shackles on. They won't let me move."

Shaeleen paced for a few moments and then turned to Shem. "How are your acting skills?"

Shem raised his eyebrows.

"You're going to pretend to capture us. Aaron and Harold will help." Shaeleen revealed her plan as it came to her mind. "You will push through the castle and toward the TruthSeer Justyn, and I will yell out, demanding to see him."

"But—but—I don't know where Justyn is. He is old and sends Erwin to do his bidding," Shem said.

"It won't matter," Shaeleen continued. "We'll cause enough ruckus that he will find us. Get me above ground and to some light, and I will find him." She didn't know if she could do it again, but she would try. It was the only plan she had at the moment.

The three men nodded, and Shem headed to the door.

"And, Shem," Shaeleen said, "this must look real."

Shem's eyes opened wide.

"I mean it!" Shaeleen said. She wasn't going back to that dirty cell. *We have to see the queen and then get out quickly.*

Shem nodded and opened the door.

"Help!" Shaeleen screamed and struggled away from Shem, running down the hallway. "Let me go!" Her heart pounded, and she put all she could into it. She hoped Shem would play his part.

"Get back here!" Shem yelled. "Where are you going?"

Shaeleen turned her head back to him with a look telling him to do better. "I must see the queen," she yelled out.

Orin ran after her. "Shaeleen!"

Coming to the end of the hall, two other guards met them at the same time that Shem, Harold, and Aaron caught up.

Shem grabbed Shaeleen, and Aaron grabbed Orin, who kicked Aaron in the shins.

"Aaaargh!" Aaron yelled out and grabbed Orin tighter.

Shaeleen struggled, but Shem put his arm around her neck and Shaeleen let him hold her there.

"I caught these prisoners," Shem said to the two new guards—his acting ability shining forth. "I'm taking them to the TruthSeer. He will find out what's going on here once and for all."

"They should go back to the prison cells," one of the guards said.

Shem shook his head, and Shaeleen stomped on his foot to make things look good. One of the other guards slapped her across the face. She spat at him.

"Upstairs, now!" Harold said. Being older than the other four men, he brooked some level of respect, and they all obeyed. Coming to a flight of stairs, they pulled Orin and Shaeleen up to the next floor—the ground floor of the castle.

Early morning light brightened the candlelit room they stood in. A few servants scattered in front of them, busy with their own duties and not wanting to get involved with the guards' affairs. Shaeleen was sure it was beautiful, but she didn't have time to look around.

"The queen!" Shaeleen yelled out, still playing her part. They only had a few minutes left to see whether the ruse would work or not. "I want to see the queen!"

Shem smacked the back of her head and then clamped a hand over her mouth. She bit it, and he pulled it back, roaring in pain. A few drops of blood dribbled down his wrist. At the same time, Orin somehow pulled free from Aaron and began running up another flight of stairs—a wide, carpeted staircase that obviously led to better rooms.

The two other guards raced after him, and Shem pulled Shaeleen along. "That wasn't necessary," he whispered in her ear. "That hurt."

Shaeleen didn't say anything, but turned her head and tried to convey an apology with her eyes. Shem didn't look altogether convinced.

Orin arrived at the next landing before the guards caught up to him—which Shaeleen thought must have been on purpose because Orin was quick enough to outmaneuver them, even without his powers, she was sure.

At the top of the landing stood wall-sized windows, looking south into the Bay of Jalen. Light from the newly risen sun, in the east, sparkled along the top of the blue water, and, in response to the light, Shaeleen felt her powers rise up within her. But surprised onlookers—from below them and on their floor—stared at the group of five soldiers holding on to the two youths.

Shaeleen turned her head up. She could see three more levels of rooms above her. Closing her eyes for a brief moment, she called the light to her TruthStone and felt the entire castle around her. She used the morning sunlight to search for Justyn. While still struggling with the guards, it was difficult.

Without giving her full attention to the light, she used both of the stones to use the light to sense where TruthSeer Justyn was. With a few interruptions to keep the guards at bay, she found Justyn, in a far corner of an upstairs room, just before Orin called out to her.

"Shae, Shae," he whispered loudly, still struggling against the guards—both real and pretend.

She opened her eyes and looked at Orin.

"You're glowing again," he said.

Everyone below, on the main floor, and those on the landing, with them, were staring at her. For a moment, all was quiet.

Then, on the floor below them, Erwin strode in. He walked with arrogance and confidence, but his face was stern, and his cheeks were red.

He is not happy.

"Bring the prisoners down to me!" his voice bellowed.

Shaeleen couldn't let that happen. In a moment of silence, she pulled away from Aaron and dug deep inside herself to reach the power of the TruthStone. "I call upon TruthSeer

Justyn," she said, her voice echoing off the walls. At the same time, she had pushed her wishes of truth into the light and up the stairs.

"I am a TruthSeer," Erwin said, his rage seeming barely held in check. "Bring her to me!"

"Erwin!" an old, yet strong voice sounded from above.

On the landing three floors above Shaeleen stood a man that looked like the oldest person she had ever seen. He had long, white hair that was flowing softly down over a blue robe, his thin arms poking out the edges. His face was calm, but his light eyes—even from three floors away—flashed in anger over the assembled crowd.

Erwin took a few steps toward the bottom of the stairs and, looking up at his master, said, "TruthSeer, the prisoners have escaped."

"Bring them to me," Justyn said.

"But, sir, you don't need to worry about these small children," Erwin whined. "You need your rest."

"TruthSeer," Shaeleen said, speaking for the first time since Justyn's arrival. "I need to speak to your queen."

Justyn glared down at her, and she could feel his penetrating gaze probing her mind for the truth. *Such power he has!*

"I will see you first, my dear, before the queen," Justyn said in a softer voice, with a trace of admiration. "You did call out to me."

His words brought a smile to Shaeleen's lips. *It worked again.*

"Erwin, please have your guards take their shackles off before they leave," Justyn said. "I have this handled."

"But…" Erwin tried to push things. But Justyn beckoned Shaeleen and Orin by crooking his fingers. They held still for a moment while a nearby guard took a key out and unlocked the shackles around their wrists.

Shaeleen rubbed her wrists with her hands while looking back down at Erwin. She saw the tendrils of darkness around him once again and, in the lightened room, knew them for what they were—powers of the shadow. She had read about that power somewhere in the *TruthSeers' Journal*. But she would have to deal with that later.

Before leaving the landing and moving up the stairs, Shaeleen leaned in toward Harold. "Thank you, Harold. Thank you for all your family has done. I won't forget it. I bid you safe travels."

He smiled at her and then motioned for Aaron and Shem to follow him. The two other guards also descended the stairs behind them. Shaeleen hoped nothing would happen to her newfound friends. She felt grateful for them.

Orin walked next to her as they ascended the wide staircase, floor by floor. Servants stopped and stared at them, whispering to each other afterward—as if wondering who these two were for them to be summoned so by the ancient TruthSeer. Each floor up grew in its adornment and wealth. Shaeleen noticed that thin flooring turned into plush carpets. Simple walls turned into walls filled with expensive portraits and paintings. And basic wood furniture became exquisite woodwork. Shaeleen ran her hands over the smooth banister lovingly. The wood grain in the maple had been stained to standout perfection.

After three flights, she was breathing harder but finally standing in front of the TruthSeer. But he turned and walked down the hallway.

Orin turned to Shaeleen with a questioning glance, and she shrugged before following the TruthSeer down the hallway into a room. The room had a group of plush-cushioned chairs set against the backdrop of a large window overlooking the Bay of Jalen, to the south. Two floor-to-ceiling curio cabinets, full of rare seashells and obsidian rocks, took up one wall. Another wall held a tapestry depicting Mount Eyvindr, on Verlyn, with the image of a man standing at the base of the mountain—a man all knew to be King Wayland, the founder of their kingdoms.

"Please sit." Justyn motioned both of them toward the chairs. Off to the side was a tray, holding cups, some type of drink, and a few pastries. Shaeleen turned away so she would not be tempted by these. Orin rolled his eyes at her and sat down in one of the chairs. *Now is not the time to think about food.*

The TruthSeer turned to Orin first. "I hear you caused quite a bit of trouble for the commander." The man's voice seemed to hold a hint of amusement.

"He wasn't very nice, and we needed to get away," Orin said matter-of-factly.

The TruthSeer smiled more fully now. "Well, I'm glad you enjoy telling the truth. Doing so will be much easier on me and on your friend here."

With that, he turned to Shaeleen. He stared deep into her eyes for a moment. And it took all the courage she had to hold his gaze, but she did. She knew she had to tread carefully around this TruthSeer. Traveling with Erlinda had taught her a few things.

"It was you who reached out to me, wasn't it?" Justyn said.

"It was," Shaeleen admitted.

"A skill most TruthSeers take a lifetime to learn, if they ever even do," Justyn said. "Many never discover the connection between truth and light. But that conversation will have to wait for another time. I fear my apprentice will not let matters drop so easily. Why do you need to see Queen Victoria?"

CHAPTER TWENTY-SIX

Shaeleen took a deep breath. She had told the TruthSeer of her trip to North Bay, of Prince Calix's plans to attack Stronghaven, and of Commander Kerr's traitorous deeds and his plans to ally himself with Prince Calix. She had also mentioned traveling with Erlinda and her well-wishes to Justyn himself. Throughout the story, she had left out any mention of the stones, the secret about Prince Basil and Prince Calix, and Orin's speed, though she did suspect that the TruthSeer knew about Orin's speed already.

"You bring us grave tidings," Justyn said. "The commander's influence has been growing in strength recently. I fear that even my apprentice believes him to be the solution."

"I think your apprentice may be the power behind Commander Kerr," Shaeleen said.

"No. That can't be right." The old TruthSeer steadied himself against a doorway, the pain of his words obvious to Shaeleen. "Erwin is just a young TruthSeer apprentice."

Shaeleen took a deep breath to steady her own pain. "Twice I have seen black tendrils of power coming from your apprentice. He is more dangerous than you have realized."

Justyn nodded. "I have spent much of my time with the queen, and have ignored my apprentice and his apparent greed and growing powers."

"Speaking of the queen, I must see her."

The TruthSeer shook his head. "I'm afraid she is too weak to see you. Now that you've brought this news to me, I can take care of things."

Shaeleen did not feel any lies in his words, but she did feel he was hiding something. "You're not telling me everything."

Justyn smiled. "And neither are you, I surmise."

Shaeleen blushed and looked down. Turning her mind inward for a moment she thought about what to do. Suddenly she felt a new sensation in her mind. *Another stone.* Her powers were pointing her somewhere—to a place of strength. She stood up promptly and turned around with her power focused outward now.

Orin jumped up also, as if ready for danger. "What is it, Shae?"

As Shaeleen took a few steps around the room, the TruthSeer watched her from his seated position. All of a sudden, she knew the source of what she was looking for. She felt strength radiating from nearby. The Red Jasper StrengthStone—it was near!

Now more than ever, she knew she needed to see the queen—the owner of the StrengthStone. She walked over to Justyn and looked down on him in the chair. "I really do need to see your queen, sir. I cannot take no for an answer. I will not!"

Justyn stood and pulled himself up to his full height. He was thin but tall. His pale blue eyes flashed darkly at her, but she held her ground. "A TruthSeer is second only to the queen or king. I assure you, things will be taken care of."

"Orin!" Shaeleen called out to her friend. "I need your assistance."

Orin rushed to her side and reached for her hand. By the look in his eyes he knew what Shaeleen wanted.

But Justyn was quicker, and he grabbed her wrist instead. He brought his eyes down to meet hers, and she felt his power trying to enter her mind.

"How dare you!" She tried to pull away, but he held her tight.

"You will tell me the truth of why you want to see the queen, Shaeleen," the TruthSeer demanded.

Shaeleen felt this command begin to control her mind. She *wanted* to obey him. She *needed* to obey him. The compulsion was becoming too strong for her.

She'd opened her mouth, to tell Justyn all, when Orin grabbed her other hand and, with the other TruthSeer also in tow, used his power of speed. Orin pulled the two of them with him, back out into the hallway. Then he ran in and out of each room's doorway, searching for the queen.

They soon reached the northeast corner of the castle, where two guards stood in front of a door. But that barrier was nothing for Orin. Through the door he went, with both Shaeleen and Justyn still in tow. Then Orin stopped.

Shaeleen stood up with her mouth agape. They were in a dimly lit room with an enormous four-poster bed in the corner. Two servants were in attendance, and they yelped at this intrusion, backing away into a corner. One servant had been putting linens away, while the other had been tending someone on the bed.

"This is outrageous!" Justyn's face was beet red. He stared hard at Orin. "You have no right to interrupt Her Grace's intimate privacy. You will be punished for this."

"No, he won't," Shaeleen said more calmly than she felt. "I told you I needed to see the queen. If you were as strong as a TruthSeer as you should be, you would've known I had spoken the truth."

Justyn's face went from red to pale white, and he put a hand on the edge of the large bed. "I hadn't noticed..."

The two servants skittered around to the other side as Shaeleen walked around the bed. Reaching the head of it, she looked down. The woman lying there with closed eyes must be Queen Victoria, longtime queen of Gabor. Her hair was short and gray. A tint of rose makeup on her cheeks was the only other color on her face. And a red blanket was pulled up and tucked under her chin.

Shaeleen reached her hand tentatively forward, and one of the servants let out a gasp. The queen's eyes flickered open—and were empty for a moment—but then she held Shaeleen's eyes with her own. A thin smile crossed her lips.

Justyn came up next to Shaeleen. "I am sorry, Your Highness. I tried to stop her. I apologize for this intrusion."

The queen motioned for her servants to help her sit up in the bed, and then she dismissed them out of the room. After doing so, she pulled her attention back to Shaeleen.

Shaeleen bowed to the queen—her presence seemed to palpably demand respect. "Your Highness, I bring you news of Commander Kerr's treachery."

The queen eyed Justyn for confirmation, and he nodded his head.

"Where is your heir, Your Highness? The heir should be here running things for you in your weakened condition."

The queen coughed a few times then, in a low voice, said, "My heir is my granddaughter. She has been on Verlyn preparing to become a queen, and is to be engaged soon."

Flashes of intelligence flowed into Shaeleen's mind, and she understood. "To Basil," she whispered in understanding, but felt a growing pain in her gut once again.

"To *Prince* Basil, yes," Queen Victoria said, subtly chastising Shaeleen for not using the prince's proper title. "To the heir of Galena."

At that, Shaeleen almost fell to her knees in pain. Doubled over, she put her hands on the side of the bed to keep from falling.

"Shae!" Orin rushed to her side and held her up.

Out of the corner of her eye, she saw that Justyn also was bending over—pain evident in his face. Then he glared at her with eyes wide and round.

"Tell them, Shae," Orin said. "Maybe they can help us."

Shaeleen was torn inside. *It is not my secret to tell.*

She'd purposefully avoided thinking about it—revealing the secret would have too many painful outcomes. Even now, her head and gut seemed about to burst. She tried to push the pain down, something she was learning to live with.

Orin helped her to stand back up, saying, "I hate to see you in so much pain, Shae."

"If some secret involves my granddaughter, Diamonique, you must tell me. She is my only kin left and is the hope of Gabor," the queen pleaded. "If something happens to her, Commander Kerr will take over the kingdom and take all the remaining strength with him."

Justyn glared at Shaeleen as if daring her to not tell the truth now.

Shaeleen took a deep breath and decided to speak the words that could shatter Galena, Gabor, and all of Wayland.

"Prince Basil is not the true heir; Prince Calix is the oldest," Shaeleen said, having to push the words out past her lips quickly. The truth in this matter hurt no less to say than a lie might have. *How am I ever going to tell Basil?*

The queen coughed again, and Justyn moved to her side to comfort her.

"That monster," Queen Victoria whispered. "We've heard of his deeds even here in Riverton. Why isn't anything being done?"

"Only a few know the truth," Shaeleen whispered. "It could rip apart Galena."

Justyn turned to Shaeleen and said, "And Gabor with it."

Tears came to the queen's eyes. "My kingdom! I have failed her. I don't have enough strength left."

The queen's words pulled at Shaeleen's heart, but they rang true. "Show me your StrengthStone, the Red Jasper. It is here, isn't it?"

Justyn sucked in a breath. "No one sees the stone."

The queen sat up a bit more and put her hand on Justyn's arm. "It's all right, my faithful TruthSeer. It is time for all secrets to be revealed."

Justyn looked at his queen questioningly and shook his head. "No. We can't. It will destroy us."

Just then, the sun streamed in through a window, sending a stream of light into the room. The light settled on a portrait in the corner, and they all turned their heads.

"It's in there," Shaeleen said, her words barely audible.

The queen nodded and then turned to Justyn with stern eyes. He walked slowly toward the portrait and took it carefully off the wall. Behind it stood a small cupboard in the wall.

"Please, young man, help me over there," the queen said to Orin, who snapped instantly to the queen's side. He held her hand as she swung her legs around and put her feet on the floor. Shaeleen retrieved a pair of golden slippers that sat in the corner and put them on Queen Victoria's feet.

With Shaeleen and Orin on either side, they escorted the elderly queen to the small cupboard. Her elegance showed forth even in her weakened condition. "It needs to feel my power to open," the queen said, running her fingers over the wood.

There was a slight click, and then a small door swung open. Reaching inside, the queen pulled out a little bag with a drawstring—not unlike the one that Prince Basil had kept the IntelligenceStone in.

Shaeleen took a deep breath and leaned closer. She could feel the pulsating power of the StrengthStone calling to her TruthStone. The queen emptied the contents of the bag into the palm of her own hand. A reddish glow grew out from the center of her palm, where there sat a small Red Jasper stone—it was hardly bigger than the blue Labradorite IntelligenceStone Shaeleen had received from Prince Basil.

Tears dripped from the queen's eyes. "This is all that is left. We have given so much away through the years. Now I fear it is not enough."

Shaeleen reached into her own pocket and took out her bag. Opening its drawstring, she reached her hand inside and pulled out the Moldavite TruthStone. A bright green light pulsated from it.

Justyn gasped. "It's so large. How did you...?" The power of the stone dropped him to his feeble knees.

"She is the one, Justyn," the queen cried. "The one I told you about. She is the one to save the kingdoms. The prophesied one!"

Shaeleen reached her other hand down to raise Justyn back upon his feet.

He moved over and sat on the edge of the bed. "But there is only one TruthSeer per kingdom." He put his hand on the footboard to steady himself.

"I represent all of Wayland." Shaeleen smiled and raised her hand out in front of her. The light of the TruthStone grew larger and swirled through the air. It made its way over to Queen Victoria's outstretched hand, and then the green and the red light swirled together until a purplish light sat in the middle of all of them.

Tears dripped down the old queen's face, but she appeared more excited and alive than she had moments before. "It's yours." She held the Red Jasper StrengthStone out for Shaeleen. "Take it."

Justyn jumped up off the edge of the bed and said, "No, Victoria. That belongs to Gabor. You can't give it away. It's all we have." The TruthSeer's face was stern, and he reached out to take the stone from the queen's hand.

But Orin moved swiftly, appearing between the queen and her TruthSeer. "Let it be," Orin said with more authority than his years would give him. "It is her right."

Shaeleen smiled at Orin's protection of her and cocked her head to the side. For a brief moment, she saw Orin as something more than he was: almost princely in appearance. She returned her attention back to Queen Victoria.

The queen reached her hand toward Shaeleen and dropped the Red Jasper stone into Shaeleen's hand. A bright light exploded from her upturned palm. Green, red, and blue light—then a brilliant yellow!

The four people in the room had to turn their gazes away. When they looked back, the small Red Jasper StrengthStone was gone. Now imbedded inside the TruthStone, it sat next to the blue IntelligenceStone from Prince Basil.

Shaeleen audibly gasped and had to take in a deep breath to control so much power. Shaeleen could now sense how the light in the room was moving from where the queen was toward Shaeleen as the sun slowly shifted its position outside. Pure euphoria surged through Shaeleen's body, and she shuddered at the power she now held in her hand.

Closing her eyes, she traveled upon the stream of light once more—out of the queen's bedchamber and up over the city, the powers of truth, intelligence, and strength coursing through her mind and body—and riding on the stream of light.

She could see everyone in the land—felt a connection to all that had shared even a modicum of strength from the stone over the years. Her mind flew far to the west in the midday sun, until she saw the city of North Bay—with half a dozen warships in its usually peaceful harbor.

"Kerr!" Shaeleen gasped.

She had to warn Basil about the treachery of his brother and the commander from Gabor. *Basil!* Her heart lurched in thinking about him. He was such a good man, a leader the people loved. *But...* She groaned with the weight of the secret held by only a few. *What will I do? What should I do?*

Before leaving North Bay, she searched out her brother. Cole stood in a room with the wizard Faegon. Shaeleen noticed that TruthSeer Erlinda was back and stood in the corner of the room. The queen mother stood by her side and held her hand. Their eyes were red and tired, a resigned look filling their faces.

Oh no! What have they done?

Prince Calix sat on a small throne and directed the group. Commander Kerr stood by his side. Cole stood at attention in front of the leaders.

"Cole!" she called out in the light.

Cole glanced around him, a frown forming on his face.

"Cole," she called to him again. "Meet me in Stronghaven."

Cole nodded his head slightly and looked around again. "Shaeleen?" His mouth formed the word, but no sound came out.

Then the prince addressed him. "Wizard Cole," the prince called out, and Cole turned his attention away from Shaeleen's voice. "I have a special task for you."

Cole didn't speak but stood waiting for the prince's orders.

"Do you serve your prince? Do you recognize my authority in the kingdom?"

Cole bowed his head and nodded. "I serve the truth, Prince Calix."

"Oh Cole!" Shaeleen shouted. *Why did I leave him there all alone?* She watched as Cole frowned slightly and shook his head.

"Is something wrong, Wizard?" Prince Calix asked. "Faegon tells me you are learning quickly. You say you serve the truth. Then I have a quest to test your loyalty to the truth."

Shaeleen knew that her brother was being manipulated by Prince Calix appealing to Cole's sense of duty and honor.

"Sir?" Cole said, standing at attention.

"I need you to go to Verlyn and find Princess Diamonique of Gabor. She is to marry the heir of Galena, and her engagement will be announced soon." The prince smiled and rubbed his hands together.

Cole stood still for a brief moment, thinking. "She is to marry Prince Basil, then?"

Shaeleen's stomach turned over and she grew queasy. *Even in the light I feel the pain of lies!*

Prince Calix stood up and threw a glass of wine to the floor, the shards spreading in a hundred pieces across the marble floor. The group in attendance took a few steps back.

"No, she will not marry my self-righteous brother. I will tell you why," Prince Calix yelled out. The room stood in total silence except for his voice echoing off the walls. Then he crooked his finger toward Cole.

Shaeleen felt herself grow tired. The light in the room had shifted, and shadows began to fill the prince's room in its stead. She fought to stay there one more minute. She wanted to hear what the prince would say to be sure, but she knew what his words would be. *He now knows he is the oldest.*

"Shae!" a voice called, deep in her mind. It was Orin, calling her back.

"No. Leave me be," she cried out, trying to hold on.

The scene in North Bay was fading. She saw her brother walk slowly toward the prince. The prince took a step forward, leaned close to Cole's ear, then whispered something so softly that no one in the room overheard his words—including Shaeleen. But Cole pulled back with a confused and surprised look on his face.

"Oh no," Shaeleen said out loud. "Cole!" she screamed through the light. But it was no use, for she was being pulled back to Riverton. And the last thing she saw there was Cole bowing low to Prince Calix.

His darn sense of honor!

Shaeleen was slammed back into the queen's room in Riverton. Her knees buckled, and she started to fall, but Orin was there to hold her up. As she closed her hand around the stone, the light diminished and then was gone. She sat down on the edge of the queen's bed and put the stone back into the pouch.

"Calix is going after your granddaughter," Shaeleen finally said to the queen. "He is sending my brother to fetch her, and Calix intends to marry her."

Hearing this, the queen fell to the ground. Justyn ran to her side. From the floor, she peered up at Shaeleen and said, "You must save her, Shaeleen. Please, you have to find her first," she begged, her voice catching with emotion.

Shaeleen looked at Orin. "We do have the means to travel faster than my brother does."

Orin smiled. "Just say the word, Shae!"

Justyn helped the queen back to her bed and helped her lie down. Then he turned to Shaeleen and Orin and said with a stern look, "You two are trifling with powers you know nothing about."

"Shaeleen knows what she's doing," Orin said, defending her.

Justyn pinched his lips hard. "I've been a TruthSeer for fifty years—"

"And yet," Shaeleen interrupted, "your apprentice dabbles in the power of the shadow and supports Commander Kerr's thirst for power and treachery. Where does that leave your kingdom now, TruthSeer?"

Justyn's face went white. He opened his mouth to respond, but the queen put her hand on his arm.

"Justyn, Shaeleen, Orin—now is not the time to assign blame. We must save my granddaughter and the kingdoms. And Shaeleen is the only one that has the means to do that."

Justyn said nothing, but he didn't look happy.

The queen coughed and then continued talking. "She already has three powers and the use of a fourth power, through Orin here. Never have we heard of such a coalescence of powers before. Go, Shaeleen, and save my granddaughter. Will you do that?"

"I serve all the kingdoms, Your Highness. However, I feel your granddaughter is important to the future of Wayland. First, though, I must return to Prince Basil. He sent me and my brother on this errand, to discover what his brother was doing. I need to warn him. I owe him that."

"And, will you tell him?" the queen asked, referring to the birth order of Prince Calix and Prince Basil.

Shaeleen shook her head. "I don't know. I really don't know."

"If you don't, the pain will destroy you," Justyn said. "You don't have enough experience to handle it."

Shaeleen gave him a dark look. She didn't like his condescending attitude toward her—though she could understand a little how he must feel. A TruthSeer was used to being the most powerful person in the room—and now, he wasn't.

"We will see," Shaeleen said.

"My servants will get you a change of clothes and secure a ship for the journey," the queen said before laying her head back down and closing her eyes. "I'm so tired."

Shaeleen and Orin followed Justyn out of the room. Their trip from Riverton to Stronghaven would take a few days. *A few days for me to decide whether to tell Basil or not.*

CHAPTER TWENTY-SEVEN

Three days later, Shaeleen and Orin disembarked from their ship and stepped onto the docks of Stronghaven. During their journey home, Shaeleen had still not come to grips with what she should do. The TruthStone sat heavy in the pocket of her dress—a beautiful, light blue gown with a gold-rimmed, red cloak falling over her shoulders—a gift from the queen.

Shaeleen was beginning to feel as if the weight of Wayland's future had fallen into her hands. And it was strange to watch others—people walking around, captains yelling at their crews, and kids running through the streets—all with no thoughts of what was happening in the world around them.

Shaeleen was aware that Galena had been blessed with relative peace for so many years that people usually just went along with their daily business with no thoughts of trouble. Periodically, a small border dispute or a minor aggression of an enterprising noble would occur, but the power of the stones had always protected Wayland.

"I need to go and see my father," Orin said, bouncing on his toes. "He won't believe the adventures I've had without him."

"Orin." Shaeleen grew serious. "I don't know what I would have done without you. You saved me more times than I can count."

"And you thought I was just some thieving street urchin the first time we met, didn't you?" Orin laughed and pushed his blond curls out of his eyes.

Shaeleen joined in with a laugh of her own and a nod of her head. "I admit, I might have been a bit judgmental…but you *were* stealing things."

"If your brother wouldn't have caught me, I would have gotten away with it too."

Shaeleen frowned a bit, thinking about Cole. She hoped he had heard her plea for him to return to Stronghaven.

"Just be careful, Orin," she said. "You are going with me to Verlyn, aren't you? I mean, if your father allows it?"

"Of course I am." Orin bobbed up and down on the balls of his feet. "Once he knows what's going on, he won't be able to stop me."

"You can't tell him everything," Shaeleen said, looking around her and lowering her voice. The sounds of gulls flying overhead and of seamen yelling had helped to keep their conversation private, but she still needed to be careful.

Orin peered down at his shoes. "I know, Shae. I know. I will be careful. Can I tell him I helped you and met the queen of Gabor?"

"Yes, that's fine. As long as he doesn't know about *you know what*." Shaeleen looked around her again. That was a secret that could rip peace away from her beautiful city without a moment's pause.

Orin nodded.

"Now, go get a bath, eat, and see your father. I'm going home to see my family, and then I will meet you in front of the castle tomorrow morning." Shaeleen shooed Orin away, but she could tell he was anxious.

Orin took off, running north through the docks, while Shaeleen turned toward the south part of town. She had not gone more than a few blocks, when she heard a carriage coming up behind her. She moved to the side but hardly paid it any attention.

"Shaeleen!" a shrill voice shouted out from the carriage window.

Shaeleen turned, and immediately she let out a long groan.

"Where have you been?" Clarise's high-pitched voice flew out of the carriage.

"Stop!" came another voice from inside it.

Lady Judith.

Shaeleen groaned again. *I don't have time for this.* Without thinking, she smoothed down her hair.

Lady Judith, with her head sticking out of the stopped carriage, glared at Shaeleen for a moment, her eyes nearly popping out of her head at the clothes Shaeleen now wore. The queen of Gabor had also provided Shaeleen with a silver headband that she now wore on her forehead, just under her hairline. It was to be a gift from the queen to her granddaughter Diamonique when Shaeleen met her in Verlyn.

"Where have you been? And where did you get those clothes?" Lady Judith whined.

"Aren't you off to the charity event for the prince?" Shaeleen asked. "Enjoy your day with the commoners." Then Shaeleen turned away from the carriage and, with her head held high, continued walking forward down the street.

"How rude," Lady Judith mumbled. "Driver, stop that girl for me."

The driver hopped down to obey, and Shaeleen breathed out a rush of air. *I'm not letting that woman capture me again!* Hiking up her dress with one hand, she took off, running down the street, swerving between townspeople out shopping. But she could hear the footsteps of the driver, who was gaining on her. Breathing hard, she wondered if she could make it home before he could catch her.

Turning around a corner, she ran into a man and knocked him flat on his back. Stopping momentarily, to check if he was all right, Shaeleen saw a familiar face peered up at her with surprise that mirrored her own.

"Shae!" Cole gasped out loud.

Just then, the man that was chasing her grabbed on to her hand and pulled her toward him. "Lady Judith would like a word with you."

Cole stood up and turned with an angry look at the driver. "Let her go."

The man stared hard at Cole, obviously trying to decide if avoiding facing this young man was worth Lady Judith's displeasure.

Cole stood with a fire in his eyes that Shaeleen hadn't seen there before. And she noticed a small sizzle of light at the tips of his fingers as he drew his sword.

Shaeleen thought about using her TruthStone's power on the driver, but knew she needed to be careful with that. Instead, she pulled upon the small StrengthStone. She felt her muscles bulge, and she pushed the driver away on her own, with more force than she'd intended. He landed against a wall and slumped to the ground.

"Tell Lady Judith I have nothing to speak to her about." Shaeleen stood over the man, her cloak swirling around her. "I am on an errand for the prince."

Looking from Shaeleen to Cole and back again, the driver slowly stood up and held his hands in the air as he backed up and then ran back the way he had come.

Shaeleen turned around and saw Cole staring hard at her. He appeared to be in shock.

"I could always take care of myself," she said, trying to lighten the mood.

That brought a small crack to Cole's lips, and he almost smiled. "You look amazing, Shaeleen!"

Shaeleen grabbed him hard and hugged him. "I'm so sorry I had to leave you, Cole." Pulling back out of his warm embrace, she noticed he, too, was dressed far better.

He now wore a new, crisp uniform—blue and black, the colors of Galena's IntelligenceStone. His hair was styled a bit more neatly than when she had left him almost two weeks before. But the biggest differences were in his eyes and his demeanor. Two weeks had brought power and confidence to his usually shy persona. *I guess I've changed too.*

"I just came from Gabor," Shaeleen said.

Cole's eyes grew wide. "I thought I felt you in North Bay. But, afterward, I didn't know if it was my mind playing tricks on me or not."

"That was me," Shaeleen admitted.

"How?" Cole let out a deep breath. "I can tell a lot has happened."

Don't I know it! She wanted to tell Cole about her travels to Gabor, but now was not the time—the thought of what to tell Basil still consumed her mind.

"We need to report back to Basil," Shaeleen said, but she started walking in the direction of their home. "I think it would be nice to go home first, don't you?"

Cole's eyes had flashed at her not using Basil's title, but he let it go for once. They walked in silence for a moment. Then Cole spoke. "Shae, Prince Calix has asked me to do something for him."

Shaeleen nodded. "Bring Diamonique back to him?"

"How did you know?" As Cole's eyes grew round with surprise, Shaeleen noticed the power he seemed to hold behind them now.

"I was in the room with you, Cole," Shaeleen said with excitement. "It really is quite amazing. Truth and light go together. That is the strength that holds Wayland together: light and truth and the power of the stones."

"Slow down, Shae." Cole laughed. "What are you talking about?"

"I can travel on the rays of light," Shaeleen said. "Well, not physically, but I can see things."

Cole scrunched up his face. "Well, I don't quite understand what you're saying, but I am glad you're back." His smile grew wide, and he put his arm around her shoulder for a moment.

Turning back to their new task at hand, Shaeleen grew more serious. "About Diamonique? Are you going to bring her back to Calix or to Basil?"

"Shae, we serve the truth, don't we?" Cole's demeanor seemed to grow solemn. "Why didn't you tell me you were leaving North Bay before you left?"

Shaeleen wondered about the change in subject. She realized her brother was most likely facing his own internal questions of what to do. *How could I have left my brother there all alone?*

Shaeleen looked away from Cole's eyes. "I couldn't risk others finding out, Cole. I still don't know what to do."

"What do you mean *you don't know what to do*?" Cole said, raising his voice. He took a step away from her. A few townspeople walking by turned in their direction. He lowered his voice as he continued, "We serve the truth, Shae."

"But Basil should be the king," Shaeleen began to whisper. As soon as she had spoken this, pain erupted throughout her body. She almost fell over.

"Shae!" Cole said as he grabbed her and held her up. "You can't mean that. It would kill you to live that lie. Besides, that's not your call to make. The truth is the truth."

Shaeleen took a moment to compose herself. They were only a few blocks from their home. She breathed deeply and continued walking, although somewhat slower.

"But I can't let Calix rule," she said finally. As her head began to pound, she knew that Cole was right. *How can I live with this pain?* "You do know what Calix is intending, don't you? Siding with Commander Kerr is not very smart of him."

Cole laughed. "Commander Kerr was not very happy with you or Orin. By the way, where is that little scoundrel? Is he still stealing and causing problems?"

Shaeleen stiffened. "That *scoundrel*, as you call him, saved my life more than a few times over the past two weeks—something that you should have been doing." She knew she didn't really mean to blame her brother, but she was tired and in pain. Cole was being so infuriating: putting his sense of honor and truth above the best interests of the kingdom—or of all Wayland, for that matter.

As they turned a corner, Shaeleen could see their house farther down the street. Their father stood outside, unhitching his horse from the wagon. *He must have just finished making a delivery.*

Cole put a hand softly on her arm to stop her in the street. She flinched and pulled away at his compassion. *I don't want to feel better right now.* She wiped new tears away from the corners of her eyes.

"Shae," Cole said, clearly confused at her reaction. "What has gotten into you? I am here to help and protect you. I would have gladly gone with you."

I need to get home. Shaeleen started walking again, faster and more deliberately. "I had no choice, Cole—I told you that. Then I needed to get to Gabor and see the queen. And you seem to be doing just fine running Calix's errands for him."

Cole was almost running to keep up with her. "Shae, please stop and talk to me. I'm your guardian—your protector. But how can I protect you if you don't let me know what you're going to do? Aren't you going to tell Prince Basil about his brother being the true heir?"

The question stopped her in her tracks, and Cole took a few steps past her before he noticed she had stopped. *That is the question, isn't it?* That is what she had been wrestling with for over the past week. Would she tell Basil and destroy him and possibly the kingdom, or let the secret linger longer and destroy herself?

Looking past Cole, she saw their father stop what he was doing and look down the street at them. He yelled for their mother, and soon their father, their mother, and Alva stood in front of the house.

"Aren't you, Shae?" Cole asked again. "Please listen to reason. We were sent to find the truth. Prince Basil is an honorable man. He will listen to the truth."

"But I didn't know telling the truth would be this hard." Shaeleen felt the tears run hot down her face. "I never asked for any of this. How can the fate of a kingdom fall on my shoulders?"

"Honor and truth are never easy." Cole sighed deeply and looked at his family down the street then back at Shaeleen. "But I am here for you, Shae. Talk to me."

No one could understand what she was going through. The internal struggle was killing her. Why didn't her brother see what was best for the kingdom? The truth wasn't always the best way, was it? But, then again, she was supposed to be above the kingdom and represent all of Wayland. She growled in frustration as her stomach groaned and her head pounded.

"I…" She paused, still not knowing what to do. The IntelligenceStone was telling her to do one thing, but her heart was telling her to do another—and right now in the middle of the pain, the anger, the frustration—*I will side with my heart!* "I will tell Basil that his brother has sided with Commander Kerr and that they intend to take his throne," Shaeleen said. Then her head exploded in pain.

Cole reached over and held her up, his eyes searching hers for understanding. "But the throne belongs to Prince Calix," he seemed to plead with her to understand reason. "That is the truth and the law that we must uphold."

Shaeleen didn't want to hear reason or honor or truth right then. It was all too much for her. "Basil will make a better king." Shaeleen pushed away from Cole and stood on her own. Cole backed away from her as she pushed her next words out through the pain. "He will be king!"

Instantly, Shaeleen leaned over and vomited at the strength of the pain from her lie. Three times she retched.

Her mother came running up to her. "Shaeleen, Shaeleen, what's wrong?" her mother said as she came up next to Shaeleen. "Cole, go get her some water!"

Cole looked at Shaeleen with compassion in his eyes, but she only glared at him—she didn't want his compassion at the moment. She wanted his understanding. They both knew she had lied. Shaeleen's father joined her mother, and they helped her to the house. Her sister, Alva, took the water from Cole and handed it to Shaeleen.

She drank it down quickly, feeling it soothe her sore throat. Making her way to the kitchen table, she sat down.

"You look horrible, Shae," Alva said.

"I'm fine." Her head throbbed with the pain, but it wasn't as bad as her stomach had been. She took a few deep breaths and tried to relax. It had been foolish to speak as she had; she knew the truth of it deep down. *I just need some rest.*

"Cole," their father said. "What happened to Shaeleen? Didn't you take care of your sister?"

Shaeleen looked up at Cole. She couldn't tell what he was thinking, other than that he had seemed hurt by her decision to not tell the truth.

"We got separated," Cole said. "But she was able to take care of herself."

Shaeleen let out a deep breath. At least he didn't tell their father that she's a TruthSeer and is sick because she just lied, or that Calix would be their next king. He was too honor-bound for that. He was still her protector even though she had treated him so badly. Awkward silence filled their small kitchen.

"Well, it's almost suppertime," their mother said. Turning to Cole and then to Shaeleen, she added, "Get cleaned up, then come back in to eat. We can talk about what happened then."

"I'm not hungry," Shaeleen said. In fact she was starving, but she couldn't face sitting around the table with her family right then—the questions that would be thrown at her would be too much. She would have to lie again and again and again. It would be better to be alone.

"Neither am I," Cole said and began to walk to his bedroom.

"We will meet the prince in the morning to report," Shaeleen called after Cole. The pain from her earlier lies barely allowed her to think at all. "I expect you to be there with me."

Cole turned around so fast he knocked a small wooden carving off a shelf—a carving that he had made when he was a small boy. Picking it back up, he said, "I will be there to report, and I expect you to tell him the truth of it all. That is what he sent us to find out."

Shaeleen headed to her own bedroom, closing the door behind her. Then she slumped to the floor, her back to the door, and cried softly.

What will I say to Basil tomorrow? Is there anything to say that will save him and the kingdom?

CHAPTER TWENTY-EIGHT

Shaeleen looked out of a window of her home and sighed. A storm had come in from the east during the night and had continued into today. With Stronghaven being at the end of a peninsula, it was hit roughly on all sides by the unrelenting rain and wind. To Shaeleen, the foul weather seemed to reflect her mood that day.

She dressed slowly, putting the pouch with the TruthStone into a pocket in her dress before pulling on her warmest cloak—which she knew would do nothing for her in this type of storm. It might keep a bit of water off of her, but wearing it would be close to unbearable with the humidity.

The weight of the TruthStone in her pocket was not only physical, but she felt as if the entire future of Galena and the continent of Wayland weighed her down. Sighing again, she then took a deep breath and opened the door of her bedroom. Two large candle lamps were lit in the main part of the house to offset the gloomy darkness from outside.

Shaeleen's mother, Gleda, leaned over the counter in the kitchen as she kneaded bread. Alva sat at the table, a book open in front of her. She'd glanced up when Shaeleen had entered the room, but Alva didn't say anything.

Shaeleen gave a half smile. "What're you studying, Alva?" Shaeleen said, wanting to reestablish some sense of normalcy compared to the previous evening.

"History," Alva responded, looking up through her long, straight, brown hair. "Boring as always. Why do we need to know about King Wayland and his founding of the kingdoms?"

"History is part of who we are, Alva," Gleda, their mother, said without turning around.

Alva looked up at Shaeleen. Shaeleen thought about what sat in her pocket and about her last few weeks of travels. *I have helped some people.* "You never know, Alva, when you might become a part of history."

Alva furrowed her brows and mumbled. "Verlyn, gemstones, King Wayland... I just don't get why it matters."

Shaeleen perked up. "What does it say about the gemstones, Alva?"

Alva pushed her book toward Shaeleen. "It's all right here, if you want to read it. The gemstones came from Verlyn and were given to King Wayland to help keep peace in the kingdoms when he died."

"I'd almost forgotten..." Shaeleen mused to herself. She needed to find Diamonique, the princess of Gabor, in Verlyn. Maybe she could find out more about the gemstones while she was there. She thought about Melindra, the keeper that had thrust the stone on Shaeleen only weeks before. *Maybe I could find her or others like her. They could help me figure out what to do.*

Shaeleen patted Alva's head. "Thanks, Alva. Keep up your studying."

Their mother turned around and smiled at Shaeleen. "Nice to see you are in a better mood this morning, Shaeleen."

"I'm sorry," Shaeleen said.

"Care to talk about it?" Her mother took a few steps toward Shaeleen, her hands still dusted in flour.

Shaeleen shook her head. "No. I can't right now. Maybe later. Where's Cole?"

"He already left—told me to tell you he knew his duty and would meet you at the castle," her mother said.

Shaeleen frowned and mumbled, "His stupid sense of honor."

"What was that?" her mother asked.

"Cole. He has to be right about everything." Shaeleen gritted her teeth to try and keep from having thoughts of her brother spoil her mood once again. "His honor and sense of duty sometimes make me so mad."

Alva nodded in agreement. "He never gets in trouble for anything."

Just then, their father walked into the house. He looked soaked. Taking off his hat, he shook it out by the door. Then he eyed his daughters and asked, "Who never gets in trouble?"

"Cole," Alva and Shaeleen said at the same time.

"Ahh." Their father smiled at both of them. "He does have a propensity for telling the truth and for following orders."

"Telling the truth isn't always the best thing," Shaeleen said. A slight throbbing started at the base of her skull. She pushed it back down. She needed to be more careful about the words she spoke.

"I think the truth is always the best," her mother said.

"What if telling the truth hurt someone you cared about or even hurt the entire kingdom?" Shaeleen asked.

Her father and mother looked at her with surprise.

Her mother rinsed her hands. Then she came and stood by Shaeleen's father. "Lies hurt people."

Shaeleen grimaced at her mother's words. *A truth I know all too well.* "What if a lie only hurt one person—terribly hurt them—but the truth could hurt thousands? Then what would you do?"

Shaeleen's mother put an arm around her. "Shae, what is bothering you so much? Do you know something that could hurt someone? Does this have something to do with the prince and your errand for him?"

Shaeleen's eyes filled with tears, and she blinked a few times to hold them back. Before she could answer, a knock sounded at the door.

Her father turned and pulled it open. Standing at the door was a boy, his unruly hair wet and plastered to his head.

"Orin!" Shaeleen rushed forward and pulled the boy inside, hugging him profusely.

He pulled away and asked, "Shae, are you all right?"

She only nodded and then turned to her family. "This is Orin." She struggled to know the right words to say. She couldn't tell them about his speed or the times he had saved her. "We met on our trip to North Bay."

Orin nodded his hello to her family. Then Shaeleen glanced past Orin as her father closed the door. She saw a carriage outside, so she gave a questioning look at Orin.

"I thought it would be better than walking to the castle in this weather," Orin offered.

"And where did you get it?" Shaeleen asked.

Orin shrugged. "I don't think you would like my answer if I told you, Shae."

"Well, that's the truth at least," Shaeleen said. She turned to her family. "I have to go to the castle and report back to Basil. I hope to be back later, but then I have another errand to run that may take a few days."

Her father raised his eyebrows at her. "Is Cole going with you again?"

"I don't know," she stated flatly. "It depends on where his honor leads him."

"Well, I would feel better if he did," her father said. "I don't like you suddenly traipsing around. You're too young for this, Shaeleen. I know Prince Basil has asked, but I do worry."

"I love you, Papa," Shaeleen said and gave him a hug. "You just need to trust me for now."

Her father opened the door for them, and she and Orin ran to the carriage. A driver sat up front, under a small covering of his own. But, by the look of his clothes, it didn't seem like the covering protected him from the weather.

Sitting in the carriage, Shaeleen hardly noticed the finery of it all. The curtains stayed closed, and she sat deep in thought.

"Shae?" Orin turned to her with concern in his eyes. "Everything all right?"

No, everything is not all right!

She took a deep breath and tried to stop wringing her hands. It wasn't fair to take her frustration out on Orin. "Just trying to figure out what to say to Basil."

"Ahhh," said Orin, nodding his head to tell Shaeleen he understood her dilemma.

The rest of the ride to the castle went by in a blur for Shaeleen. Scenario after scenario played out in her mind. None of which were good for everyone. Someone would suffer in all of this—her, Basil, the kingdom. She couldn't stop all the pain.

* * *

Twenty minutes later, they pulled up at the front of the castle. They waited in line for a few other carriages to drop people off under an overhang. Shaeleen took the few minutes to compose herself. She straightened her clothes, wiped her eyes, and tried to put a smile on her face. Whatever happened today, she needed to be strong.

As they climbed out of the carriage, a guard came up to them. "State your business."

"Shaeleen, for Prince Basil," she said, for she did have the intelligence and good graces to use his proper title when necessary.

The guard looked through a list of names on a small piece of paper and nodded his head. "This way, then." He waved his hand toward the door to the castle.

Shaeleen thought back to being brought here with Lady Judith, just over two weeks earlier and laughed. The release felt good. *How my life has changed since then.*

After they waited for a few minutes in another room, a servant came and led them to the throne room, where they waited again. Shaeleen was getting restless, and needed all of this to be over. She hadn't seen Cole yet. After another hour, it was their turn.

Just as they stood to approach the prince, Cole joined them from behind. "Shae," he said with a short nod of his head. "You look nice today."

"I'm glad you're here, Cole," Shaeleen said, ignoring the compliment at first. Then she thought better of it and realized that Cole was trying to smooth things over. "I was worried about you. Are you all right?"

Cole sighed deeply and nodded his head. "You are my sister, Shae, and I am also your guardian. We must stick together." He had smiled as he said it, but there was also a warning in his undertone. Then Cole noticed Orin, standing on the other side of Shaeleen. "And what is he doing here?"

"He is my friend, as I told you, Cole."

"Friends or not, we are here to see the prince," Cole replied. "This is *our* business."

"Hey, I'm a part of this too, Cole—like it or not," Orin said, trying to stand up for himself.

Cole shook his head. "Fine, fine."

As they entered, the prince stood up and motioned to the three of them, giving Orin a questioning look. "I will speak with you three in my private office."

An officer of the castle led the three of them, walking behind Prince Basil down the hall. Shaeleen listened to their footsteps echoing off of the marble floors. She turned her head to the right at the sound of rain splattering on tall windows. Between the windows hung finely-made tapestries. Each step brought her closer to the point of decision. Each step she took seemed harder and harder, and she fell farther behind.

"Shae!" Cole called out to her. "Hurry up."

Once the prince and they were inside his private office, Regent Warin joined them before the officer closed the door. All five stood in silence for a moment, and Shaeleen just looked down at the floor in a daze.

"And who do we have here?" Prince Basil asked Shaeleen, indicating Orin. His words pulled Shaeleen from her daze, and she looked him in the eyes for the first time since arriving. The tenderness and compassion they held almost made her fall to the floor. But she sucked in a deep breath and pushed forward with the answer.

"Orin is a friend we met on our travels," Shaeleen began. "Basil—"

"*Prince* Basil," Cole interrupted. "I disagree with having him here. I caught him stealing, and he holds certain powers that cannot be trusted."

Shaeleen turned to Cole, with hands on her hips and a scowl on her face, and said to the prince, "Orin is my friend, has saved my life countless times, and has proven his worth to me. I can vouch for him."

Prince Basil smiled and reached his hand out toward Orin. "Well, if you vouch for him, then I trust that is the truth of the matter. Let's sit, and you can report to me what you've found on your travels." Prince Basil led them to a group of chairs.

"Is this wise?" Regent Warin asked the prince. "He's just a young boy, and these two—"

"These two are the age that I myself am, Regent," Prince Basil said. "I have sent them on an errand of great importance. I trust them fully."

Shaeleen turned away, feeling guilty. He trusted them, but she didn't even trust herself. She fingered the TruthStone through the pouch in her pocket, but it did nothing to lift the weight she felt.

The regent only nodded his head to Prince Basil.

The prince sat opposite Shaeleen. He was dressed immaculately in royal blue—which set off his dark blue eyes. He was quite handsome. When he glanced her way, a small grin formed in the corner of his mouth—setting off his dimple. And his eyes sparkled in her direction. Her heart pounded, but she turned away quickly. She couldn't stand looking him in the eyes, not right now. What would he do when he found out the truth about his brother...if he found out?

Maybe he doesn't need to ever know. Maybe something could happen to his brother. Thoughts swirled around in Shaeleen's head as different scenarios played out again in a matter of seconds. But once more, she couldn't think of an option that would solve all her problems. *Oh Basil!*

"Shae, the prince is asking you a question." Her brother's voice brought her out of her private thoughts.

"What?" Shaeleen blinked her eyes a few times.

"Tell me what you have learned about my brother."

Shaeleen felt panic rise inside of her. *What do I say?* She glanced at Cole, who pierced her with his eyes—obviously wanting her to tell the truth. She looked at Orin, and he lowered his head as if he couldn't face it either, but was letting her decide on her own. This was the point in time that she had to decide.

"Shaeleen?" The prince scooted up in his seat. "Is it that bad?"

She couldn't put it off any longer. She pushed all thoughts from her mind and drew on the feelings of her heart and without any more delay pushed the words out: "Your brother, Calix—"

"*Prince* Calix," her brother interrupted.

She glared at him. "Prince Calix has sided with Commander Kerr from Gabor—against the queen's knowledge or support," Shaeleen said, the words coming more quickly now that she had decided what to do. "There are already Gaborian warships in North Bay. They plan on taking the throne of Galena and then turning their sights back to Gabor. Prince Calix intends to rule here, with Commander Kerr ruling Gabor."

The prince sighed and leaned his head back in his chair.

Shaeleen breathed a sigh of relief. She had spoken her words without telling any lies.

"My lord." Regent Warin stood up at the news. "We must prepare for war. Your brother could be here soon."

The prince glanced up at his regent and then back to Shaeleen. "And my mother? Did you see her?"

Shaeleen nodded.

"Is she well?"

"She is well, and I can tell she loves you and misses you very much." Shaeleen had to hold back her tears.

"Then why does she stay there with my brother?" His tone showed a deep hurt at the thought of his mother siding with his brother.

Shaeleen's heart almost broke at Prince Basil's own pain. She looked at Cole, who only nodded his head toward her as if to say to do as she pleased. She dabbed at her eyes with a finger, to clear away the tears.

Shaeleen only shrugged at the prince's previous question, but she would not say anything more. She knew that, if she told Prince Basil the news, he would do the honorable thing and step down, allowing his brother, Calix, to have the throne of Galena. But, if she didn't tell him, maybe there was still a solution she could come up with that would allow Prince Basil to become king. *I have less than six weeks to find an answer.* A pounding started at the base of her skull and spread up through her head, settling more fully in her temples.

So much pain to try and hold back, she thought.

"Shaeleen, what is wrong?" the prince asked.

"It was a difficult trip, Prince Basil," Cole jumped in.

"I told you not to send them, Prince," Regent Warin said. "They are too young to handle this."

The prince shook his head. "No. They are the right ones. I just can't figure out what went wrong." He shook his head. "I just can't seem to think as clearly as I used to."

Shaeleen felt her eyes go wide. Giving up the IntelligenceStone—as small as it was—must have dimmed the prince's ability to think. He was still more intelligent than most, as the power flowed in his blood, but he was not as quick-thinking as when the stone was in his possession. Maybe, given the circumstances, that was a good thing. Hopefully he would not guess at what she was hiding.

Shaeleen felt tears well up again, and in anger she pushed them away and continued speaking. "He plans to attack before betrothal," Shaeleen said.

"That's barely six weeks away." Regent Warin put a hand to his head. "We really must warn Lord Gregory. The day of betrothal is the day you become—"

"I met the queen of Gabor," Shaeleen blurted, jumping out of her seat before the regent could finish his sentence. She knew what he was going to say, and she was not sure she could handle the pain from it right then. Shaeleen hoped to change the direction of the conversation.

"And Cole?" the prince asked.

"He stayed behind in North Bay to keep an eye on your brother," Shaeleen admitted.

The prince eyed Cole but didn't ask him anything.

Then the prince looked up at Regent Warin. "Please go and tell the council we will meet in one hour. I want to know all the options we have to avoid war and to keep as many people safe as possible. I love this kingdom and intend to protect it. I will stay and say a few more words to my friends."

His friends? What kind of friend am I if it don't tell him the truth?

Before the regent could leave, Shaeleen called him back. "Regent, some of the prince's lords are not loyal to him. I saw Lord Bancroft and others at a dinner with Prince Calix. You should be careful."

The regent only nodded, clearly not enjoying getting suggestions from a young woman. After he left, Prince Basil leaned forward in his chair.

He eyed Shaeleen intensely. "And, did the queen give you anything?"

Shaeleen nodded. Off to the side, she could see Cole's questioning eyes. She reached into her pocket and pulled out the pouch. She opened it up, pulled out the TruthStone, and held it out in her hand. The stone began to glow—green, at first, then the small IntelligenceStone and StrengthStone glowed their blue and red and joined with the green light. The entire effect gave off a greenish-purplish glow that spread out from Shaeleen's hand.

Cole sucked in a breath. She had not told him about the StrengthStone the previous evening.

Prince Basil nodded and motioned for her to put it away. "That much power makes me nervous. It must be hard for one person to hold it." His eyes searched hers with apparent sympathy. "It must be hard to know the truth of everything."

Shaeleen turned away, her heart feeling about to burst. *Am I doing the right thing here?* She steeled her mind with her decision. She couldn't let the goodness of Prince Basil be destroyed. Now that she had made the decision, she had to deal with the pain it would cause her.

"Well," the prince continued, "I must ask you—the three of you—to go on one more errand for me. I trust you will keep this a secret."

Shaeleen and Cole looked at one another. They both had made other pledges: her, to Queen Victoria; and him, to Prince Calix.

"What do you ask of us, my prince?" Cole asked.

"I need you to go and bring my betrothed to Galena in safety," Prince Basil said. "She is Princess Diamonique of Gabor. She is currently on the island of Verlyn, completing training in Sylvermoor. She has been taught the intricacies of being a queen."

Shaeleen, Cole, and Orin all glanced at each other in turn, eyebrows furrowed and mouths held grim.

"Well?" the prince asked. "Will you accept this quest from me, as prince of Galena?"

Cole nodded. Orin nodded, a small grin trying to burst out on his face. But Shaeleen sat in thought for a moment longer. It wasn't that she wouldn't accept, but it was the growing importance of the princess that caught her mind up in deep thought. *What does she have to do with all of this?*

Prince Basil seemed to misunderstand her hesitation. "I know, Shaeleen, that I released you from allegiance to only Galena. Your powers must aid all of Wayland. If there is some reason you cannot—"

"No." Shaeleen shook her head. "There is no reason not to retrieve the princess from Verlyn. I would very much like to see the fabled kingdom."

"Great!" The prince stood up and clapped his hands. "I will have a ship ready for you in a few days' time."

Shaeleen stared at the floor, trying to hold the guilt in.

"And don't worry," the prince said with a smile on his face. "All will be well. You will see. Galena will continue to prosper under her new king."

At that, Shaeleen jumped up and ran out of the room. She hurried down the hallway, until she found a washroom. She went inside and retched, throwing up the small amount of food she'd had in her stomach. After a few more heaves, she stopped and washed her face.

A small mirror hung above a basin of water. Looking at her face, she noticed lines from the pain already forming around her eyes and on her forehead. Then tears ran down her face—it was becoming an annoying habit.

CHAPTER TWENTY-NINE

Three days later, Cole, Shaeleen, and Orin were standing on a ship anchored in the docks of Stronghaven. The prince had commissioned a full crew to sail them to Sylvermoor, a trip that would take them, first, south to Mistport, in Antioch, to drop off a few other nobles, and then on to the island of Verlyn, to the southeast.

Orin wandered off, looking for something to eat, which left Shaeleen and Cole alone at the railing, looking back at the city of Stronghaven.

"I still don't know why you didn't tell Prince Basil, Shae." Cole turned his head to look at her. "He deserves to know the truth of things."

"We've been over this numerous times, Cole. I just couldn't – not yet. He is too good of a person. He would step aside for Calix. Basil is the best king for Galena." She pushed away the pain in her gut.

"But, the pain," Cole said in sympathy and moved closer to Shaeleen. "It will kill you."

Shaeleen whirled to face him. "What do you care, Cole? You've sided with Calix—even though you know the type of man he is."

Cole's lips thinned, but he held his apparent anger in check. "Shae, I am here with you, aren't I? We'll figure this out. I have not sided with anyone—only the truth. I thought you of all people would understand my supporting the truth. The truth is..." He looked around, and, with the breeze off the sea and the sound of the crew readying the ship for departure, no one was near enough to overhear his words. "The truth is Prince Calix, as the oldest, is the next king of Galena. You can't change that!"

And that was the crux of her dilemma. That was why she was angry. It wasn't at Cole or even Calix—but at herself. How could she hold the TruthStone and not uphold the truth? *I will deserve the mockery of TruthSeers for generations to come.*

"Aren't you my wizard, Cole?" Shaeleen's eyes filled with tears. "Aren't you supposed to protect me, help me, support me—and keep me from pain?" she asked, her voice coming out louder than she'd intended.

Cole's face fell, and he reached his hand toward her face. "Shae, if I could take your pain, I would. I hate to see you suffer. But you needn't do so. I am your guardian wizard and your protector. But, to support you *means* supporting the truth, something that is bigger than both of us—than all of us."

Shaeleen wiped her eyes and knew that her brother spoke the truth.

He waved his arm out over Stronghaven. "No one—not even you, with all your growing powers—has the right to manipulate the truth of things or the order that is meant to happen. Even the stones are governed by an order of things. You told me that truth and light work with, and control all the powers of stones."

"I already have three powers, Cole. What happens when I get all the rest of them?" Shaeleen felt tortured inside thinking about all that power. "What will I become?"

Cole shook his head. "I don't know, Shaeleen. But you must be careful."

Shaeleen shook her head at the thought of all she could now do already. "I'll tell you what could happen, Cole. I could become all-powerful and make anything happen that I want to happen: I can ensure that Basil takes the throne. I can crush Commander Kerr's army. And I can destroy Calix if need be."

"Shae!" Cole hugged his arms around himself with obvious worry. He gazed around the ship and then turned back to her. "You're distraught. Do not think such things. That's blasphemy to Wayland and her kingdoms."

"Then take it from me!" she wailed, reaching inside her dress and bringing the pouch out. She held it in front of him. She could see the response to temptation cross her brother's face and then his desire for honor and truth. *Maybe he would be a better TruthSeer than me.*

He took two steps back and shook his head. "I...I can't," Cole said, conflicting emotions still crossing his face. "Don't tempt me like that," he choked, his voice becoming more quiet. "Don't ever tempt me again with so much power, Shae. I might not be able to resist it next time." He backed up farther, still shaking his head. Then he turned and left.

Alone at the railing, she slumped to the deck of the ship, her back to the railing, and took the TruthStone out of its leather pouch. She rolled the smooth, almost round, greenish stone in her small hands. Black lines crossed the stone and joined with the small Red Jasper and Labradorite stones, now embedded there.

Shaeleen held the TruthStone carefully in both hands and sobbed. She cried for the pain it had already caused her. Cried for the pain it would cause her still. And cried for the pain it would cause the kingdom of Galena and all of Wayland in the weeks and months to come.

* * *

This is the end of *TruthStone,*
Book 1 in The TruthSeer Archives.
To continue the adventures of Shaeleen, Cole, and Orin,
read **TruthSpell**, Book 2 in the TruthSeer Archives

Forcing someone to tell the truth…

…Can have painful and devastating results.

But is it worth it?

Thrust into the role of saving the stones of power, Shaeleen is still learning how to manage the magical abilities she has been given.

As the holder of a TruthStone, every lie she hears or tells causes her immense physical pain.

Sent to prevent a civil war, her journey veers off course when she discovers an evil shadow power threatening the magic of Wayland.

As Shaeleen gathers the other stones of power, she discovers a TruthSpell that can force others to tell the truth and force them to follow her will.

Will her newfound powers help her save Wayland's magic? Or will she become a monster worse than the one she is fighting against?

Read book 2 of the TruthSeer Archives to continue on an epic magical quest with exciting adventure, moral dilemmas, powerful magic, and evil wizards.

***

Other Series By Mike Shelton
The Alaris Chronicles

For 100 years it protected them…

…and now the magical barrier is about to fail.

What waits on the other side?

Bakari is nerdy and awkward. At 15, he's lived at the Wizard Citadel for most of his life. Everything seems to be working out like he'd hoped. He just got promoted to Level 1 and despite being painfully shy, he has a friend.

Kharlia knows medicine. And he really likes her.

When Bakari finds an ancient map that marks a source of power, he must check it out. With Kharlia by his side, they wander through the Kingdom toward the spot on the map. The trip isn't what they expect.

Magical creatures have made it through the barrier. Should they fight or flee?

Bakari knows they are in trouble. He isn't a battle wizard. As they struggle against the beasts, the worst thing Bakari can imagine happens.

Will they survive?

You'll love this first book in *The Alaris Chronicles*, because of the beautifully woven story with diverse characters, great adventure, and political intrigue.

Sign up on Mike's website at www.MichaelSheltonBooks.com and get a copy of the prequel novella e-book to The Alaris Chronicles, Prophecy of the Dragon.

Protect the youngest heir of the Dragon King. That is the mission given to Imari in this prequel novella to The Alaris Chronicles.

The Cremelino Prophecy

A Prophecy.

A Powerful Sword.

A Reluctant Wizard.

Wizards and magic have long been looked down upon in the Realm. So what happens when you find out you're a wizard?

Darius San Williams, son of one of King Edward's councilors, cares little for his father's politics and vows to leave the city of Anikari to protect and bring glory to the Realm.

But when a new-found and ancient magic emerges within him, he and his friends Christine and Kelln are faced with decisions that could shatter or fulfill the prophecy and the lives of all those they know.

Trying to escape fate, Darius learns that no matter where he goes, prophecy and destiny are waiting to find him.

If you love magic, sword & Sorcery, wizards, and epic fantasy don't miss this first book in The Cremelino Prophecy-- and discover what remarkable destiny awaits Darius.

Sign up on Mike's website at www.MichaelSheltonBooks.com and get a copy of the prequel novella e-book to The Cremelino Prophecy, The Blade and The Bow.
Follow Darius and Kelln in one of their more fantastic adventures prior to The Path Of Destiny.

The Wizard Academies

He lost his family...

...He's got voices in his head.

And he's more powerful than they ever imagined.

Fifteen-year-old apprentice Kyril is sick of being bullied. And after a tragic fire leaves him orphaned with out-of-control thoughts and powers, he can't wait to escape constant taunting at the wizard academy. So when a dicey faction entices him with companionship, he ignores the grim warning signs.

Even as Kyril's power grows within the group, he's left out of the crew's dangerous plans to derail the authorities. And when being accepted comes at the expense of making questionable choices, he fears his newfound friendships aren't worth the deadly price.

Can Kyril master his new magic before his shady companions send him to his doom?

Mark of the Medallion is the spellbinding first novel in The Wizard Academies YA fantasy series. If you like sword and sorcery, enchanted adventures, and suspenseful coming-of-age stories, then you'll love Mike Shelton's action-packed tale.

About the Author

 Mike was born in California and has lived in multiple states from the west coast to the east coast. He cannot remember a time when he wasn't reading a book. At school, home, on vacation, at work at lunch time, and yes even a few pages in the car (at times when he just couldn't put that great book down). Though he has read all sorts of genres he has always been drawn to fantasy. It is his way of escaping to a simpler time filled with magic, wonders and heroics of young men and women.

Other than reading, Mike has always enjoyed the outdoors. From the beaches in Southern California to the warm waters of North Carolina. From the waterfalls in the Northwest to the Rocky Mountains in Utah. Mike has appreciated the beauty that God provides for us. He also enjoys hiking, discovering nature, playing a little basketball or volleyball, and most recently disc golf. He has a lovely wife who has always supported him, and three beautiful children who have been the center of his life.

Mike began writing stories in elementary school and moved on to larger novels in his early adult years. He has worked in corporate finance for most of his career. That, along with spending time with his wonderful family and obligations at church has made it difficult to find the time to truly dedicate to writing. In the last few years as his children have become older he has returned to doing what he truly enjoys – writing!

mikesheltonbooks@gmail.com
www.MichaelSheltonBooks.com
https://www.facebook.com/groups/MikeSheltonAuthor/
https://www.facebook.com/mikesheltonbooks/
http://www.Twitter.com/msheltonbooks
http://www.Instagram.com/mikesheltonbooks
https://www.pinterest.com/mikesheltonbooks/